BOTH ENDS OF THE WHIP

Brenda Murphy

A NineStar Press Publication

Published by NineStar Press
P.O. Box 91792,
Albuquerque, New Mexico, 87199 USA.
www.ninestarpress.com

Both Ends of the Whip

Printed in the USA
First Edition
May, 2018

Print ISBN: 978-1-948608-61-9

Also available in eBook, ISBN: 978-1-948608-59-6

Warning: This book contains sexually explicit content, which may only be suitable for mature readers.

To C, always.

Chapter One

"DID YOU TELL her?" Bridget's voice was hoarse.

Octavia leaned down and touched her cheek. "No." The springs squeaked when she left the bed. She stretched and walked to the window. With two fingers, she pulled the curtain aside. Cool air seeped in around the window frame. Her skin and her nipples pebbled. *Fuck. Why didn't I? What am I waiting for? Say something.* Bridget's silence was worse than if she had pleaded. The warm smell of their afternoon tryst filled the small bedsit. She glanced over her shoulder at Bridget. She lay on her back with her eyes closed and her hands clasped over her stomach. Her long red hair curled around her head and spilled over the white pillowcase. Octavia wanted to crawl back into the small bed and kiss each freckle scattered over her naked body. She wanted to lose herself in the softness of her skin and make her beg for release. *She's angry. Sad. What am I waiting for? Fuck me, I need to get it together.*

She turned back to the window and looked out. Early morning mist hung over the grass surrounding the manor house. A long black car pulled into the circular drive. A lone woman exited the car. Tall and willowy, she glanced about her before she lowered her head and hurried across the pavers. *Not a guest. Visitor? Solicitor?* Octavia let the curtain fall back into place. *Say something. Anything.*

"Today. I promise." Octavia turned to Bridget. She was sitting up now. She had pulled on Octavia's shirt and was leaning against the brass headboard.

"You said that yesterday." Bridget looked down at her hands. "I've told Cook. She's gone out of her way to be crueler than usual to me." She twisted her fingers together. Her shoulders were slumped making Octavia's shirt appear even larger on her small frame.

Octavia crossed the room and took Bridget's hand in her own. "Look at me love." She rubbed her thumb over the skin of her knuckles. Bridget raised her chin, her eyes bright with unshed tears. Octavia leaned down and brushed her lips with a kiss. "Today." She kissed Bridget again, deeper this time.

Bridget settled her hands on Octavia's hips. "I can't stand the idea of anyone else touching you. Every day we're here, I hate it. I hate worrying someone will ask for you and you'll go because you think you have to."

"I go because I made an agreement. I owe Martha. It doesn't mean anything."

"It does to me." Bridget pinned Octavia in place with her hard expression. "If you want me to be committed to you, to kneel to you, to be yours, you need to understand I want the same from you. I'm not a toy or a doll to be played with until someone better comes along."

Octavia held Bridget's gaze. "I know, love. I know. Today. I promise." She lifted the edge of her collar and the number tag jingled. "Today is the last day I wear this."

"YOU'RE SURE? WHAT if you went on holiday? You haven't taken any time off in years. A break would do you good." Martha smoothed her hand over Octavia's shoulders before she tugged at the neckline of her shirt, straightening it. She flattened her hands on Octavia's chest and leaned in to kiss her.

Octavia pulled back, avoiding the kiss. "No. It's more than that, Mistress."

Martha lowered her hands. Her gaze was steady and her eyes dark. "You're done then?"

Do it. Now. For Bridget. For both of you. Octavia kneeled at Martha's feet. She lowered her head until her forehead touched the toe of Martha's boot. She pulled her thick single braid to the side. *How many times have I kneeled this way aching with need and want, wanting only to be under her hand? Begged to feel the sting of her lash, to be allowed to serve her. Begged for a kiss. When did it change?*

"I want to be free, Mistress. Please release me." Sweat trickled down her back. She waited in silence, her breathing rough. Martha rested her palm on the crown of her head, her touch igniting a wave of desire in Octavia. Her body warred with her mind. *Hard. So hard. So much I want. So much she can't give.* Octavia blinked away the tears that burned the back of her throat. She heard the rustle of fabric. Cold metal pressed against her neck, the sharp edge scraping her skin and she shivered. Her collar fell in two pieces onto the floor, the brass tag clinking on the tiles. Octavia exhaled. She raised her head and sat up. She picked up the remnants of her collar before she rose and stuffed the pieces into her front pocket. Her palms were sweaty and she wiped them on her jeans.

Martha stepped away and turned her back to Octavia. "Have you thought about where you'll go? What to do with your accounts?"

The chill in Martha's voice made Octavia's heart ache. "I've been looking. No firm plans yet. I thought I'd leave the accounts with you until I'm settled."

"Bridget as well?"

No secrets at Rowan House. Nothing to hide. Not now. "Yes. She's told Cook."

Martha turned and looked at Octavia. She rested one hand on her hip. "I'm surprised she lasted as long as she did. Last time I trust Cook to hire someone."

Octavia pursed her lips. "Jealous of a sub?" She rocked back on her heels and crossed her arms. "This has got nothing to do with Bridget. This is about us."

"Because I refused give over to you? To give you control?" Martha quirked her mouth.

"Because you refused to understand I wanted more, needed more from you."

"Eight years and it comes to this? You're leaving me for what? A woman-child? A soft sub? She can't give you what you need. You'll be bored in a year."

"Maybe. But at least I'll be happy."

Martha's face flushed and she inhaled sharply before she smoothed her features. Her manner cool and haughty, she lifted her chin. She met Octavia's hard look with one of her own. *Angry. So angry. And hurt. Fuck. I hurt her. She'd never acknowledge it. Still holding back.* Octavia turned away from the hurt in Martha's eyes. *She loves me. But not enough. Not enough to give me control.*

"Fuck you. You asked for my ownership. You begged me for it. I didn't force it on you."

Octavia winced at the edge in Martha's voice. "I did." She met her gaze. "People change. I've changed. I should've told you about Bridget. I owed you. I'm sorry."

"I knew. I knew when you didn't ask me for permission it was more than play." Martha clasped her hands behind her back. "I expect you to stay through the end of the month. You'll need to train one of the others to manage the stable until I can hire someone." She pinned Octavia with her glare. "You're excused from your other duties."

"I signed a contract. I'll honor it."

"You are not to play with any guests or other staff. Honor our past. Honor my last command."

Martha turned and squared her shoulders. She walked away, her footsteps loud on the tile floor. Octavia stood in the center of the room. She closed her eyes, trying to shut out the ghosts of memories of their time together that swirled around her. Her heart ached for what had been and what would never be. She thrust her hand in her pocket, pulled the pieces of her collar out. She fingered the smooth edge of her number tag. *I'm free. Free to follow my own path. With Bridget. But where?* She touched her neck, the bare skin where her collar had been. She swallowed the dry-edged pain in her throat, willing the tears away.

"THERE'S FRESH TEA in the pot." Bridget stirred a pan on the stove, her back to Octavia. The warm smell of butter and olive oil heating filled the kitchen. Octavia poured herself a cup of tea and sat at the long worktable.

"Cook's out?" Octavia scanned the large kitchen, wary of the tyrant who ran it.

"At the fishmonger's, showing my replacement the routine." Bridget moved the pan she had been stirring to the back of the stove top. "Hungry?"

"I'm ready for second breakfast." Octavia sipped her tea. "I only had a bit of toast before I mucked this morning."

Bridget turned to her. She wiped her hand on her side towel. "I've a mountain of prep to do but I could make you some eggs if you want."

A flash of flame erupted from the sauté pan behind Bridget. Octavia stood up and her chair clattered to the floor. "The pan."

Bridget spun to face the stove and stared. Black smoke filled the small space and the fire alarm sounded loud in the small space. *Fire. Fuck. Why isn't she moving? What the hell? Lid? Flour? Salt? Lid.* Octavia clambered over the table and pushed Bridget to the side. She grabbed a large lid off the counter and dropped it on the pan. She turned to Bridget, clasped her shoulders and looked into her eyes. They were glassy and her face was fixed in a blank stare.

"Hey. Bridget. Hey. Look at me." She pulled her away from the stove.

The rest of the house staff arrived. The smoke alarm was shrill. Martha pushed past the others. She swept her gaze over the scene. After snatching a side towel from the counter, she wafted it in front of the alarm until it stopped its harsh sound.

Octavia helped Bridget to a chair. She kneeled and clasped her hand tight. "Bridget." She touched her chin and peered into her eyes. "Are you okay?"

Bridget shook free of Octavia's touch and looked down at their hands. "Yes. I'm sorry." Her voice was quiet.

Martha came to stand behind them. She rested her hand on Octavia's shoulder. "Did she get burned?"

Octavia looked up. "No. She... I don't know what happened. She froze."

"I'm fine. I need to finish the prep. Cook'll be back soon." Bridget rocked in the chair. "Cook'll be back soon. Need to clean up my station."

Martha leaned down and assessed Bridget's appearance. "I'll deal with Cook." She turned her head and met Octavia's gaze. "Take care of her. Rebecca can handle the stable this afternoon."

She hesitated. Yesterday she would have known how to answer her former Mistress. *What to say? Yes, Mistress? Yes, Martha? I asked to be free. I need to own it.* "I'll take her to my room."

Martha looked down and away from Octavia's eyes. "I'll have one of the others bring your food. You both are excused from staff meals for the rest of the day."

Octavia helped Bridget to her feet. She slid an arm around her waist. "I've got you, love."

Bridget leaned into her shoulder. Octavia led her away from the kitchen and through the halls and across the courtyard to her bedsit over the stable. Bridget did not speak and her steps were mechanical. *What the hell? What happened?* Octavia replayed the events leading up to fire. When they arrived at her room, she guided Bridget to a battered wingback chair and made her sit.

Bridget avoided her eyes, her gaze focused on the floor. "Sorry." Her voice was tight and small.

"Are you back?" Octavia smoothed her hand over Bridget's hair.

"Yeah. Sorry. I'm so stupid."

"It was an accident. It could have happened to anyone." She rubbed Bridget's shoulder. "You're not stupid. Don't talk about yourself that way." She placed a kiss on the top of Bridget's head. "I shouldn't have distracted you."

Bridget hugged Octavia around the waist. "If you hadn't been there..." Her breath hitched and there were tears in her voice.

"But I was. And we're safe." Octavia rubbed the back of Bridget's neck.

Bridget leaned her forehead against Octavia's hip as quiet sobs racked her body. *This is about more than the fire. What?* She replayed conversations they had about their lives before Rowan House, searching her memories of quiet afterglow talks and the deeper moments after a session when buried feelings surfaced. She found no explanation for

Bridget's actions and reactions. *Later. I'll ask.* She held tight to Bridget until the tears stopped bearing witness to a pain she didn't understand but wanted to.

BRIDGET DROPPED TO her knees. Her hair spilled forward and brushed the top of Octavia's boots. Octavia admired the delicate curve of her spine, letting her submission soothe the rough edges of her day and giving over to the side of herself that craved control and Bridget's offering of obedience. She leaned down and wrapped her hand in Bridget's hair to pull her head up. With her other hand she clasped Bridget's chin, the skin blanching under her fingertips. She took her mouth with firm lips and tongue, goaded by the soft whimpers of need pouring from Bridget. She growled low in her throat in answer. *Yes. This. Power. Control.*

Octavia broke their kiss. She straightened and cupped Bridget's face with both hands. "Look at me." She smoothed her thumbs over her cheekbones. "What have you chosen for your punishment? My hand or the belt?"

"Whatever pleases you, Ma'am." Bridget's eyes were bright, and Octavia grew wet listening to the eager quiver in her voice. *Willing. Wanting. Mine.*

Octavia released her. "Stand for me. Bend over and clasp your ankles."

Bridget rose and set her feet shoulder width apart before she bent from the waist and wrapped her fingers around her ankles. Her core glistened with wetness. Octavia steadied Bridget with a hand on her hip, digging her fingers in hard enough to bruise while she traced the wet seam between her legs and stroked her clit with one finger. A low groan shook Bridget's frame. Working slowly, Octavia delighted in her small moans and the way she relaxed, opening herself to

Octavia's touch. Bridget squeezed around Octavia, her body shuddering and signaling how close she was to coming for her. She took her time drawing out Bridget's pleasure, edging her closer.

"Please, Ma'am. I can't. Please let me come for you."

Octavia pulled her hand away roughly and slapped Bridget's ass, leaving a bright red mark on her freckled skin. The sharp squeal from Bridget made her clit hard, and she drew back and slapped her ass again, harder this time. She smoothed her hand over the mark it had left. Bridget panted. She leaned down and pressed a kiss to the mark. "I love the way your skin takes my marks." Bridget trembled under her hand. "Ready, love?"

"Yes." Bridget's strong voice sent a curl of desire through Octavia, and another surge of wetness spilled from her.

"Yes, what?" Octavia spanked her hard, and her palm stung with the impact.

"Ahh. Oh. Yes, Ma'am." Bridget struggled against Octavia's grip.

Her feigned resistance heighted Octavia's desire. *Wanton. Beautiful slut. Mine.* She raised her hand and spanked Bridget, hard, blow after blow until her hand ached and the cheeks of Bridget's ass were bright red. Deep groans of pleasure mixed with squeals of pain and orgasmic cries filled the air. Each groan and sharp cry soothed the ache in Octavia's soul—the part of her that craved obedience, needed to cause pain and control pleasure. Bridget's thick thighs were wet to her knees with her desire. Octavia listened and watched, careful to bring Bridget to the edge but not over. Bridget's voice changed as she begged for mercy, tears now, wetting the floor in front of her.

"Please, Ma'am. Please. Let me. Please. I can't. Let me please you. Please." The ragged edge in her voice made

Octavia's clit harder, and she ached for Bridget's mouth on her. She stopped and smoothed her hands over Bridget's ass.

"Do you want to pleasure me? Taste me? Do you want me to come in your mouth?"

"Yes. Please, Ma'am. Please let me."

"Say the words. Ask for what you want." She scratched her nails over the red marks on Bridget's ass.

"Ow. Oh. Please. Please, Ma'am, let me taste you. Let me give you pleasure. Please, Ma'am. Come in my mouth. Please."

She waited, listening to Bridget's shuddering breaths as she came down from her spanking. Octavia pinched her hip hard. "I don't know. Are you sure?"

"Ahh. Please. Ma'am. Oh please." Her voice was rough, and her body trembled under Octavia's touch as she begged.

Octavia released her. "Turn and stand for me."

Bridget straightened, and Octavia made sure she was steady on her feet. She turned slowly toward Octavia.

"Look at me."

She raised her head and met Octavia's gaze. Tears streaked her face. Her eyes were bright. She opened her mouth and licked her lips and leaned forward. "Please, Ma'am. Let me taste you. Please." Her voice was soft now as she whispered her desperation in Octavia's ear.

"Kneel."

Bridget lowered herself gracefully to her knees. *Lovely. Beautiful. Mine.*

"Eyes to me. Hands behind your back."

She lifted her eyes to Octavia's face. She clasped her hands behind her back, the movement thrusting her breasts forward. Octavia caught Bridget's nipples between her thumbs and forefingers and squeezed hard, watching as pain and pleasure swept over her features.

The deep groan from Bridget's lips sent waves of need through Octavia.

"Please, Ma'am. Please let me taste you. Please."

Octavia looked into Bridget's eyes as she would a still pool into which she had dropped a precious object. *Want. Need. So much. She wants me. Loves me.* She stood, spreading her legs wide before she cupped the back of Bridget's head. "Pleasure me."

Bridget moaned as she took Octavia with her mouth. Reverent, she licked and suckled Octavia's clit. She drove her tongue hard and deep, sending waves of sensation through Octavia. She looked down and the vision of Bridget kneeling between her legs made the sensation so much more. She held tight with both hands wrapped in Bridget's hair, and her gratification gushed into Bridget's greedy mouth. Bridget swallowed and licked and sucked, and an undertow of pleasure pulled Octavia under and held her down until she was gasping. She closed her eyes and rocked her hips into Bridget's face. Love squeezed Octavia's heart as Bridget attended to her, slowing her movements, licking gently, and murmuring soft sounds of satisfaction. She stroked her hair.

"Enough now."

Bridget sat back on her heels. Her face and chin gleamed with wetness, and her pupils were dilated with desire.

"To the bed. Lay back. Hands over your head. Feet on the floor. Legs wide. Hips off the edge of the bed."

Octavia turned her back to Bridget. She picked up the strap-on she had prepared and buckled it in place. The base pressing against her swollen clit sent a current of desire through her.

Turning, she stopped to appreciate the vision of Bridget splayed out for her. Her nipples were hard and stood up from her large breasts. Dark red curls between her thighs shone wet with desire, her thick thighs and broad body a delectable buffet spread for Octavia. *Mine. Mine alone. All of this is for me.* Octavia stroked the phallus. She stood between Bridget's wide-spread legs. She dragged the tip of the sex toy along her wet folds, drawing a sigh from Bridget before she pushed the thick head in a bit and pulled back slow.

"Please, Ma'am. I need. Please fuck me." Bridget shifted her hips and groaned.

Octavia rubbed her clit with her thumb as little by little she worked the thick cock deep until it was buried to the hilt. She drew back and sank in again, the pressure and vibration on her clit exquisite. *That's it. So good. My sweet girl. Give it to me.*

"Oh yes. Ma'am. Please. Like that. Pleasepleaseplease."

Slow and deep, Octavia fucked her, timing her strokes, pressing and rubbing Bridget's clit and drawing deep groans from her. Desire filled Octavia's heart.

Breath ragged and body shaking, Bridget whispered, "May I, Ma'am? Please let me come for you? Oh, please, Ma'am."

Yes. For me. Mine. Octavia rolled her hips and sped up her strokes. Bridget thrashed and lifted her hips and arched her back to take more. She wrapped her legs around Octavia's hips, locking them at the ankles. *Beautiful. Mine. So beautiful.* Octavia watched her face, knowing Bridget would lose the battle soon. She was clearly unable to hold back. Her breathing was rough, her hands clenched the sheets, and a fine sheen of sweat covered her skin. Octavia struggled with her desire to make her beg and her own desire to come again, her clit winning in the end. She shifted her hands to Bridget's hips, cupping her ass and gripping hard.

"Come for me. Now." She jacked her hips harder, pushing deeper and stroking faster. She fucked herself into her own orgasm as Bridget broke for her, bucking her hips and meeting Octavia's thrusts.

They rode out their pleasure together, their groans giving way to soft sighs and moans as they came down. Octavia stilled. She withdrew slowly and leaned over to drag her tongue over Bridget's clit, causing her to come again with a sharp intake of breath. Octavia unbuckled the harness and laid the strap-on aside. She helped Bridget up into the bed. She leaned down and kissed her, and Bridget opened her eyes.

"Did I hurt you, love?" Octavia brushed her knuckles over Bridget's cheek.

"No more than I wanted." Her mouth turned up in a soft smile. "That thing you do with your hips. You undo me." She shivered, and Octavia pulled the covers over both of them. Bridget tucked her head into Octavia's shoulder and draped her leg over Octavia's.

Octavia held her close, searching for the words to say everything she wanted to tell her. Finding them all inadequate, she settled on a deep kiss.

Chapter Two

"VIVIAN ABIOLA—" MARTHA inclined her head toward Octavia. "This is Octavia Vargas. She's been my stable manager for the last eight years. I can't say enough about her skills with horses. I think she would meet your needs."

Octavia's face grew warm at Martha's praise.

"A pleasure to meet you." Her voice was boarding schools and high tea, underlaid with old family money. She was as tall as Martha, and Octavia had to look up to make eye contact. She shook hands with her. Vivian's skin was soft, but Octavia appreciated the firm way she took control, her grip sure and confident. The subservient side of her quivered at her touch.

A hint of memory tugged at Octavia. Vivian's face was familiar. Octavia searched her memories, trying to place her. *A former guest? No. Where do I know her from? The circuit? No. Where?*

"And this is Bridget Murray. She's worked as assistant head chef here and comes with Cook's recommendation."

Vivian shook hands with Bridget, and Octavia glanced at Bridget, noting the way she lowered her gaze beneath Vivian's cool appraising gaze. *She feels it too.*

"Martha has spoken highly of you both. I'm in need of a stable manager and a cook. I will match your salaries here and provide living quarters on the property. I will arrange for the proper work visa and any other immigration paperwork necessary and pay for your relocation expenses and travel to Franciacorta. I don't expect an answer today, but I need one by the end of the week."

"Why come all the way here to hire us?" Bridget raised her eyebrow. "I'm sure there are stable managers and cooks in Italy."

"I need staff I can trust." Vivian looked between them, meeting their gazes in turn.

"I don't want to work at another whore house." Bridget turned to stare at Martha and met her glare with one of her own.

Octavia opened her mouth to speak and closed it when Vivian raised her hand. *Those eyes. I know her. How?*

"I live alone on my estate and travel frequently. I don't desire any services beyond what is normally expected from a stable manager and a cook." She squared her shoulders, a cool expression on her face. "If you have any other questions, I will be here until Saturday. If you want to accept my offer, I'll have your contracts drawn up." She turned and nodded at Martha and favored her with a quiet smile. "I'll see you at dinner." She left them, walking away as graceful and unhurried as a queen leaving court, and closed the door behind her. The solid sound of the door latch clicking into place was loud in the wood-paneled room.

Martha walked to her desk and sat down. She steepled her hands and rested her elbows on the jade-green blotter set in the middle of the dark walnut desk. Bridget shifted and stood away from Octavia, her lips pursed, arms crossed in front of her chest. The tick of the mantel clock was loud in the silence that rose between the three of them. Octavia walked to stand in front of Martha's desk.

"Thank you."

Martha did not raise her head. "No need to thank me. I didn't do it for you. Vivian is one of my oldest and dearest friends. Have you given any further thought about your accounts?"

Octavia sensed Bridget's eyes on her, watching her, waiting for her. "Would you mind managing them? Until we're settled? I'm not sure if it's for us."

"It is not my concern. You are free. You and your—" She glanced at Bridget. "—friend are free to do what you want. Cook has found a replacement, and Rachel seems to be handling the stable. I'll mange your accounts until you make new arrangements."

She waved her hand, dismissing them. Bridget's sharp snort underlined her desire to end the meeting.

Dismissed. Shut out. But I asked for this. I asked to be free. She stepped back from the desk and turned to leave. Bridget reached out for her hand as she walked past, and Octavia took it, the clasp of her hand steady and reassuring. *We. Mine. Us. Together.*

"WHAT WAS THAT all about? 'I don't want to work in another whore house'?" Octavia sat on the edge of the bed facing Bridget. Their knees touched. "I can't change what I've done. There is nothing wrong with sex work."

Bridget looked away from Octavia. "I was angry."

"Because Martha is trying to help us? What the fuck?"

"Because she is trying to control you, us, still."

Octavia chewed her lip. "The choice is ours."

"What if I don't want to do it?"

"You have another plan? Because I don't."

"No. I've applied to twenty hotels and resorts. I haven't been called back for an interview." Bridget twisted her shirt in her hands. "I suspect Cook has given less-than-glowing references."

Octavia raised her eyebrow. "Well, you might have stepped over the line when you told her she cooked like a shoemaker."

"How do you know about that?"

"No secrets here. And Sarah couldn't wait to tell me."

Bridget blew out a breath. "I let my temper get the best of me."

"What do we have to lose taking this gig? Have you ever been to Italy?" Octavia smoothed her hand over Bridget's thigh.

Bridget snorted. "No. None of my foster homes were in Europe."

"Is it Vivian?" Octavia suppressed a shiver as she said her name.

Bridget looked away from Octavia's eyes.

Doesn't want to tell me. She's keeping secrets. Does she want her? Want to serve her?

"She's like Cook squared. I..." Bridget tucked her hands under her thighs. "Her eyes. I had to stop myself from saying yes to whatever she asked." She slumped her shoulders. "It was how I ended up here. I didn't mind being owned but I wanted to be the only one." A frown spoiled her face. "I didn't understand it wasn't Cook's way."

"Vivian will be our employer. Nothing more." *Unless it becomes more. Does she want more? Do I?*

Octavia took her hand. "Look at me." Bridget raised her eyes and held Octavia's gaze. "You're mine. But you always have choices. Why don't we try it? If it's horrible, if we hate it, we can always leave."

Bridget nodded. "Right. We can." She turned and kissed Octavia on the cheek. "Together."

VIVIAN SAT BEHIND Martha's desk. She wore a fitted dress that hugged her slim frame. The low-cut neckline displayed her modest cleavage, and the lilac color set off her amber eyes. Her hair was close-cropped and natural. A touch of silver shone on some of the curls. Octavia tilted her head, studying her face. The nagging feeling of knowing her was back. Vivian's skin was only a shade darker than Octavia's, her features suggesting a complicated heritage. She met Octavia's gaze with a cool expression and Octavia shivered as Vivian raked her eyes over her frame. *Should have changed my clothes, maybe dressed up. Left my hair loose. Where do I know her from?*

Bridget was at her side. Her hands were clasped in front of her waist. She was dressed in her starched and pressed chef's jacket. It gleamed white in stark contrast to Octavia's outfit of faded jeans and gray T-shirt. The vine tattoos winding around Octavia's forearms stood out against her dark skin. She sensed Vivian's gaze lingering on her tattoos. *Does she like them? Hate them? I should have put on a long-sleeve shirt. What the hell? Why do I care what she thinks of me?* She clasped her hands behind her back and squared her shoulders, setting her feet wide. Her gaze was drawn to the thin gold chain with a tiny gold Magen David centered in the hollow of Vivian's throat. *Lyceum? It can't be. How the hell could she be here?*

Bridget spoke first. "We accept your offer."

Vivian sat back from the desk. "You're both sure?"

"Yes." Octavia pushed the wisp of hair that had worked loose from her braid out of her eyes. "We've read through the specifics."

Vivian lifted her chin, her gaze steady. "I have the contracts here. They're for six months. That should be enough time for all of us to decide if the arrangement is acceptable." She lifted an elegant black fountain pen from the desk and uncapped it. With a flowing hand she signed her name to each document. She held the pen out, and Octavia walked to the desk. Her fingers brushed against Vivian's as she took the pen, and a tingle of desire worked its way to her core. Octavia signed her name on the contract. *Damn. Get it together. This is trouble. So much trouble.* When she was finished, she laid the pen on the desk and glanced up into Vivian's eyes. The tingle turned into a strong wave of heat. Looking away from Vivian, she stepped back.

Vivian picked up the pen and held it out for Bridget. With slow steps Bridget walked to the desk, her focus fixed on Vivian's face. Octavia noted the small tremor that shook her hand as she took the pen from Vivian and the way Bridget lowered her gaze when Vivian looked at her. After signing her name, Bridget held the pen out with both hands, palms up, an offering. Vivian's lips curved into a smile as she took the pen from Bridget's uplifted hands.

She didn't smile at me. What the hell is wrong with me? So what? Get it together. She's our employer. Nothing more. Damn, she gets to me. And to Bridget.

OCTAVIA CUPPED THE back of Bridget's neck and pulled her in for a kiss. She nipped her lower lip, and Bridget moaned against her mouth. Sliding her hand down, Octavia palmed Bridget's breast, enjoying the way her nipple hardened under her hand. Bridget relaxed under her grip, and Octavia shifted her weight, pushing her back on the bed. Pressing her down, she sank into the softness of her body. She drew back and looked into Bridget's face. "Hands over your head. Keep them there."

Bridget gripped the rails of the brass bedstead. Using her knee Octavia pushed Bridget's thighs apart and lowered herself to grind against Bridget, rolling her hips. A soft groan from Bridget made her want to hear more. She pushed her hands under her skirt and hooked her fingers in her underwear to draw them down Bridget's legs. She tossed them to the floor. A hint of Bridget's honeysuckle perfume filled her nostrils, and she inhaled the soft innocent scent, a sharp contrast to the wanton expression on Bridget's face. Octavia lowered her head and took Bridget in her mouth. Her clit hardened under her tongue, and Octavia sucked hard and lashed her tongue over Bridget's clit, taking her up hard and fast to the edge. She held back, waiting for the desperate sounds of Bridget's need to caress her ears.

Bridget thrashed on the bed. "Mercy, Ma'am. Please. I can't. I'm going to come."

Octavia raised her mouth. "Yes, you are. When I want you to."

Bridget squirmed, and Octavia held her down and set to work, ruthless, hungry. Her need to have Bridget come under her ratcheted up the longer she feasted.

Bridget moaned. "Please, Ma'am. Please let me come."

Octavia lifted her mouth. "Not until you tell me what you thought when you took the pen from Vivian." She lowered her head and went back to work, giving Bridget enough to keep her on the edge but not enough to come.

Shrill wails shook Bridget's chest. "Nothing. Please. Let me come for you."

Octavia brought her hand up and slipped three fingers deep, teasing them over the spot that made Bridget shudder and shake.

"Oh. Oh, please, Ma'am. Oh. Please. I can't. I need."

"Liar. Tell the truth or you don't come." She kept her motions steady and held Bridget still with the other hand, preventing her from obtaining what she needed. "I saw you tremble, the way you held the pen out, like an offering. I know you. Tell me the truth."

"Aah. I wanted to kneel. To kiss her feet. To let her do. This. To serve her—oh Ma'am, please let me come. Please." The last "please" came out like a scream, and wetness surged between Octavia's thighs. Her clit was thick and hard.

"No."

"Please, Ma'am. Pleasepleaseplease." Bridget struggled, trying to arch up to meet Octavia's slow thrusts.

"Look at me."

Bridget opened her eyes and held Octavia's gaze.

"No secrets. No hiding from me. Own what you are. Secrets kill everything good."

"Yes, Ma'am." Tears spilled down her cheeks. "Sorry, Ma'am." Her voice was soft, and Octavia's heart ached at the misery in her tone.

"Truth. Always." Octavia dropped a kiss on Bridget's thigh as she pushed away the guilt that nipped at her.

"Yes, Ma'am."

"Now. Give me what's mine. Come for me." Octavia pressed hard and deep, her thrusts pushing Bridget over as she screamed, and liquid silk flowed over Octavia's fingers.

Octavia slowed her strokes, letting Bridget cool down for a moment before driving her back up and over again. Her soft groans and whimpers made Octavia shiver, and she did it twice more to hear Bridget beg for mercy.

"That's it, love. All of it. All of you belongs to me. Every drop of sweetness that flows from you." She licked and suckled her clit, gorging on the sweet salty taste between Bridget's legs. Her own clit ached for Bridget's attention.

Octavia pulled her hand away and left the bed. Standing in Bridget's line of sight, she stripped. Bridget's eyes were glazed. Octavia poured her a glass of water. She sat on the edge of the bed and helped her drink, holding her close, letting her recover. Bridget rested her head on Octavia's shoulder. *She wants to serve Vivian. Will she be able to resist? Will I? Let it go. She's mine.*

Bridget smoothed her hand over Octavia's stomach and down through the tight curls covering her clit. "Please, Ma'am, may I please you?"

Octavia wrapped her fingers in Bridget's hair and arched her neck back to look into her eyes. *She wants forgiveness. Wants to prove to me she's mine.* She tugged hard on Bridget's hair before she kissed her and nipped her lower lip. A punishment. A penance. The salty copper taste of her blood welled up and flavored their kiss, filling Octavia with need. With bruising pressure, she plundered her mouth, taking what she wanted, what she needed, before she forced Bridget's head lower.

"Do you think you've earned it?" She gripped her hair and held her back, preventing her from reaching her clit, treasuring the sensation of Bridget straining to get her mouth on her body.

"Please, Ma'am. Please let me taste you. Truth always. Please. I'll be good. Let me please you. Please." The desperate edge in her voice made Octavia close her eyes against the rush of desire that flooded her. She released Bridget and shoved her back on the bed. Planting her knees on either side of her head, she lowered herself onto Bridget's mouth.

The first touch of her tongue on her aching clit wrenched a deep groan from Octavia. Bridget's tongue swirled in soft circles before she thrust it deep. She returned her attentions to Octavia's clit. *So good. More. Yes. Like that. Mine.* She reached down and pinched Bridget's ear. "More. Fuck me. Slow."

Bridget brought her hand up and pushed deep, thrusting her fingers hard.

Octavia rocked her hips, craving her touch. "Yes. Ah there. There. More."

Bridget moaned low in her throat. She sucked hard and Octavia came, the rush of her come covering Bridget's face. She slowed her movements and licked Octavia clean with soft sounds of satisfaction. *Mine. So sweet. So good. Mine.*

"DO YOU NEED more time?" Bridget held tight to Octavia's hand.

Octavia looked around the barn. Her barn. The two mares and four geldings she had cared for every day the last eight years were each in their stalls. Heads lowered, they were all busy with their evening feed. She had spent the afternoon telling Rebecca everything she could think of about each of them. All their quirks, health needs, and little secrets about them that made managing them easier. Rebecca had been patient, taken notes, and worked hard to reassure Octavia the horses were in good hands.

"No." She huffed out a breath and turned away from the barn. "I'm ready. I take it you've said your goodbyes to Cook." She smiled at Bridget, desperate to stave off the sadness settling in her soul.

Bridget snorted. "She didn't even bother to acknowledge me when I said goodbye."

Octavia brought their hands up and kissed the back of Bridget's hand. "She's an ass."

They walked away from the barn, and Octavia fought the urge to look back, knowing if she did the tears she had managed to swallow would overflow.

Chapter Three

THE LINE THROUGH passport control was long, and Octavia remembered why she had not left Scotland in the last ten years. She rested her hand in the small of Bridget's back as they waited. "You okay, love?"

Bridget fidgeted with her passport. "Yes. I hate this. Dealing with people in uniforms."

An alarm sounded, and glass doors closed off both sides of the passport control booth. Octavia groaned. "Fuck." She looked around, as she considered waiting or trying to merge with another line. Bridget trembled, and Octavia rubbed her back. "It's all right. We aren't in a hurry. Most of the time these things are resolved pretty quickly."

Bridget's mouth was set in a thin line. "I always pick the wrong queue."

"I picked this time. Don't worry."

They watched as two more border agents arrived and escorted the young man away from the booth. The light over their line turned green, and people started moving forward once more.

Octavia patted Bridget's hip. "See? We're all set. Remember what to say?"

"We're here on holiday. Staying in Milan."

"Right."

The passport agent, a thick-set woman with her hair pulled into a tight bun, waved them forward. Octavia handed over her passport. The woman took it and swiped it through the machine in front of her. She frowned as she handed it back. "Why are you traveling to Italy?'

"I'm on holiday."

The woman tipped her chin at Octavia. "For how long?"

"A month."

The woman raked her eyes over her. "Alone?"

"No, with my friend." Octavia pointed to Bridget. The woman shrugged and pressed her stamp to the passport. She handed the passport back to Octavia and waved her through.

Octavia waited for Bridget on the other side of the glass booths. They joined the crowd at baggage claim and collected their bags. Two oversize suitcases and two carry-on bags held all they owned between them. *Not much to show for ten years of work. Better money in the bank than stuff to move.*

The sidewalk was crowded with travelers negotiating taxies and looking for hired cars. A driver held up a sign with "Vargas/Murray" written on it. Bridget pointed it out to Octavia. "That's us."

They pulled their suitcases over to the man. Octavia pointed to the sign and to the two of them. "*Buongiorno.*"

"*Buongiorno.* Ms. Murray? Ms. Vargas?

"*Si. Sei il nostro pilota?*" Octavia answered for them.

"*Si.*" He smiled at them, confirming that he was their driver. "Miss Abiola looks forward to seeing you. This way."

He led the way across the parking lot to a long black car.

Oh no. Fuck. Why is it always black cars? Why can't they be white? Or blue. Fuck. Get it together. She clenched her hands into fists.

The driver opened the door and went to load their bags. Bridget entered first. Octavia stood on the curb. She rubbed the back of her neck. *You can do this. Take a breath.*

Bridget leaned forward in her seat and looked up at Octavia. "Coming?"

"Yes. Watching the bags."

The driver finished loading the bags. He walked back to the door and gestured for Octavia to get in the car. Bridget frowned at her. Octavia chewed her lip. *Now. Get in now. You're safe. She must think I'm nuts. Maybe I am.* She slid into the seat, and the driver shut the door.

Bridget took her hand. "I thought I was a nervous traveler. Regretting our decision?"

Octavia squeezed her hand. "No. This is the right thing to do. I— I don't like limos." *Black cars. Death cars. The car ride you never come back from.*

Bridget pushed Octavia's hair back from her shoulder. She leaned in and kissed her cheek. "I'm glad we're here." She slid closer on the seat and pressed the length of her thigh against Octavia's leg. "I can't wait to get you alone." Bringing her lips close to Octavia's ear, she whispered, "Ma'am."

Octavia rested her hand on Bridget's knee and squeezed. "That's my girl. Distraction is wonderful." She lifted her hand and brought her knuckles up and under Bridget's chin. She tipped her head back and kissed her. She closed her eyes. Bridget's nearness and touch soothed her.

THE CAR PULLED down a long, unpaved drive up to a white house. On the hills surrounding the house, neat rows of grapevines were terraced, their dark green leaves contrasting with the brick red soil. In the distance, the Alps that bordered the valley were capped in white above their gray-green sides. Bridget shifted away from her, and the absence of the press of her body made Octavia regret not taking advantage of the long ride and Bridget's willingness. She opened the door while the driver unloaded their bags. The air was warm and held the smell of growing things, and over it all hung the odor of a stable not tended to. Octavia scanned the area, looking for the barn. A low-roofed gabled stable was set back about two hundred meters from the house. *Who the fuck let it get so bad I'm smelling it from here?* The rank odor had Octavia fighting the urge to get back in the car as she imagined what the state the barn would be in and the amount of work it was going to take to put right.

Bridget's hand on her arm interrupted her thoughts. "What is that smell?"

"Bad management."

Bridget waved her hand in front of her face. "Ugh. I hope it's not like this inside."

"No. I keep the windows closed on that side of the house." The icy tone in Vivian's voice let Octavia know she had heard their comments. She turned as Vivian handed the driver a wad of bills. He nodded, speaking in rapid Italian. He got back in the car and drove off slowly, kicking up a small cloud of dust.

Vivian had on white loose pants and a soft coral-colored blouse. Her hair was covered by a wide headband, the fine angles of her face on display. She raised her chin and raked her gaze over them. Octavia squirmed under her scrutiny. *Is it her?*

"Bring your bags. I will show you to your quarters." Vivian walked to the house, not concerning herself with whether they followed.

She met us herself? No staff to take care of this? Why no housekeeper?

Bridget sighed as she watched Vivian walk away from them. Octavia raised an eyebrow at her. "You can't help it, can you?"

Bridget quirked her mouth at Octavia. "Does it matter where I get my appetite as long as I eat at home?"

Octavia laughed and picked up her carry-on. She loaded it on top of her roller bag. "No. I guess it doesn't, love."

They dragged their suitcases over the rough flagstones, following the path Vivian had taken into the house. Two wide six-panel wood doors were open, and they rolled their bags into the foyer. The wheels of the luggage were loud on the tile floor. They closed the doors behind them, shutting out the light of the day.

The interior of the house was dark after the bright sunlight of midday. Modestly elegant, the foyer was cool in contrast to the heat of the drive. Hallways split off from the large entryway. Built in the style of a Roman villa, the house was constructed around an open courtyard filled with a lush garden, and bright blooms were visible through floor-to-ceiling windows. The sound of a fountain and the hum of insects filtered through the windows that let in the light from the atrium.

Vivian waited for them, her arms crossed. Octavia studied her from under her lashes.

Vivian's face betrayed nothing as she uncrossed her long arms and pointed down the hall to the left. "This is the way to the kitchen and the dining room. The house is built in a square surrounding the courtyard, so you can't get lost." She led them to a thick door patterned after the style of the foyer doors. "This is your suite, a sitting room and a bedroom." She glanced between them. "There is a connecting door, and the bathroom is between them. There's a guest house closer to the stable that was occupied by the last stable manager, but I thought you both would prefer this arrangement."

"If they kept it like they kept the barn…"

"This is fantastic, very generous." Bridget spoke over Octavia's words. "Thank you."

Octavia frowned at Bridget and blew out a breath.

Vivian looked away from Octavia and inclined her head at Bridget. "You're welcome. I'll leave you here to settle in. My office is two doors past the kitchen. Meet me there at three, and we will go over my expectations."

She left them, and Bridget opened the door. The walls were white like the rest of the house, the accents a pale green. A king-size bed with a brass headboard and matching footrail took up most of the room, and a small walnut wood armoire and matching chest of drawers were set against the wall. A heavy ornate chair with thick legs and curving armrests filled the far corner. Bridget rolled her bag to the middle of the room, and Octavia rested her bag next to it. She opened another door. It led to a bath larger than her room at Rowan House. Gold fixtures gleamed against custom tile.

Octavia whistled. "If this is for the help, imagine what her bath looks like."

She opened the door to the connecting room. A large heavy-frame sofa, decorated in a rich brocade, and two leather-covered wingback chairs surrounded a butler's table. Two wide bookshelves covered one wall. Octavia walked over to the shelves and turned her head to read the titles. The first shelf held cookbooks, modern and vintage. The second held books on equine science, stable management, horticulture and gardening. Octavia ran her fingers along the spines. She bent to peer at the oversize books on the bottom shelf and read the titles. *Sudan: Vivian Abiola. Conflict: Vivian Abiola. Collateral Damage: Vivian Abiola. Portraits: Vivian Abiola. Leather and Lace: Vivian Abiola.*

Photographer. She's a photographer.

"Check this out." She pulled the last book off the lowest shelf and held it out to Bridget.

Bridget took the book and read the title. "*Obsession: Vivian Abiola.*" She flipped it open. She stared at the page before she turned the book so Octavia could see the image. In the black-and-white photograph, a shirtless woman dressed in jodhpurs and boots leaned over another woman bound to a chair, their lips almost touching. Backlit, the bound woman's face was in shadow. The energy between the women was palpable. Bridget turned the book back to herself and flipped through more pages. She stopped and studied a photograph. She traced her finger over the image, her face a bright red, and chewed her lower lip.

Photographer. Lyceum. Yearbook photographer. She didn't look like that then. Bloody hell. Does she know? Does she recognize me? Fuck. "Oh. Hell."

Bridget looked up from the book and frowned. "What?"

"Uhm. I thought I knew her. It must be because I've seen her in work in magazines."

"Truth." Bridget narrowed her eyes. "'That's what you said to me."

Octavia looked down and away. *Truth. Unless it's dangerous. Unless it could kill you.* "I think I know her from outside Rowan House. I don't know where." *Liar. She can't know. Does Vivian know it's me? Fuck.* "Does looking at her photographs get you hot?" Octavia pinned Bridget with her gaze.

"No." Bridget flipped the book closed and bent over to replace it on the bookshelf.

"Liar." Octavia closed the distance between them. Grabbing Bridget's hips, she ground against her ass. Dropping the book to the floor, Bridget straightened and leaned back against Octavia. The book fell open to a photo of a woman wearing a white blindfold and bound with green satin ribbons to a Saint Andrew's cross. Her face was beatific, trust and surrender etched on her features. Octavia's clit responded, and wetness flooded her briefs.

She wrapped her arms around Bridget, pinning her arms to her sides. With a deep groan, Bridget tipped her head back, offering herself to Octavia. Octavia brushed her lips over Bridget's mouth and then moved lower and scattered sharp nips and kisses under her ear and along her neck. She held her tighter and moved her hands up and cupped Bridget's breasts and teased her nipples, pinching and rolling them between her finger and thumb over her shirt. Bridget shifted her feet, spreading them wide. Octavia swept her hand down and unbuttoned Bridget's pants. A soft moan of encouragement sent waves of want through Octavia, and her clit ached. She moved her hand lower and pushed past the waistband of Bridget's silk panties. *So wet. So much. Give it to me.* Dipping her fingers in, she paused to enjoy the sensation of Bridget's excitement and wet heat before she dragged the slickness between her legs up and over her clit. Bridget groaned and rocked her hips against Octavia's hand. Her jeans slid down to her knees, trapping her legs. *Such sweet surrender. So beautiful. Mine.*

"Truth. Those pictures made you hot. Didn't they, naughty girl? Tell me." Octavia pulled her hand from Bridget's panties. She held her fingers up. Bridget's desire glistened. "See how wet you are." She brought her fingers to Bridget's mouth. She opened to her and sucked Octavia's fingers deep. Need flowed from Octavia as she watched Bridget's mouth work her fingers. She pulled them free and lowered her hand to finger Bridget's clit.

Octavia moved her hand up and gripped Bridget's throat, an informal collar of hard flesh and bone. Bridget squirmed in her arms, the feigned struggle sending waves of want crashing through Octavia.

"Yes. Ma'am. Please, Ma'am. Please let me come. For you. You, Ma'am. Yours." Bridget's breath was rough, and she rocked her hips, seeking what she wanted.

"Who do you belong to?" Octavia ground against Bridget's ass.

"You, Ma'am."

Octavia tightened her fingers around Bridget's neck enough to send Bridget over the edge. "Come for me then. Show me."

Bridget stilled and shook as she came quietly in Octavia's arms, her core tightening around Octavia's fingers. *More. I want more. Need more. Need to hear her. Scream for me. Let me hear you.* Octavia thrust her fingers deep and fucked her hard and fast, bringing Bridget off, driving her up and over, reveling in her scream as she came again.

Panting, Bridget sagged against her. "Mercy, Ma'am."

Octavia relaxed her grip on Bridget's throat and pulled her hand from between Bridget's legs before she turned her in her arms. She held her close and kissed her, drinking in her surrender. She tugged Bridget's pants up and refastened them before she walked them over to the sofa. Octavia sat and pulled Bridget into her lap. She stroked her hair, waiting for her breathing to return to normal.

A soft sigh escaped Bridget. "I'm a terrible liar."

"True. But it's a joy making you tell me the truth."

"Let me pleasure you, Ma'am. Please. May I? I've wanted to since the airport. Please."

Octavia looked at the wall clock. *Just enough time.* She shifted Bridget to the floor and sat back on the couch. She toed off her shoes. Bridget sat on her heels, her hands resting on the seat cushion on either side of Octavia's legs. She watched Bridget's face as she unbuckled her belt before she opened the buttons of her jeans. She slid them off and added her briefs to the pile. Bridget's gaze was fixed between Octavia's legs. *She wants. So much. She wants me. Hungry for me.*

She moved to the edge of the cushion. Remembering her training, Bridget waited for permission.

Cupping the back of her head, Octavia pushed it between her legs. "Lick me." She closed her eyes as Bridget took her in her mouth, and the world ceased to exist. Desire built and spun out as her pleasure showered over Bridget's face and chin.

VIVIAN'S OFFICE WAS full of light and plants. A simple teak desk held an open laptop. Matching bookshelves lined the walls. Vivian sat behind her desk. Two chairs stood facing it.

"Sit, please." She gestured to the two chairs in front of the desk. "Would you like something to drink? Water? Wine?"

"Water would be wonderful."

Vivian poured them each of them a glass of water from the pitcher on the credenza behind her desk.

After taking a sip, Octavia sat back in her chair.

Vivian cocked her hand to the side, her gaze fixed on Octavia's face. "I will be honest. I expect and demand the same from both of you."

Here it comes. She's going to say she knows who I am. Fuck. Bridget's going to be angry I didn't tell her. Fuck. Sweat tickled between Octavia's shoulder blades. *What am I going to do?*

Vivian shifted her gaze to Bridget. "There have been incidents since I spoke with you on Skye. I want you to be aware, and if you change your mind about working here, I'll not hold you to your contracts."

Octavia relaxed in her chair and took another sip of her water. *She doesn't recognize me. Doesn't remember.*

"What kind of incidents?" Bridget placed her water on the floor beside her chair. She knotted her hands in her lap.

"Some equipment was damaged. The guesthouse was vandalized. A fire was set in a storage building."

"Fire?" Bridget moved to the edge of her chair. Octavia shifted closer to Bridget. She reached over and took her hand.

"It was contained, but we had enough damage I won't have much of this year's crop to sell to my neighbor."

"Where are the other staff? When do we meet them?" Octavia squeezed Bridget's hand.

"I dismissed them all after it was clear the fire was not an accident."

"And the guesthouse vandalism?"

"It occurred before the fire. The police thought it was a random act, but I don't believe it."

"Why?"

Vivian brought her amber-colored gaze to Octavia's eyes. "Sometimes the past intrudes on the present. I haven't always run a vineyard."

She knows. Fuck. She knows. She's not saying anything. What the fuck? Change the subject. Octavia studied Vivian's expression. "We noticed your books in our room. "

Vivian looked down and away from Octavia's eyes and shifted in her seat.

"Do you still work as a photojournalist?"

"No. After..." She glanced at her hands before she brought her gaze back to Octavia's face. "Everyone with a phone is a photojournalist now. I do portraits. Private events. I work when, and if I choose."

Pain. Sadness. So much sadness. Let it go. Octavia wanted to cross the room and take away the sadness in her eyes, wanted to kiss her perfect mouth until she was breathless. *What is the story there? Why so much pain?*

Bridget made a soft sound, breaking the moment. "What time would you like your breakfast...? Um, what should we call you?"

"Vivian is fine. I'm not as—" She focused her gaze on Bridget's face, and Octavia's stomach tightened with desire watching the exchange between them. "—formal as Martha, although we are alike in other ways."

Bridget's face flushed. "Could I see the kitchen, please? Vivian."

How long? How long will it be before she offers herself to her? Will I be there? I want to be there. Octavia stood up. "I think I can find the barn, if you two don't need me."

"Need and want are two different things." Vivian raised her gaze to Octavia's face, a half smile playing over her lips. "Come to the kitchen with us, and then I will accompany you to the barn while Bridget prepares dinner."

Power and control flowed from Vivian like water over smooth rocks, washing way any doubts Octavia might have had about what they had signed up for, leaving no uncertainty who was in charge. *Martha was a rushing battering wave of power, a flash flood sweeping me away in an instant. Vivian's power is quiet, a relentless stream, the kind that can wear away huge canyons. Fuck, I'm as intrigued as Bridget.*

Vivian stood and walked to the door. Bridget let go of Octavia's hand and followed in her wake. Octavia picked up her glass and Bridget's to place them on the credenza. Next to the tray holding the water pitcher and glasses was their boarding-school yearbook. The black cover with "The Lyceum" in gold print labeled with the year she had graduated tempted her. Octavia placed their glasses on the tray before she picked up the yearbook. She flipped through the pages until she found the one with Vivian's senior photo. A thin dark-skinned girl with oversize glasses stared back at her, a lone brown face among rows of white ones. She flipped to her own senior photo, as alone in her brownness on the page. She traced her finger over her real name. Her father's name. A name she had given up long ago. Her heart ached when she remembered how proud her father had been. Honor roll. Equestrian team captain. She closed the book before the tears started and carefully placed it back where it had been on the credenza.

HERBS GREW IN small pots on the windowsill, and the smell of fresh basil filled the kitchen. An eight-burner Viking stove dominated the wall opposite the entry. Bridget turned in a slow circle, her mouth open. "This is magnificent. Did you design this?" She ran her fingers over the granite countertops.

"Yes." Vivian rested her hand on the maple work island. She pulled open a drawer. "The knives are here. If you find you need any equipment, purchase it." She pointed to a door. "The pantry and dry storage is there." She swept her hand in an encompassing gesture. "This is your space. Rearrange as you see fit."

Bridget flushed. "Thank you." She smiled at Vivian. "What time would you like your breakfast?"

"I like to have a light breakfast. Pastry, fruit, and coffee is adequate." Vivian pursed her lips. "I don't keep regular hours. I'll let you know when I want something. I don't like celery but eat almost anything else. If I have guests, we can plan the menu together. I expect that you are able to manage purchases and a budget?"

"Yes. I did all the procurement for Rowan House."

"I'll want you to manage the household as well as my calendar."

Octavia leaned against the stainless-steel walk-in refrigerator, the metal cool through her shirt. She watched Bridget and Vivian. They stood close to each other, heads together as they discussed the intricate details of farm-to-table cooking with enthusiasm. In her element, Bridget met Vivian's gaze, her confidence and intensity matching Vivian's. They were standing by the window, and Vivian pulled a leaf from the basil and held it out for Bridget. She leaned in to smell the herb, her gaze fixed on Vivian's face.

"Mmm. This is perfect. I love working with fresh herbs. Would you like some hand-made pasta with a basil pesto for dinner?" She glanced at the large clock on the wall. "I have time to make it. Please. Let me make it for you."

The earnest desire in Bridget's voice sent a wave of want through Octavia. *Does Vivian hear how much Bridget wants to please her? Does she care?* Octavia folded her arms and waited for Vivian's response, not wanting to disrupt the heat that flowed between them. *Say yes, Vivian. Please give her want she wants. Let her serve you.* Bridget needed to serve as much as she needed air. Octavia tilted her head and studied the women. She imagined Bridget on her knees next to her, their heads bowed, together, serving Vivian. Her gut tightened with desire, and she shifted her position, trying to ease the ache and pressure between her legs.

"Yes. It sounds divine. Eight? I have some work to do before then." Her tone was cool, a sharp contrast to the passion in Bridget's voice. Vivian turned away from Bridget and focused her gaze on Octavia. "And now the stable."

Chapter Four

THE STABLE WAS about two hundred meters from the house. Far enough Octavia was comfortable Bridget would not overhear their conversation on their walk. The sun was setting. The guest house threw long shadows on the path. The silence between them stretched thin.

"It's a long way from Buenos Aires to Skye." Vivian's voice was quiet, and she kept her head down as she walked. "Anna."

"I might say the same of Abuja." Octavia tucked her hands in her pockets. "Did you recognize me at Rowan House, or did Martha tell you?"

"I recognized you." Vivian stopped walking and turned to face Octavia. "Did you know it was me?"

"I wasn't sure. I wondered when I saw your Magen David. Bridget doesn't know." Octavia held her gaze. "I want to keep it that way."

"I read about your father. I wrote. My letters came back unopened." Vivian reached out and rested her hand on Octavia's arm. "I'm so sorry. I can't imagine how hard it was for all of you. The article didn't mention your mother. Is she...?"

Octavia looked down at Vivian's hand on her arm. "Mama died a few years ago." Her chest was tight. She swallowed on a dry throat. "My uncle got us out of the country the day after they took my father. We changed our names."

"Your father's the reason I became a photojournalist." She tightened her grip on Octavia's arm. "You're safe here. I'll keep your secret."

"What's your connection to Martha?" A tiny flare of jealousy burned in her heart.

"Do you know of the Onyx? Madame Givernay? We met at one of Madame's occasions."

The Onyx. Why did I ask? Of course they met there. Martha's annual trips to the Onyx without Octavia had been a sore point in their relationship. "That's hell of a way to meet." *Damn, she's more a Mistress than I thought. Maybe Martha gave over to her. Maybe she couldn't be that way with me because she had Vivian.* She thought back to what Martha had said when she'd introduced them to Vivian. *One of her oldest friends, my ass. I bet they were lovers. Fuck.* She shoved her hands in the back pockets of her jeans to stop them from trembling. *Get it together. Because they were there at the same time doesn't mean anything.*

Vivian smiled. "And you? How did you come to belong to her?"

"I was working as a groom on the Grand Prix dressage circuit. At the Hartpury Festival, she followed me to my trailer. Taught me more about my desires in thirty minutes than I had learned in thirty years."

"But not everything." Vivian raised an eyebrow. "Else you'd still be with her."

Octavia pressed her lips together. "No." She reached up and touched the bare place on her neck where her collar had been. "Not everything."

Vivian's gaze was steady as she returned Octavia's eye contact. *She gets it. Gets it wasn't anyone's fault. Gets me. Those eyes. I want to lose myself in her eyes. See her over me. See her under me. Damn it. What am I going to do?*

Vivian looked away and swept her arm in a broad arc. "All of this is mine. I sell my crops to my neighbor, there." She pointed to the green tile roof barely visible against the backdrop of the maze of grapevines. "There are well-maintained trails between our farms. Good riding in the morning. Hot as hell in the afternoon this time of year." She started walking toward the barn again, and Octavia followed, taking a few quick steps to catch up.

EIGHT STALLS LINED each side of the wide center aisle in the barn. The rank smell that had greeted them had dissipated as the heat of the day gave way to the cool of the early evening. Octavia walked the center aisle, making a mental list of where to start. This place had been neglected and was a far cry from the neat and tidy barn she kept at Rowan House. The rear door opened out on to a fenced pasture. Three horses stood close to each other in the shade of the lone tree in the field. A small gray donkey picked up his head and looked in their direction.

"Is that all of them? This is a lot of mess of for three horses and a donkey."

"I had all the stalls filled until the fire. I asked my boarder to make other arrangements. I didn't want to be responsible for her horses. There was a woman who mucked for me, but she found another job. I've tried to keep up the barn, but with my travel schedule it's been hard, and the temporary workers I hire do the minimum."

Octavia chewed her lip. The despair in Vivian's voice was unsettling. The knowledge she was comfortable enough with Octavia to drop her Mistress role and appear weak was even more unsettling.

"So how did you come to own a vineyard? I never figured you for a farmer."

Vivian laughed. "I'm not. This was one of my father's ideas. He bought it. He and my mother lived here exactly one season. He gave it to me five years ago, along with a big lecture about not giving him grandchildren. We built the barn and added the indoor ring."

We who? Ask. Don't ask. Octavia cocked her head to the side. "I'm not getting the connection. What does owning a vineyard have to do with having children?"

"I don't get it either. You know how dramatic he can be."

"Remember the time he called the head of the school, convinced you were dead because you didn't answer the phone when he called?"

Vivian snorted. "I had forgotten that."

A bray interrupted their conversation as the donkey sounded his displeasure. Ears back, he glared at Octavia and brayed again.

"Easy boy. I'm not going to hurt anyone." Octavia turned to face Vivian. "Trouble with dogs?"

"Not since I bought the donkey." She opened the gate, and the donkey charged toward Octavia.

"Hey." Octavia climbed up to the top of the fence and sat on the rail to get away from the furious animal. "He's like Cujo in a donkey suit."

Vivian laughed again, and Octavia remembered why she had worked at being the class clown to make her laugh in high school.

"Victor. Halt!" The donkey shook his head and brayed at Octavia again. He glared up at her and turned his hindquarters to her. He kicked the fence where Octavia sat. Vivian clapped her hands and he stopped. With a huff he turned to her. "*Komm doch zu mir.*" Obeying her call to come to her, he trotted over and leaned his head against her leg. She scratched between his ears. "We bottle-fed him. He's quite sweet once he knows you." A wistfulness swept over Vivian's face and was gone so quickly Octavia wondered if she had imagined it.

We again. Ask. Don't ask. She would say if she wanted to. She said she lived alone. Octavia climbed down off the top rail, resting her hand on the fence. She kept the donkey in her line of sight in case he decided to come after her again. She watched Vivian rub the donkey's ears. "Does he only listen to German? Can't you teach him Italian? Or Spanish? My German is the worst."

"Only German. I haven't had the need to teach him anything else."

Octavia rested her hands on her hips. "I guess I'm going to have to brush up on my German."

In high school, they had bonded over the lack of heat and spices in the dining hall food. Images of them huddled in the back of assemblies speaking to each other in Spanish and making each other laugh filled her memories. Not a secret language, but at their Swiss boarding school it might as well have been. Vivian had been the only person to understand how much Octavia missed home. They had spent more than one holiday together at the mostly empty school, the trip home too far for short breaks, their brown skin making them not particularly welcome at most of their schoolmates' homes.

Octavia walked over and rubbed the donkey's back. He settled under their hands.

"See, Victor, *sie ist ein Freundin*, she's a friend."

The donkey shot Octavia a wary glare. They stood petting the donkey between them. Octavia watched Vivian's face, noting the fine lines at the corners of her eyes. The years they had spent apart seemed so long, yet the intimacy between them was as strong as it had been in their boarding school. So far from their families, alone in their otherness, they had survived the wrenching loneliness with each other.

Too fearful of rejection and of being dismissed from school to act on her desires, all Octavia wanted to do now was to reach out and touch Vivian, to hug her body close, to feel the shape of her in her arms, to make Vivian forget the lingering sadness hovering beneath her smile. The shy girl with glasses had grown into a lovely powerful woman, but in this moment, she reminded Octavia of the girl she had waited for outside the library and the dining hall and arranged her class schedule just to be near. So many memories. She blinked away her melancholy over the years lost between them.

"Have you been bringing them in at night, or do you let them stay in the field?"

"We've had such good weather I've let them stay out. I don't worry about them with Victor around."

Hearing his name, the donkey rubbed his head hard against Vivian, knocking her off-balance. Octavia reached out and caught her arm to keep her from falling. Her skin was warm under her fingertips. The donkey pushed between them on his way back to the field. Octavia held on to Vivian's arm. Then they were standing so close the heat from their bodies blended into one.

Octavia brought her gaze to Vivian's amber eyes. Heat flared between them and threatened to turn into a bright flame. Octavia brought her hand up and clasped Vivian's shoulder and pulled her full against her. Everywhere their bodies touched she ached with need. Vivian relaxed against Octavia's body, her surrender making Octavia's breath catch in her throat. A moment. A lifetime. Memories of one desperate encounter in a dorm room fumbling in the dark, finding each other the night before graduation, bubbled up, sending a wave of want through Octavia.

Vivian shifted her hips and pulled back. She placed her hand on Octavia's chest, her fingers spread wide. "Bridget will be missing us." The resignation in her voice, and the way her eyes shuttered, doused the spark between them.

Octavia dropped her hands to her side and stepped back. *Bridget. Damn, I got so caught up I didn't even think of Bridget. Fuck. What Vivian must think of me. Damn it, what is wrong with me?* "Right. She will." She turned away from Vivian and closed the gate. "Why don't you go ahead? I want to poke around a bit. Make a plan for tomorrow."

Vivian opened her mouth as if she wanted to say something before she pressed her lips together and nodded her agreement. She turned away from Octavia, her steps quick. Octavia stood there and watched her walk away. *What the hell am I going to do about Vivian? If she wanted me, she would have kissed me. This is trouble. I'm in so much trouble. Bridget. Do I tell her? She'll be pissed I didn't tell her before. She's gonna be pissed anytime I tell her. Damn it, I should've told her before. Fuck, now what do I do?* She kicked a loose stone along the path back to the house, turning her thoughts over in her head, finding no answer.

"I CAN'T BELIEVE you brought it with you." Bridget rolled over onto her stomach. She pillowed her hands and rested her chin on them. Her broad shoulders, sculpted forearms, and thick hips, leading to a perfectly shaped ass, made Octavia's mouth water.

So much I want to do to her. So much I want to have with her. "As much time as I've spent wearing this strap-on, my name should be engraved on the harness." Octavia tilted her head to get a better view and memorize every inch of Bridget's body.

"I should be jealous but I appreciate the results of all the practice." She shot Octavia a wicked grin.

So beautiful. And mine. I could come looking at her body and stroking this thing. Octavia rubbed the strap-on, covering it in lube and watching the expression on Bridget's face. "Mmm, I like the way you look at me in this. Like you've never seen one before and you can't take your eyes off it. What do you want, my love?"

She walked to the edge of the bed and ran her hand over Bridget's back. She trailed her fingers along Bridget's spine, stopping at the dimple over her ass. Bridget trembled under her hand. Octavia mounted the bed and sat between her legs. She dipped her fingers between Bridget's legs and gathered the evidence of her desire. She smeared it over her clit, drawing a deeper moan from Bridget.

"On your elbows, raise your ass for me." Bridget complied, resting her forehead and forearms on the mattress. Her obedience ratcheted up Octavia's desire, her clit throbbed against the base of the phallus. Octavia pushed two fingers in slowly and pressed down, rubbing the spot that made Bridget sigh and arch her back in a silent plea for more. "What do you want, love? You want me to fuck you?"

She pulled back slowly before she pushed deep, drawing a loud moan from her. A shudder shook Bridget's body and sent a bolt of desire straight to Octavia's clit.

"Please, Ma'am. Please fuck me. Please."

Octavia pulled her hand free and brought the head of the strap-on up, stopping short of entering her. Desire coated Bridget's thighs, and Octavia traced a finger along her crease. "I don't think you mean it." She pushed forward, rubbing the slick phallus against Bridget's clit. She pulled back and thrust forward slowly, edging her with the thick shaft against her clit.

"Oh. Please. Please, Ma'am. Fuck me. Please." Bridget thrust her hips back. "Please."

Octavia wrapped her hand in her hair and pulled her head up. "Look at me." Their gazes met in the mirror Octavia had moved so it reflected the bed. Bridget flushed, her freckles lost in the redness of her skin. "Ask me again. Look at me. Ask me for what you want." She punctuated her request with a tug on Bridget's hair. "Exactly what you want."

Bridget's blush deepened, and she closed her eyes.

"Open your eyes." Octavia yanked hard on Bridget's hair. "No. No hiding from me. From what you want." She stilled, waiting for Bridget to own what she wanted.

Bridget opened her eyes wide, her lips pulled back in a feral smile. *Push back. That's my girl. Mine.*

Her gaze steady and her voice sure, she spoke the words Octavia needed to hear. "Fuck me. Fuck me, Ma'am. Fuck me. Please."

Octavia held her gaze as she brought the thick phallus up and sank into Bridget. The pressure on her clit and the vibration up the shaft as she thrust deep made her want to fuck Bridget hard, to fuck them both to orgasm, until they were lost in each other. She pulled back and pushed forward again.

"Oh, more. Please, Ma'am. More." Bridget shook under her. Octavia slow-fucked her until tears of frustration and want tracked down Bridget's face. With one hand on her hip and the other still wrapped in her hair, she watched the flash of ecstasy on Bridget's face in the mirror as she sank deep. The vibration and pressure on her clit was delicious.

Bridget rocked back, meeting Octavia's thrusts. "Please, Ma'am. Please. I need. More. Please."

Octavia pushed harder, slamming into the soft flesh of Bridget's ass. "Is this what you need?"

"Yes. Oh please, Ma'am. Faster." Her eyes were wide. "Please."

It was the tear-choked "please" that tripped Octavia's trigger, the desperate need in Bridget's request as she saw the truth of her desire reflected in her eyes, the trust she had in Octavia to give her what she needed. What they both needed. *Mine. So beautiful. Mine.*

"Like this?" She pulled back, teasing with another slow stroke before she worked the strap-on hard and deep, watching the storm in Bridget's eyes as she edged her closer to coming.

Her breathing was ragged. "Yes. Oh yes. More like that. Please, Ma'am."

Deep groans and panting breaths filled the room as wetness flowed from Octavia as she fucked Bridget. Her own pleasure building, she held back, wanting to watch as Bridget tumbled over in ecstasy.

"Let me. Please let me come for you, Ma'am. Please. I can't. Oh please." Her eyes were bright, her gaze locked with Octavia's in the mirror. Bridget's body was shaking as she fought herself, fought to give Octavia what she needed.

"Come for me then." And Octavia rolled her hips and increased her pace, hammering into Bridget, bringing both of them off. She drove the shaft deep and shifted to increasing the pressure as she slowed her pace, riding out her own orgasm and aftershocks of pleasure. They shuddered together, moans giving way to sighs as they came down.

She draped herself over Bridget's back and relaxed her grip on her hair. Octavia pressed her face against her shoulder. Bridget lowered her head until it rested on the sheets, her hair spilling forward, exposing her neck. Unable to resist, Octavia nipped and licked the tender skin of her nape. She reached under Bridget and smoothed her hand over her stomach, down through the soft curls between her legs. Bridget's clit was thick and swollen. Octavia fingered her and forced her to come again. Her soft whimper as she came filled Octavia with want. She shifted her hips and stroked slowly in and out, letting Bridget recover, keeping her on the edge of another orgasm.

Bridget groaned, a deep sound that made her body vibrate. It shook Octavia to her core. "Oh Ma'am, please. Mercy. I don't know if I can come again."

Octavia scattered kisses over Bridget's back. "You underestimate yourself. And me." Octavia fucked her slowly, matching her deep stokes with the jacking of Bridget's clit, letting the pleasure build. Bridget stilled under her. The deep shuddering breaths she took told Octavia she was close. "Come as you wish."

Soft groans gave way to deeper ones, until she brought her head up and met Octavia's gaze in the mirror. "For you, Ma'am." She screamed her release, wetness spilling over Octavia's fingers, matching the love that spilled over in her heart.

WHAT THE HELL? Octavia woke to Bridget thrashing in the bed, soft cries and mumbled words poured from her mouth. *Dreaming. She's dreaming. Nightmare. Again.* Octavia listened, pushing away the urge to wake her up, trying to make sense of the torrent of garbled words pouring from Bridget's mouth. *Wake her. What is she saying? Wake her. Now.* Guilt and the sounds of Bridget's distress and suffering overrode Octavia's curiosity about her dream. She reached over and touched Bridget's shoulder.

"Bridget. Wake up. Hey, love. Wake up." She patted her shoulder.

Bridget started awake. Her breathing was rapid. "What?" She grabbed Octavia's hand with both of hers.

Octavia squeezed her shoulder. "You were dreaming. It didn't sound good. I woke you."

Bridget snuggled closer. "I was. It was awful."

Octavia shifted her arm and held her tight. "You want to talk about it?"

"No." The sharp tone in Bridget's voice pricked at Octavia. "I don't."

"I wasn't trying to piss you off. Talking about it might make it better."

"If it bothers you, I can sleep in the other room." Bridget sat up, pushing away from Octavia.

"For fuck's sake." Octavia bolted upright and turned on the light. She squinted against the flare of brightness. "What the hell, Bridget? I wasn't trying to start a fight. I thought it was the right thing to do to wake you up."

"I don't want to talk. It doesn't help." Her voice was flat. She lay down, turning away from Octavia. "Sorry I woke you."

What the hell? Why won't she talk to me? Octavia stared at the tight set of Bridget's shoulders. *What to say? Say nothing. Let it go. She'll talk to me when she wants to. Or she won't.* Octavia stifled a sigh and turned off the light. She flipped her pillow over and lay down before rolling on to her side to face away from Bridget and the distance between them.

Chapter Five

THE EARLY MORNING light filtered into the kitchen from the wide windows, casting a soft glow over the dark-wood table. Octavia finished her tea as she watched Bridget bustle about the kitchen. She opened the pantry door and surveyed the shelves and pulled boxes and cans off the shelf, inspecting each one before she replaced it. She was dressed in jeans and a dark blue T-shirt, and her thick red hair was pulled back, a mass of curls at her neck. The light showed off her cheekbones and the fine freckles scattered over her cheeks and the bridge of her nose. She stopped and scribbled notes on a legal pad.

Octavia poured herself a second cup of tea and stirred a small bit of milk into it. *Dark circles under her eyes. She didn't go back to sleep last night.*

Bridget frowned and held out a package toward Octavia. "Can you read the date on this?"

Their unresolved fight in the middle of the night had made the morning tense and filled with awkward attempts at normalcy. Octavia set her cup down and walked over to Bridget. She took the package and turned the end toward the light. "Nope. It's is too faded."

Bridget sighed. "I can't do a proper inventory. I can't read the dates on half the things here." She leaned her head on the door. "I don't know why I thought I was ready to be head chef of anything."

The defeat in her voice made Octavia's heart ache. *Dark circles. The tightness around her mouth. Her voice. Even during the worst of times at Rowan House, she didn't look like this.*

She came close and reached out to touch Bridget's chin, drawing her gaze. "We don't have to stay. But we've only been here two days."

Bridget's eyes filled with tears. "I'm sorry. I think I'm tired."

Octavia reached out and pulled her close, wrapping her arms around Bridget's waist. She leaned back to see into her eyes. "Yes. And it's all new. We are making our way here without anyone to help us or tell us what to do. It is liberating as hell and also stressful. I feel like Sisyphus and that fucking rock trying to get the barn clean." She pushed her hand under Bridget's hair and cupped the back of the neck. "You're perfectly qualified to do this job. You're brilliant and a wonderful cook."

"I keep hearing Cook's voice in my head, and I worry she was right. What if I screw up? What if after our trial period she boots us out?"

"We've already established Cook is a jealous asshole. If it doesn't work out here, then we go somewhere else. It's not all on you."

Bridget leaned her head against Octavia's chest and pressed herself tighter into Octavia's arms. "I'm sorry about last night. I'm glad you woke me."

Octavia opened her mouth to speak but shut it when she heard Vivian clearing her throat as she entered the kitchen. Breaking their embrace, they turned as one to face her.

"Is there coffee?" Her voice was rough around the edges. Her tight curls were swept up in a head wrap, showing off her profile. She wore a silk thigh-length aqua-blue dressing gown that clung to her. Her dark nipples were visible through the thin fabric. The shortness of the robe displayed Vivian's long legs. A wide keloid scar blossomed in the center of Vivian's calf and crossed the front of her knee before it disappeared under her gown.

Nothing on under there. Damn. What the hell made that scar? Car accident? Damn. Don't stare. Too late. Octavia's cheeks grew warm, and she shifted her gaze to Vivian's face. The raised eyebrow and cool look in her eyes let Octavia know she had noticed her staring. Octavia glanced at the floor and tucked her hands in her back pockets. She watched Vivian's face from under her lashes.

Vivian turned her gaze to Bridget. "If the coffee's not ready, bring it to my room." Not waiting for Bridget to respond, she turned away from them.

"Ma'am? How do you take your coffee?"

Octavia's heart squeezed hearing Bridget call Vivian "Ma'am." She swallowed the anger that bubbled up. *Fuck that. "Ma'am." What the hell? Does she want to be hers?*

Vivian turned back to face Bridget. "Call me Vivian. I'm not your Mistress—" She glanced at Octavia. "—or your lover. If it is too casual for your comfort, you may call me Ms. Abiola. I take it black. Get the coffee going. Bring it to my office." She nodded at Octavia before she turned her back to Bridget.

Bridget moved to the counter. Her face was a dark red, and she avoided Octavia's eyes as she measured the coffee for the press.

Say something. No. Fuck that. Does she even know what she's doing to us? Does she care? The thick silence between them built until Octavia ended it by slamming the door on her way out to the barn.

OCTAVIA SCOOPED THE pelleted feed into three large buckets for the horses and a smaller bucket for Victor. The small herd gathered at the gate. Ears up, they shuffled and watched as she approached with their breakfasts. Victor brayed a good morning, and Octavia's foul mood started to melt away. She hung his breakfast bucket on the fence first to silence his noisy greeting. She worked her way along the line, clipping each horse's bucket to the fence. She spoke to each one, calling them by name before giving them a quick neck rub.

The largest of the group was Max. A red gelding, he reminded Octavia of the horse she missed the most from Rowan House. The two small gray mares, Sassy and Carmel, completed the herd. Rangy and quick, they had the tough build of working horses. All of them were well-mannered. *I'll work them this afternoon. She said it'd been a while since they've been ridden. Lunge them a bit. Get them in shape.* She missed Rowan House. Missed the horses she had cared for. A deep longing for the familiar whinnies and nickers that used to greet her every day filled her. *It will be like that again. They need to get to know me.*

She walked along the fence and stopped to smooth a hand over the neck of the gelding. "Right, Max?" He flicked an ear forward and then back as he continued to chomp through his bucket of food.

Leaving them to their breakfasts, Octavia opened both ends of the barn. A small breeze blew through, pushing stray bits of sawdust ahead of it. *At least they built it right. If I can get these stalls down to the floor, they'll dry out. Even Rowan House was not this nice. The indoor ring is regulation. What the hell happened to her leg? She's so different and so much the same as when we were in school. Hell, I'm different. What's up with Bridget?*

She worked steadily, shoveling, loading the wheelbarrow with muck before she rolled it to the manure pit. *Need to find some farmer what wants this stuff. Bridget wants a kitchen garden but we've got enough manure for ten gardens. Should've brought some water with me. Damn it, I don't want to go back to the house yet.*

She had been able to clean two stalls yesterday down to the floor. Sweaty from her shoveling, Octavia took her shirt off and worked in her tank top. Her thoughts formed an endless loop of questions, the upside and downside of her work, the hours of time she had for thinking. She pushed another load of manure to the pit. She swiped at the sweat on her forehead, missing a stray drop that rolled down her face and stung her eye.

When she got back to the barn, she sat on the built-in bench outside her office to rest. She stretched her legs out in front of her and crossed them at the ankles. The familiar smell of honeysuckle carried over the smell of sweat and horses.

"You forgot this." Bridget held out a stainless-steel water bottle to Octavia. Her gaze was soft. "Ma'am."

Octavia leaned back against the wall. She pinned Bridget with a hard look. *Trying to make it up to me. Not so easy. Not ready to forgive yet.* "Thank you." She took the bottle from Bridget, ignoring the spark of heat that flared between them when she brushed her hand. "Finish your inventory?"

"Yes. Can we talk?"

"Can you tell me why you called Vivian Ma'am? I know I haven't collared you, but I thought we had an agreement."

"I don't know. It slipped out."

"Like how you stare at her? Like how you lower your gaze when you speak to her? Like how you tremble when she accidentally brushes your hand? I see how much you want to please her. Do you? Are you aware?"

Bridget twisted her the hem of her shirt in her hands. "Yes. I don't know why."

"Not true. It's how you ended up at Rowan House. It's how you fell for Cook."

"I love you."

"Don't change the subject. What has love got to do with anything? You want to belong to her. You want to kneel to her, submit to her, beg her to let you serve her, and you can't even bring yourself to admit it."

Bridget's face flushed. Her eyes were dark. "You don't get to tell me how I feel."

"No, I don't. But you don't get to call me Ma'am until you figure out who you want to belong to or if you want to belong to anyone. It's not a kinky sex game to me, Bridget. It's who I am. If you're playing in this world, say the word. Ownership is sacred. It means something. I turned my life upside down and left the only place I've been able to be myself twenty-four seven to be with you. I'm not going to take what you give me if you don't even realize what it means to me."

"I didn't want to be part of Rowan House. I didn't want to be a whore."

Octavia sat up and uncrossed her legs. "At least I was an honest whore. It was play when it was play, and it was real when it was real. It was honorable, and it was my choice. Eyes wide open. I didn't lie to myself about what I was doing or why I was doing it. I liked it. You say you want to be exclusive, you want to belong to only me, and then you turn around and call Vivian Ma'am. What the fuck, Bridget? If she hadn't set you straight, you'd be in there now kneeling, bringing her coffee, begging her to let you kiss her foot."

"I'm sorry." Bridget stepped back as if she had been struck. "I don't know what to say."

Octavia looked away from Bridget and took a long drink from her water bottle. *Fuck, does it matter? You want Vivian too. You almost kissed her the other night. Be honest.* She looked back to Bridget's face sweeping her gaze over her body before settling on her eyes. "Don't say anything." She placed the water bottle on the shelf behind her. She stood up and crossed the space between them. Bridget looked down. Octavia wrapped her arms around her and pulled her close, grounding herself in the way Bridget clung to her.

"I don't know how to handle this." Bridget pressed her face into Octavia's neck. Her voice was a whisper. "I want you, to be yours. But she has a way about her. You're right. It was like this with Cook at first." She pressed a kiss to Octavia's neck. "I love you, but what Vivian brings out in me, I don't know what to do with."

Bridget's hot tears tracked a trail down Octavia's collarbone and wet her tank top. *Like you could give her advice on what to do with feelings about Vivian.* She rubbed Bridget's back. "I think she made it clear how she wants to proceed. She's old-school. If she wants you that way, she chooses you, not the other way around."

Bridget snorted. "Like you chose me?" She pushed away from Octavia. "If I had waited for you to choose me, we'd still be at Rowan House."

Octavia pressed her mouth in a thin line. "Vivian is a Mistress. She's not Cook, nor is she Martha. And she is not me. And you need to get it together if we are going to stay here. I don't care if you want to be with her, but for fuck's sake, be honest with me and yourself."

"I don't know what I want." Bridget flattened her hands against Octavia's chest.

Octavia released her and stepped back. She rested her hands on her hips. "Until you can tell me, until you can figure it out, you don't get to call me Ma'am." She turned away from Bridget and picked up a pitchfork. She placed it in the wheelbarrow.

"Lunch is in an hour." Bridget's voice was hollow. She hesitated, one hand on hand on her hip. "If you want any." She walked out the door with quick steps.

Octavia watched her walk away. *What the hell am I going to do? Why did I leave Rowan House? Fuck this freedom. For Bridget? For myself? I'm not a Mistress. Maybe she needs more than me. I want more. I want to kneel, to lose myself in the sweetness of pain, to be marked, bruised, cherished. She loves me but she can't give me that. It's not in her.* Octavia's head hurt as she turned the possibilities over in her mind. She longed for the simplicity of letting someone else take control, letting Martha make the decisions, resting at the feet of a strong woman, letting her command her pleasure, taking what she needed, letting Octavia focus on serving. *Safe. Cherished.* A wave of longing swept over her. *Cherished. That's what's missing. I'm loved. She loves me. But she can't ever give me the comfort of being owned. And Martha could never give me the gift of her trust and her surrender, even for a moment.*

One of the barn cats, a long rangy gray-and-black tabby, brushed against her legs on its way to the stairs leading to the hay loft. *Not a stray but not owned either.* Octavia brought her hand up and touched the bare skin of her neck, the place her collar had been. *Will I ever get used to not being owned?*

OCTAVIA WASHED UP in the sink in the mudroom. The house was cool after the heat of the barn, and she shivered as she pulled her shirt on over the tank top she wore. She walked into the kitchen. The table was set with two place settings. In the center rested a crystal water pitcher and a large platter filled with thick wedges of tomatoes and fresh mozzarella slices drizzled with balsamic vinegar and fragrant green olive oil. Dark green basil leaves were scattered over the top and stood out against the bright red of the tomatoes. She inhaled the smell of Bridget's signature crusty bread. Bridget stood at the counter, scooping berries into dessert bowls.

Taking in the line of her thick hips, the way her broad shoulders filled out her uniform made Octavia's mouth water for more than the gorgeous lunch laid out for them. She crossed the floor and wrapped her arms around Bridget's waist to pull her against her body. She kissed the soft space under her ear. "This looks and smells amazing. Is it for us?"

"Vivian had a late breakfast and left. She won't be back until supper."

Octavia pressed more kisses along the slope of her neck. Bridget brought her hand up and cupped the side of Octavia's face, resting it there. Octavia stilled. She hugged Bridget closer. Their breathing synced, and the hurt and angry words melted between them. *Love. She does love me. As much as I love her.*

They sat and ate together, the two of them, easy and relaxed, enjoying the peace that came with knowing they would not be scolded for enjoying lunch and each other.

"You know—" Octavia dipped her bread into a small puddle of olive oil and thick balsamic vinegar on her plate. "It's customary here to rest in the afternoon." She raised her eyebrow at Bridget. "You know, to avoid the heat of the day." She popped the bit of bread into her mouth and chewed slowly, savoring the bread mixed with the rich olive oil and sweet vinegar.

"Is it?" Bridget dabbed at her mouth with her napkin. She lifted her gaze to Octavia's. "I do think I could do with a nap."

Octavia stood up. She picked up her plate. "Let's clear this up. And then we rest."

When the last plate was cleared and the kitchen cleaned, Octavia interlaced her fingers with Bridget's. She kissed the back of her hand. "Ready, love?"

Chapter Six

"I'M NOT SURE why you had to find the only mud puddle in the whole field and roll in it." Octavia brushed the mud from Max's coat. She ducked under the crossties to work on his other side.

"Do you always talk to them?"

The brush clattered on the floor. Octavia bent to pick it up, one hand on the horse to steady him. "Only when I think I'm alone."

Vivian laughed. "I'm sorry I startled you."

"It's okay." She worked the brush over Max's side and flank.

Vivian picked up a brush and worked his other side. "I've missed this."

"Grooming the horses?"

"Spending time with them, yes. I've neglected them." She patted Max's shoulder. "But that's going to change."

"What happened?" Octavia placed her brush in the grooming box. She stepped around the horse. She looked into Vivian's eyes. *Sadness. Grief. Regret. Pain. So much sorrow.* "Did you fall?" She gestured to Vivian's leg. "I noticed your scar."

"No." Vivian looked away. "I haven't had the desire. It was something I always did with my wife. Between assignments." She stopped brushing Max and held the brush to her chest.

Married. She was married. Damn. "Breakups suck."

Vivian raised her eyes and met Octavia's gaze. "She died three years ago."

"I'm so sorry. I didn't know." Octavia's cheeks grew hot. "I'm sorry."

Vivian sighed and placed the brush on the bench. She sat down next to it and looked straight ahead, avoiding Octavia's eyes, her cool mask back in place. "I don't tell people. I hate the pity in their eyes when they find out." She rested her chin on her chest. "Or looks of disapproval. People have a right to know what's going on, to read and see the truth about conflicts, not the sanitized version big media wants to tell." Her voice was a fierce whisper. "Miriam died doing what she—" Vivian's voice cracked. "What we believed in."

Anger and grief flowed from her, and the fierce determination of her voice made Octavia shiver. *Miriam? Miriam Shultz. The journalist.* She remembered photos of a bombed-out car that had been plastered on the front pages of the newspapers Martha read obsessively. Her gut roiled, and a sour taste filled her mouth. *That was her. Her car. Her photo. Just like Papa.*

Max tossed his head, rattling the cross-ties, and snorted. Octavia rubbed his shoulder. "I know you're done, Max." She leaned her head against his neck, avoiding Vivian's gaze. *Say something. No. Fuck. What to say?* Failing to find anything to say that didn't sound ridiculously stupid and trite, unsure she should say anything at all, Octavia clipped the lead on Max's halter and unclipped the cross-ties.

She led him back to his stall and gave him a bit of hay. She stood and watched as he ate. *Married. To a journalist. Not just any journalist. Miriam Schultz. Damn. Explains the German. Go to her. Say something. Be there for her. And say what? Listen. That's all anyone needs when they're grieving.*

Octavia hurried back to the grooming area. A heavy silence greeted her. The brushes and other grooming equipment were stowed neatly back in their box. Vivian was gone. *Too late. I should have stayed. I should have listened. Been present. I walked away. I left her when she needed to talk.*

"IS SHE JEWISH? I saw her necklace. Do I need to learn to make challah?" Bridget sat cross-legged on the bed flipping through a cookbook. The short robe she wore gaped open, giving Octavia a clear view of her breasts.

"I don't know if she's religious. Her mom's Jewish from New York City and her dad's Catholic from Abuja."

"Where's that?"

"Nigeria."

Bridget raised her eyebrows. "That must have made for some interesting family reunions."

"She said she's never been Jewish enough for her mom's family nor Catholic enough for her dad's family."

Bridget flipped through a few more pages in the cookbook. "She's only asked me to make this German potato soup and some rye bread."

"Did she tell you she was married? To a woman?"

Bridget quirked her mouth at Octavia. "No. You seem to have the information hookup here. She's doesn't talk to me much at all."

Careful. She'll figure out you've known her before. "It's not like we're hanging out all the time. She mentioned it when I asked her why she had stopped riding her horse."

"I think she likes you best." Bridget closed the book and placed it on the nightstand. She stretched out next to Octavia.

Octavia turned to her side to face Bridget. "Jealous?"

Bridget rested her hand on Octavia's waist. "Some." She scooted closer on the bed and leaned her forehead against Octavia's chin. "I don't know if I'm jealous because I think she likes you more than me, or because I think you like her."

"She likes you. She looks at you like she likes you."

"She always pulls away from me. Like I'm standing too close."

"Maybe she's afraid she'll like you too much."

Bridget raised her head and met Octavia's gaze. "Are you afraid I'll like her too much?"

"No." *Liar. Be honest.* "Yes."

"You were angry when I called her Ma'am. So was she."

"It means something. It's not just a word. She's a Mistress with a capital M."

Bridget trembled. "I love you. I don't know why I care so much about what she thinks."

Octavia ran her fingertip over Bridget's jaw. "Because you do. Because even if you love me, you're attracted to her. Like I am."

"It's not just me?" Bridget kissed Octavia's cheek.

"No. Not only you." She cupped the back of Bridget's neck. "Tell me what gets you about her, what makes you wet when you think of her."

Bridget's flushed and laughed. She spread her hand out wide and thumbed Octavia's nipple through her shirt. "You go first."

"Her eyes. And her long legs. And the way her mouth moves when she talks."

Bridget squeezed her fingers together, pinching Octavia's nipple hard. "Mmm yes, her eyes. Those legs. I want to start at the top of her foot and lick my way up. And her voice. I ask her things to hear her speak. Sometimes I pretend not to hear her so she'll call my name." Bridget's eyes were wide.

"Brat. Pretending not to hear." Octavia laughed and moved her hand from the back of her neck, sliding it down to cup her ass. She squeezed hard, making Bridget squirm and gasp. "Her mouth. I want to sit on her face and rub myself on her mouth."

Bridget laughed and rolled on top of Octavia, pinning her to the bed. Her eyes bright, she ground her hips against Octavia. "So naughty. How about I sit on your face instead?"

"Mmm. How about that?" Octavia moved her hands to Bridget's waist and pulled the sash to the robe. The knot gave way and the robe fluttered open, displaying Bridget's lush body. Octavia pushed her hands under the robe and smoothed them over Bridget's stomach.

Bridget leaned forward and pressed her breasts on to Octavia's face. "You like this, don't you? Me on top."

"Yes. I love you over me. Love this view." Octavia held Bridget's breasts together, running her tongue between them. Bridget groaned, and Octavia sucked each nipple until they were hard under her tongue.

Bridget ground against her. Slick with need, she rubbed her clit against Octavia's stomach. "Want me?" She rocked her hips. "Want me to come for you? Come in your mouth?"

"Come over me, love." Octavia slid down between her legs and gripped Bridget's thighs. Bridget clutched the headboard, her knees on either side of Octavia's head.

Octavia turned her head and kissed the inside of her thigh. "Give it to me. All of it." She thrust her tongue up, tasting the sweet salty flow of Bridget's need. Octavia wrapped her arms around her thighs and pushed her tongue deep before swirling it over her clit. Bridget ground herself on her face. *For me. This all of it. For me.* Working her tongue in and around, over and in, she dug her fingers into Bridget's flesh as she devoured her.

"Oh yes. That's it. Please. Don't stop. There. There. Oh. Ahh." Bridget broke, spilling wetness over Octavia's chin and face. Octavia licked and sucked the sweetness as it flowed from Bridget.

With soft lips and gentle tongue, she held on through the aftershocks as they shook Bridget's body. Lifting herself clear of Octavia, Bridget let go of the headboard and rolled to her side. She leaned over and cupped Octavia's face, nibbling her lips before she kissed her. Octavia savored the taste of her flavoring their kiss.

Bridget leaned back, meeting Octavia's gaze. "We're all right? Aren't we?"

The love reflected in her features made Octavia's heart ache. "Yes, love. We're all right. We're together. You're mine. I'm yours. I'm not going anywhere."

Bridget draped her leg over Octavia's body before she swept her hand over her shirt. She moved it lower and played with the buttons of Octavia's jeans. "May I? Ma'am?"

Octavia stretched her arms up and tucked them behind her head. "Yes."

Bridget unbuttoned the top button and tugged down the fly. She slipped her hand inside and fingered Octavia's swollen clit. "Oh Ma'am, you're so thick and wet." She pushed her fingers in deep, drawing a groan from Octavia.

Octavia closed her eyes and clasped the headboard. *Please fuck me. Don't ask. Fuck me hard. Make me come. Take control. Please. Hurt me. Tease me. Fuck me.* She arched her hips up, trying to send Bridget the signal for what she craved. Bridget worked her fingers in and out, fucking her slowly and gently. Octavia bit her lip, wanting more, unable to ask, afraid to ask, wanting Bridget to own her the way she needed. To give her the roughness she craved.

Bridget stilled. "Talk to me please. I don't know how to give you what you want. Tell me. Please. I want to make you feel like I feel."

The quiver in her voice broke Octavia. She opened her eyes. "You do, love. You do. You're doing fine." She reached down and touched Bridget's cheek. "Fuck me like you want to."

Bridget leaned in and kissed her and fucked her then, bringing her off but missing the desperate need in Octavia's body for roughness and pain.

Chapter Seven

"IT'S BEEN SO long." Vivian leaned down and adjusted her stirrup.

"I lunged him, so he should be ready to work. I'll hang out in the ring with you." Octavia held Max's head until Vivian tightened the straps of her riding helmet.

"Thank you." Vivian picked up her reins.

They walked to the ring, Vivian atop Max, Octavia by her side. Octavia glanced up from time to time to take in the elegant form of Vivian on horseback. She reached out and touched her thigh, drawing her attention. "Do you want me to coach you or watch?" She left her hand on Vivian's leg, appreciating the firmness of her thigh under her tight riding breeches.

"I know you well enough to know you couldn't help yourself if you tried not to."

Octavia laughed. "I can control myself much better than when we were in school. I'd respect your request."

Vivian reined her horse to a stop. "Really? After the other night in the barn, I'm not so sure." She fixed her gaze on Octavia's hand, her brow furrowed. "I don't want to cause problems between you and Bridget. I value your friendship. I want to trust you."

Octavia snatched her hand from Vivian's thigh. "Understood. I'm sorry. I don't want things to be awkward between us." She kept her head down, avoiding Vivian's eyes. "I get it."

She walked ahead to the door of the indoor ring and rolled it open. She entered the dim building and turned on the lights. *Not into me at all. How could I think she would be? If she wanted more, she'd let me know. Damn it. I need to get it together. What was I thinking?* She touched her neck, rubbing the spot where her collar had been, and wished for a moment she was back at Rowan House. *Safe. Cherished. Owned.*

Max and Vivian entered the ring. Octavia sat in a folding chair and watched as Vivian circled the ring, walking him at first and then at a trot. After he was warm, she schooled him, practicing pacing and flying changes. Octavia noted the way Vivian worked with Max, making mental notes of things she could improve upon. She remained quiet, unsure of what to say or if to say anything. She wanted to fall at Vivian's feet and beg for her to let her serve. To feel her control. She closed her eyes against the pain and ache in her heart. *Martha wasn't perfect, but damn I miss her. Miss her hand on my neck. Miss her touch. Her control. Maybe Vivian's the same. Absolute control or nothing. I need to get it together. Don't want to fuck things up. Bridget loves it here. Bridget. Maybe she truly does respect us. Or maybe she doesn't want me. Damn, this is hard.*

The sound of Max's hooves approaching stopped her rumination. She looked into Vivian's eyes. "Heels down. And bend him around your leg. Look where you want him to go. Bring your leg more forward on the flying change. Lower your hands." She kept her gaze steady and voice even.

Vivian arched a brow. "Noted." She turned Max, and Octavia studied the way Vivian followed every direction she had given her. *Would she ever do it outside of here? Let herself be commanded, let herself be taken. Let me lead? Not me. Not into me. I'm deep in the friend zone. Damn it.*

OCTAVIA SWEPT THE center aisle of the barn. Victor followed at her heels, so close that when she stopped he bumped into her. "*Was geht ab*, Victor?" He rubbed his head on her. "I can't pet you all day. I've got work to do."

Fall rains had soaked the lower fields. Worried about Victor's hooves, she had brought him into the barn. She had put him in his stall, but he kicked and brayed so much she let him have the run of the barn while she worked. The sky was a soft gray-green, and the air was heavy and smelled of rain. *Have to bring them in tonight. Too cool for them to stay out.* She stopped and studied the sky. Clouds sat heavy and dark, blocking her view of the Alps. A chill wind swirled the sawdust at her feet. *Definitely have to bring them in. Need to check the weather. Maybe I should get a smartphone. Nope, one more way to track me. I'll ask Bridget to check for me.*

Victor brushed against her side, knocking her off-balance. "They should've named you Shadow."

"Diavolo would have been more appropriate." The silky tones of an unknown voice made Octavia spin around to search for their source. The owner of the voice wore a black knee-length dress that highlighted her curves. Sleeveless, the dress displayed her toned arms. Her silver-gray hair was pulled into a loose bun. Humor filled her eyes. "*Mi scuse.* Sorry to startle you. I came to see Vivian. Is she here? She said she'd meet me at five. I'm Sofia." She held her hand out.

Octavia clasped her hand and shook it before she looked at the barn clock. "She's working out in the indoor ring with Max. Your fields are next to ours, right?"

The woman tipped her chin at Octavia. "*Si.* Vivian sells her crops to me." She looked around the barn. "The barn looks fantastic. You've done a wonderful job with it. I want to bring my horses back here. I don't like where they are." She returned her gaze to Octavia's face. "Vivian has raved about you." A smile played over her mouth as she raked her eyes over Octavia's body. "I can see why."

"Thank you." Octavia's face grew warm under Sofia's attention. Victor shook his head at Sofia and laid his ears back, showing his teeth.

"Devil. He hates me." Sofia crossed her arms and frowned at the donkey. "Still."

Octavia grabbed the donkey's halter and tugged him over to his stall. He locked up his legs at the door, refusing to move. "*Mitkommen*, Victor. Come along. Please. *Bitte.*" She rubbed between his ears. "*Please.* Be good." He snorted and followed her into the stall. She released him and closed the stall door and locked it. He spun and kicked the door, rattling the hardware and making Octavia laugh. "He barely tolerates me."

Vivian arrived on Max. *She could have been a professional. She could not look more perfect on him.* Octavia walked out to meet her. Atop Max, Vivian projected the air of a woman in command. Octavia wanted to grip her leg, to press a kiss to her thigh, to serve her, to kneel at her feet, rest her forehead against the top of her boot. *Not what she wants. So hard. Damn. She doesn't want me. Get it together.* Octavia reached up and held Max's bridle while Vivian dismounted. Her shirt was damp and clung to her body. The tan form-fitting breeches she wore were tucked into knee-high smooth leather riding boots. She pulled her riding helmet off and smiled at Octavia.

That's the smile I miss. Octavia tucked the helmet under her arm. "Good ride? He was a bit feisty when I lunged him yesterday."

Vivian handed the reins to her. "He made me work for it. We're both out of shape." She wiped at a bit of sweat on her forehead with the point of her wrist. She held Octavia's gaze. "Thank you for encouraging me."

"You have a visitor."

Vivian looked over Octavia's shoulder. "*Ciao*, Sofia. *Scusa sono in ritardo*. I lost track of time."

"*Va bene*. I was enjoying talking to your new barn manager." Sofia smiled broadly at Octavia.

"I'm sure." Vivian arched her eyebrow. "She can be very entertaining."

"When can I bring my horses back? The stable where I board them is too far and full of tourists. You've such a treasure here in Octavia. Don't be selfish."

"We can talk about it over dinner." She kissed Sofia on both cheeks before she slipped her arm around her waist. She looked back over her shoulder and met Octavia's gaze. "Do you need help with him?"

Octavia patted Max's neck. "No, he's a gentleman. I'm going to strip his tack and cool him out a bit before I put him up. Nice meeting you, Sofia."

"*Il piacere è tutto mio*. My pleasure." She held Octavia's gaze long enough to make her swallow hard. Vivian rolled her eyes and turned them toward the house.

Octavia watched them walk away, imagining all the ways things could go. *Wait till Bridget meets Sofia. Vivian was pissy. Jealous? Why? Is she with Sofia? Or upset for Bridget?* She ran up the stirrups before she walked Max, making a long loop around the barn and the indoor ring. Her thoughts twined back on themselves as she tried to figure out Vivian's attitude and her own.

"HEY, SOFIA AND Vivian have expressed a desire for our company. You wanna come to dinner?" Bridget stood with one hand on her hip, her other hand resting on the doorframe.

Octavia finished washing her hands in the sink in the barn office. She grinned at Bridget in the mirror over the sink. "Depends. What's on the menu?" She turned to face Bridget and took her time drying her hands.

Bridget came forward and stopped a breath away. Octavia set the towel aside and put her hands on Bridget's hips. "I've worked up a bit of an appetite." She leaned forward and brushed her lips over Bridget's mouth before she lowered her head and kissed her way to her ear. "Maybe I want to skip to dessert."

Bridget hooked her fingers in Octavia's belt loops to pull her forward and ground against her. "Greedy woman. I've spent all day making a beautiful dinner, and you want to skip to dessert?"

"Maybe what I'm hungry for isn't on the menu." She moved her hand to the front of Bridget's chef's coat, unbuttoned it and slipped her hand inside, palming her breast. Bridget arched into her, meeting Octavia's rough kiss with her own passion. She dropped her hands lower and squeezed Octavia's ass, digging her fingers in hard. Octavia's nipples hardened in response to Bridget's rough breathing and the way she ground her hip against her clit. She moved her hand lower, unfastened her pants, and pushed her hand inside the wet heat between Bridget's legs. *Yes. So wet. For me. For this.* She kissed Bridget, her lips hard and bruising as she fingered her. Bridget groaned and rocked her hips faster, shifting her legs so her pants fell to her knees.

Pulling her hand free, Octavia guided her across the room. When Bridget's hips bumped the edge of the desk, Octavia pushed her down onto her back. Going to her knees, Octavia pulled Bridget's pants lower, trapping her legs at the ankles. She traced a line with her tongue up Bridget's thigh before taking her into her mouth. The smooth thickness of her clit sent a wave of wetness to Octavia's core. *So sweet. Mine.* She sucked and licked Bridget's clit, matching her strokes.

Bridget squirmed and raised her hips. "We're... They're expecting us. I..." She gasped as Octavia thrust her fingers deep. "Oh. I'm going to... May I? Please let me."

Octavia lifted her mouth from her and whispered, "Come as you wish"

Bridget grabbed Octavia's head and wrapped her hands in her hair. "Now. For you, Ma'am." Shaking hard, she bucked her hips as she came.

Greedy for the sweetness flowing from her, Octavia sucked harder and made her come again. She waited until the aftershocks had finished shaking Bridget's frame. She planted a kiss on the soft curls at the top of her sex before she moved up. She put her arms on either side of Bridget, framing her as she lay on the desk, and kissed her mouth. "You were saying?"

Bridget looped her arms around Octavia's neck. "I was trying to tell you to come to dinner, they're waiting for us." She kissed the corner of Octavia's mouth. "I have to say I like this dessert-first part."

Octavia helped her up and pulled her pants up. She refastened them while Bridget buttoned her chef's coat. She glanced at the clock. "If they say anything, blame it on me." She kissed Bridget hard.

Bridget brought her hand between her legs and cupped Octavia through her jeans, making her groan. "You kiss me again, and we'll be even later than we are."

Love. The way she looks at me. Love. And desire. Love. Octavia leaned close and kissed her cheek. "Save it. I have plans for your sweet mouth."

Bridget met her gaze. "I hope so."

"Do they expect me to come to dinner like this? I need to shower."

Bridget quirked her mouth. "Evidently your charms are enough to overpower the smell of the barn. Sofia seemed most impressed. She insisted you come to dinner. Vivian got all lady of the manner and made it clear we were together. By then the old goat was three glasses of wine in, and she insisted both of us join them for dinner and Vivian caved. I think they were lovers."

"Don't be ageist. I don't think she's much older than me. Were? Or are they still?"

Bridget smoothed her hand over Octavia's shoulders. "I don't know. Whatever. You're much better preserved. And you're mine."

Octavia hugged her close. "I am." She kissed Bridget's forehead. "Come on, love. I'll shower quick."

Chapter Eight

OCTAVIA BRAIDED HER hair and secured it with an elastic band, knowing it would still be wet when she took it down. She tugged on a long-sleeve white button-down shirt and black jeans. She slipped her feet into sandals and hurried down the hall to the dining room. Vivian sat at the head of the table holding a wineglass. Sofia was holding forth about something. Bridget sat across from Sofia feigning polite interest in the conversation. Vivian's gaze was fixed on Bridget. Octavia's gut tightened as she watched them unobserved. *The way she looks at her. Vivian wants her. Why is she holding back? Respect for us. So not interested in me.* Octavia chewed her lip as she stood in the doorway.

Sofia looked up and met Octavia's gaze. She took a sip of wine. "Don't lurk. Join us, Octavia. Have some wine."

The way Sofia said Octavia's name made her squirm. *Drunk. Hope she's got a ride home. She sure as hell's in no shape to drive.* "No, thank you. Water is fine." She sat down at the foot of the table facing Vivian between Sofia and Bridget.

Vivian cleared her throat. "So nice of both of you to join us." She nodded at Bridget.

At her nod Bridget left the table. Octavia stood up. "I should go help her."

"Sit. I'm sure if she needed help she would have asked. Never interfere with a chef serving." Vivian stood up and walked to the end of the table. She placed her hand on Octavia's shoulder as she filled her water glass from the crystal pitcher on the table.

Octavia stilled under her touch and relaxed. *More. More. I want more. Of her. So fucking hard.* Vivian strolled back to her seat and sat down. Her gaze settled on Octavia. *If I look at her, she'll see. See how much I want her. Want to serve her. Damn it. I'm so fucked.* Octavia studied the pattern on the dishes, avoiding Vivian's captivating expression.

"*Allora*, Octavia, I want to bring my horses back here."

Octavia looked up and met Sofia's gaze.

Sofia narrowed her eyes at Octavia. "'Vivian says it's up to you. What do you say?"

Octavia looked to Vivian for guidance. Vivian's face was a calm mask giving nothing away. "I don't know. How many horses do you have? We've only room for two more. I need to keep a stall open for the donkey, and I like to keep a stall empty to rotate to when I muck on wet days."

"I've a gelding and an ancient mare I've had forever. The mare is retired. She needs pasture and company."

"Do you ride the gelding every day? Do you need him exercised? I don't know if I can keep up exercising four horses by myself."

Sofia placed her glass on the table and inclined her body toward Octavia. "Oh I like to ride every day." She traced a finger around the top of her wineglass. "Sometimes twice a day."

Oh hell. Just what I need, Lady Hot to Trot in the barn every day. "I also need to see their veterinary records before they come back, especially if they've been boarded in a large facility."

Sofia quirked her mouth. "I'll have their records sent." She arched a brow. "They'll be in Italian. I'd be happy to translate." She reached out and touched Octavia's hand. "Maybe we could meet at my home tomorrow to discuss it further."

A ladle clattered on the floor. "Sorry." Bridget glared at Sofia. She placed a tureen of soup in the middle of the table. She fixed her gaze on Sofia as she bent to pick up the ladle. Sofia drew her hand back and picked up her glass of wine.

"No need. Send them. I can read them."

"*Tu parli Italiano? Sei fantastico!* Vivian was right. You're amazing."

Bridget returned from the kitchen with a clean ladle and large platter of rye bread. She served the soup, coming perilously close to slopping the hot liquid on Sofia while serving her, making Octavia cringe.

Vivian cleared her throat. "Enough, Sofia. Let's enjoy our dinner. I'll call tomorrow and we can discuss it."

Octavia spooned the soup into her mouth, savoring perfectly seasoned *Kartoffelsuppe*. They ate in tense silence.

"*Molto buono.* This is perfect, Bridget." Vivian lifted her eyes to Bridget's face as she placed her spoon next to her empty bowl. "I've been craving this."

Bridget blushed. "Thank you."

Sofia snorted. "Needs salt, dear."

Vivian leveled her gaze on Sofia. "It is perfectly seasoned to me, but then I haven't drowned my taste buds in wine."

Octavia hid her smile behind her napkin. *Damn. It's about to get rough up in here. Good for her sticking up for Bridget.*

Bridget added her own hard look to Vivian's. "I cook to please the Mistress of the house." She shoved back her chair and began clearing the bowls. Once she'd picked up her bowl and Vivian's, she pushed through the door to the kitchen. The unmistakable sound of a pan being thrown rang out. Octavia glanced toward the kitchen door. *I should go to her. She's pissed as hell. But damn it's awkward.*

Sofia sat back in her chair, a sick smile on her face. "Seems your new cook is sensitive about her cooking."

Vivian tilted her head at Octavia and raised a brow before she shifted her eyes toward the door to the kitchen. *She wants me to go. To leave her alone to talk to Sofia.* Octavia pushed her chair back. "Excuse me. I need to help Bridget." She left the room without looking back. *What the hell am I going to say about her horses? I can still say no. She's Vivian's frenemy. Damn, this is complicated.*

OCTAVIA PUSHED THE kitchen door open slowly. "Hey. You okay, love?"

Bridget looked up from the dessert she was plating. "I've sat through worse dinners. I'm not going back out there with that bitch. What the hell is wrong with her? Flirting with you like I was invisible."

Octavia pressed her lips together. "She's a nutcase."

"And if her horses are here, she'll be slinking around here all the time, throwing herself at you."

"I can handle it. I'm good at dodging unwanted attention."

Bridget quirked her mouth at Octavia. "For how long?"

Octavia crossed her arms in front of her chest. "This is not Rowan House. And what the hell, Bridget? Are you going to hold it over me forever? I did what I did at Rowan House as a choice. I always had a choice."

"How much choice does any whore have?" Bridget's eyes were dark.

Octavia glanced up at the ceiling. *Why do we keep having this argument? Fuck me. What does she want? Like it's my fault Sofia is interested. Fuck.* "I'm going to say this one last time. I made the choices I did because I wanted to. I can't change my past. If you can't deal with it or are going to act like this every time some woman shows interest in me, I can't do this. I can't control other people any more than you can. What about Vivian? You think I don't see it? See the way she watches you?"

"Lower your voice. I don't want her to hear us," Bridget whispered.

"I'll yell if I want to. I don't care who hears me. Fuck this. You spend every minute of your time thinking of ways to please her. You think I don't know how much you want her? You think I don't see how Vivian holds herself back around you? I have eyes, Bridget." The anger Octavia had kept tightly wrapped boiled up. "And I'll do any damn thing I want. We're free, remember? If I want to shout or throw something or go out there and tell Sofia to go fuck herself, I will." She rocked back on her heels and crossed her arms in front of her chest.

"Too late. She's left." Vivian's cool voice cut through the angry tension of the kitchen. "And I suspect she'd ask you to help."

Bridget and Octavia turned as one to look at Vivian. Bridget flushed a bright red and stared at the floor.

Not ready to let go of her anger, Octavia fixed her gaze on Vivian. "I could have used your help out there. I don't want her here any day let alone every day if she's going to be rude to Bridget and drool over me. Was that some sort of test? To see if I'm committed to Bridget?"

"No. As stable manager, the decision is yours. As for her behavior, I addressed it." She turned her gaze to Bridget.

Her voice was soft. "I'm sorry, Bridget. I didn't know she would behave that way. It was unfair of me to allow it." The earnestness in her voice unwound Octavia's anger.

Bridget's gaze was fixed on Vivian's face. She crossed the floor and stood a breath away from Vivian. She looked up. Her eyes locked on Vivian's countenance, she licked her lip, wetting it. Vivian leaned down and brushed a kiss over Bridget's forehead. "It won't happen again."

Bridget closed her eyes. A blissful expression suffused her face before she opened them and stared into Vivian's face. Her pupils were wide. A spark of desire flared in Octavia making her want to cross the floor, stand behind Bridget, and bind her for Vivian's pleasure, to watch the two of them together. To gather the threads of their desire, weave a tapestry of intimacy and wrap it tight around them. And yet watching the two of them eye-fuck each other made her gut churn. *No room for me. Vivian made it clear. Great. I should pack my bags now. Fuck. I thought this would work out. Thought we would work out. Damn it. I should have stayed at Rowan House. The lines are clear there. What was I thinking? I'm not enough for her. She can't let go of who I was. She wants Vivian. They want each other even if they don't get it yet. Fuck this. Fuck me.*

Octavia turned away and walked to the door.

"Wait." Vivian's voice was soft. "Please."

Octavia kept her eyes on the tiles. She rested her head on the doorframe.

"No. You don't owe me anything. I need to go. Before you two forget I'm here anymore than you have."

"Please. Talk to me. Don't pull away. Anna, please."

Octavia spun on her heel. "The fuck, Vivian? You promised."

Bridget observed the two of them before she settled her gaze on Octavia. She lowered her brows, her eyes dark "Who is Anna? What are you hiding?"

Vivian covered her mouth with her hand. The guilt in her eyes made Octavia wince. She looked from Vivian's face to Bridget's. "I am. Or was. Doesn't matter now. One more thing in my past you'd have a hard time with."

"Never mind. Fuck both of you." Bridget slammed open the door to the dining room and left.

Octavia watched her go before she walked out of the back door to the mudroom. She toed off her sandals and stuffed her feet into her boots, ignoring Vivian's voice as she called her.

SHE KEPT HER head down on her way to the barn. The night had grown chilly, and a soft drizzle of rain fell around her. She wished she'd picked up her jacket. The sweat cooling on her body and the adrenaline crash made her shiver. *I should've told her. From the beginning. Everything. About me. About Vivian. Too late. She'll never trust me now. What am I going to do? Go back? Beg Martha for my collar? No. I can find a job. They'll be happy together. Vivian deserves to be happy. Bridget needs more than me.*

She flipped on the lights in her office. The only sound in the barn was the scurrying of the cats as they prowled about the loft. She sat down heavily in her chair. *I could stay. Move to the guest house. Leave them the big house. She loves me. Not enough. Did Vivian call my name to force me out? To force us apart? To force me to be honest? Or was it a mistake? She's not into me. Never was. But damn I want her. Want them both. Bridget would never go for it even if Vivian might.*

Her favorite cat, the gray tabby, slipped in the door and jumped up on her desk. She stared at Octavia, her green eyes wary for a moment before she settled in and stretched out on the desk. Octavia reached over and stroked the cat's head. The cat rolled on her back and let Octavia scratch her belly. The soft purring of the cat eased her heart and the comfort of the animal's simple affection settled over her.

She sighed. "You'd like it if I stayed here all night petting you, wouldn't you?" The cat jerked under her touch and nipped her before bolting off her desk and out the door.

"What the hell, cat?" The acrid smell of smoke wafted into the office. *Fire.* Octavia stood up fast, and her chair clattered on the floor. She ran out the door and flipped the main overhead light switch to check the barn. *Idiot. If the barn were on fire, you wouldn't need the lights. Fire. Where?* She ran out the end of the barn and scanned the shed row. She stepped back and looked at the roof of the barn. *Not the barn.*

She spun in a slow circle. *Where is it? The house? No. Guest house? No. Where is it?* On the far side of the field, she saw the bright yellow-orange glow of a fire. The small turnout shed was in flames. *Fuck. Too far from the hose. No way to save it.*

The wind brought a heavy wave of smoke to the barn. Victor's alarmed braying set the horses off, and they shuffled and stomped in their stalls. *Need to shut out the smoke before they panic.* Octavia shoved the heavy barn door closed and turned the switch for the overhead exhaust fans. *Fuck. Who set it? Sheds don't burst into flames in the rain. Good thing the ground is so wet or the field would catch. Someone set that. Who?* She walked to the front of the barn. She rolled the front door closed. *Good design. I can shut out most of the smoke. The fans will take care of the rest.*

She went to the back of the barn. The frame of the turnout shed spewed sparks as the roof collapsed. Octavia pulled the hose from the reel and turned the water on, ready to douse any sparks that might blow near the barn. *Fuck. The one time I wish I carried a phone. Come on, rain.* She looked up at the sky and said a prayer.

"Octavia! Where are you?" Vivian's voice split the night. Her tone was shrill and held an edge of panic. "Anna?"

"Here. I'm here."

Vivian arrived out of breath. She reached out and ran her hands over Octavia, touching her everywhere. "Are you hurt? I couldn't find you."

"I'm fine. I..." A crack of thunder sounded, and a flash of lighting lit their faces. Vivian grabbed her by the shoulders and kissed her. Stunned, Octavia hesitated before she wrapped her arms around Vivian and pulled her hard against her. *Me. She's kissing me. Wants me.* The taste of wine on Vivian's lips brought back memories of their one night together. Past and present melded, and they clung to each other. All the years of longing filled her, and Vivian's kiss burned away Octavia's anger and hurt, burned away her doubts, consumed her.

Vivian broke their kiss. She leaned her forehead on Octavia's brow. "Anna. I'm sorry. Please don't leave." She kissed her again. "I want you. I've wanted you since I saw you at Rowan House."

The cool rain soaked their skin, contrasting with the burning need coursing through Octavia.

"Bridget?" Octavia held Vivian by her shoulders and studied her expression, searching for what she wanted to see.

"Yes. Both of you. Please. Don't leave." She clutched the front of Octavia's shirt and kissed her way along Octavia's neck. Her lips brushed along her jaw before she kissed her again, a too brief touch that left Octavia hungry for more. "Please. Come back to the house. We'll talk." The sounds of a siren in the distance disturbed the night. They let go of each other. "Go to Bridget. Talk to her. I'll talk to the fire department. When did you notice it?"

"About ten minutes before you got here. I was in the office when I smelled it."

"Go to her. I'll make the report to them."

The sirens were closer now. Octavia nodded her agreement. She walked slowly back to the house. *What am I going to tell her? All of it. Tell her all of it. The truth. About me. My name. And Vivian.* She touched her lips. *That kiss.*

Chapter Nine

OCTAVIA PULLED HER boots off in the mudroom. The lights were dimmed in the kitchen. She passed through the dining room on her way to the room she shared with Bridget. The door was closed. She tapped on it. "Bridget? Hey, love. Talk to me." She tapped on the thick wood again. She turned the bronze knob. *At least she didn't lock me out.* The bedroom was dark. She flipped the light switch to turn on the lamp by the bed. The covers were pulled tight, the bed made as neatly as they had left it. *Where the hell is she?* "Bridget?" She walked through the bathroom connecting to the sitting room. "Bridget?" A pile of wet clothes sat atop muddy shoes on the bathroom floor. *Was she outside? Did she see us? Fuck.*

Bridget sat on the leather sofa, wrapped in a towel. Her wet hair spilled in wild curls around her shoulders. She glanced up at Octavia, her mouth pressed in a thin line. She looked away. "I'm not sure I want to talk to you."

Octavia leaned against the doorframe. "Even if you don't, we can't leave it like this."

Bridget twisted edge of the towel in her hands. "You lied to me."

"Yes." Octavia kept her voice neutral. "I did. About my name. And Vivian."

Bridget looked up at Octavia. "Why? All your talk about telling the truth always. You were lying to me the whole time."

"I want to tell you everything."

"Now you're forced to." She held one of the couch pillows in front of her body.

"No. Because now I'm ready." Octavia kept her gaze fixed on Bridget's eyes.

"What if I don't want hear it? How can I believe anything you say?"

"You don't have to believe me. If you don't, it's your business."

"So who are you? Anna? Or Octavia?" Bridget quirked her mouth.

"I was born Anna. When I had to change it I chose Octavia."

"Why? Are you a criminal? On the run?"

"No." Octavia raised her chin. "What do you know of the disappeared?"

Bridget frowned at her. "In Ireland?"

"Argentina. My father owned a newspaper. He had photos implicating people in power. They took him. I was eighteen."

"Why couldn't you tell me? That was years ago." Bridget set the pillow aside.

"I don't know if the people who killed my father don't want to kill the rest of my family to make a point. Memory is long in politics. They might think we still have the negatives my father refused to give them."

The confused expression on Bridget's face reminded Octavia of their age difference. She met Bridget's gaze. "Before digital cameras, you had to develop film images using chemicals and then print them on photo paper. Negatives are what you printed from. And the only way to make copies. If you destroyed the negatives, you destroyed the images forever."

"How does Vivian know you as Anna?"

"We went to boarding school together. In Switzerland."

Bridget inhaled sharply. "Were you lovers?"

"No. Best friends. We had one brief encounter after two bottles of wine the night before we graduated. I never saw her again until the day we met her at Rowan House. I wasn't sure it was her. I didn't know who she was until we were here."

Bridget looked down and away from Octavia. "And you didn't tell me. Even if you didn't want to tell me the other, you should have told me you had known her."

"I'm sure Vivian would allow you to break the contract."

Bridget snorted. "That'd be convenient for you, wouldn't it? You finding your long-lost love, me out of the picture."

She must have seen us. Fuck. "What makes you think I want to end us? Do you?"

"I don't know what I want. I don't know who to trust."

"I asked Vivian not to say anything. She only lied to you because I asked her to."

Bridget leaned back on the sofa. She raised her eyes to Octavia's face. "So she only lies when asked? Fuck that. Fuck you."

Octavia met Bridget's hard glare with one of her own. "You want to. That's why you're so angry. You want her. You want me. You can't figure it out. Now you have an excuse to ditch me and try for her. You don't have to. Love's not narrow. It doesn't diminish because you share it."

"Spare me a lecture. I had to share you with Martha. And the others. I hated it."

"You hated Martha. And the others were part of who I was then. It was play when it was play, and it was work when it was work. I enjoyed it. It fed a need in me." She swallowed hard. "If you want to end us, I understand. I'll go. But I want you to tell me. Be honest with yourself. And me." Octavia crossed the room and stood in front of her close enough Bridget had to look up to meet her gaze.

Bridget's eyes were dark. "Fine talk from you about honesty."

"I've never lied to you about how I feel or what I want. I've been honest in our relationship. I've loved you from the first moment we met. You fill a place in me I've missed my whole life. I wanted to protect you. I don't know how to fix this, or if you want to, but know this. I love you." Octavia risked a touch of Bridget's hair. "I love you now and always."

Bridget leaned away from her touch. "I don't know. I don't know what I want. I need to think."

She's done. What am I going to do? Her heart ached thinking of life without Bridget. Octavia chewed her lip. "I'll be in the barn if you want to talk." She left Bridget on the sofa. She went to their bedroom, where she collected her jacket. She closed the door quietly and left.

OCTAVIA SHIVERED IN her jacket. *Should've changed to dry clothes.* She hurried along the path, anxious for the warm comfort of the barn, her refuge, a consistent safe place in her world. The smell of wet burnt wood filled her nose. *Ugh. That smell. Have to clean it up in the morning. Wonder what's left. It was set. Who the fuck wants to intimidate Vivian? That was a message. If they wanted to do damage, they would have torched the barn.* Her stomach lurched as she imagined what could have happened. *I need to review our fire plan. I should sleep in the barn. Maybe they'll come back maybe they'll try again.* She balled her hands into fists. *Beating someone's ass would do wonders to lighten my mood. I'll sleep on the office sofa.* She flipped the collar of her coat up against the chill wind that sprung up after the storm. *Need a blanket. Wacky-ass weather.*

She rolled open the door to the barn and shut it after her. The door to her office was half-open. Vivian was sitting in the desk chair, her long legs stretched out in front of her and crossed at the ankles. *Vivian. Waiting for me.* Octavia pushed the door to the office open wide and stood in the doorway resting her hand on the frame.

Vivian looked up at her. On the desk were two glasses and a dusty bottle. "Do you like cognac?"

"You always keep your cognac in the barn?" Octavia moved to the chair next to the desk and sat down across from Vivian.

"Miriam liked a nip after a ride."

"She sounds like I would have liked her."

"Yes. I think you two would have liked each other very much." She filled two shot glasses.

The cognac is the same color as her eyes. So beautiful. Octavia picked up her glass. "To old friends and new beginnings."

Vivian raised her glass and touched it to Octavia's before she took a sip. She licked her lower lip. She raised her glass. "To love's memory."

They touched glasses again before they drained them.

Vivian coughed and set her glass down. "I've not done this since she passed." She picked up the bottle and refilled her tumbler.

"Drink cognac?"

Vivian held the bottle over Octavia's glass. "More?"

"Yes please."

She filled Octavia's glass. "Consider what I'm considering." She met Octavia's gaze. "With you. And Bridget."

Octavia held Vivian's gaze over the rim of her glass before she took a sip. She placed her glass on the table. She touched the back of Vivian's hand. "No pressure. I've loved you since we were girls. And I'll love you always. However that will be."

Vivian looked down at the table before she brought her gaze back to Octavia. "I was trained by the world's most powerful and impressive Dominatrix, and here I am struggling to find my way back to my life. I pulled away from everyone after Miriam died."

"A committed relationship is more than a collar. And I'm honored you're even considering whatever it is you're considering."

Vivian reached out and touched her fingers to Octavia's lips. "I wonder how it would have been if we had been bolder then. If we had understood what drew us to each other."

"We have now." Octavia caught her hand and pressed her lips to her fingers. "I talked to Bridget."

"And?"

"And she's angry as hell. At both of us. But me mostly."

Vivian pursed her lips. "She's young. And I think provincial in her outlook."

"Twenty-eight. She tell you about her life?"

"No. Martha shared her personnel record, the background check they do before they hire at Rowan House."

"A background check doesn't tell you everything."

"True. I noticed your record was sanitized. Did you ever tell Martha who you were?"

"After we were lovers, yes." She took another sip of cognac, the liquid fire settling low in her belly. "Bridget spent a lot of time in foster homes. Her parents OD'd when she was two. She and her sister lived with her grandma until she died in a house fire. Then she bounced from foster home to foster home. She ran away at sixteen. Put herself through culinary school. Met Cook. Ended up at Rowan House as sous-chef."

Vivian tilted her head. "I take it she didn't know exactly what she signed up for?" She tipped her glass back, finishing her cognac. "From her comments, she has no use for sex workers."

Octavia laughed. "Which is funny because she says she loves me. Or at least she said she did."

Vivian reached across the desk. She took Octavia's hand and squeezed it. "She'll come around. I see how she looks at you. She needs time."

The sound of the outer door rolling open startled them. Octavia stood up. "I'll go."

"Together." Vivian picked up the bottle, clasping the neck. She shifted it in her hand, holding it like a club.

Octavia walked carefully, keeping her steps light. The yellow glow of the night lights of the center aisle threw a long shadow on the wall. "Hello?"

"Jesus Mary and Joseph, you scared the hell out of me." Bridget's voice was loud. "What are you two doing out here? It's creepy as hell in the house by myself." She wore jeans and a white silk shirt, wet from the light rain. The top three buttons of the shirt were undone. She was braless, her ample breasts and dark nipples visible through the wet fabric. Damp dark red curls lay on her shoulders. She eyed the bottle in Vivian's hand. "Private party?"

"We were talking. Join us." The command in Vivian's voice was unmistakable.

Bridget rocked back on her heels and shoved her hands in the rear pockets of her jeans. The arch in her spine pressed her breasts tight against the shirt. "Or what?" Her challenging tone threaded its way into Octavia's core. *She needs a spanking. A good one. And kisses. Lots and lots of kisses. Us. She needs us. Wants us.*

Vivian placed the bottle of cognac on the bench. "Nothing." She straightened and squared her shoulders before she fixed her gaze on Bridget's face. "And that—" She closed the distance between them. "—is not what you want." She touched Bridget's hair, fingering the wet ends and twisting a bit around her finger. "Is it?"

"I don't—" Bridget voice was breathy. "—don't know what I want."

The sound of her desire laced with uncertainty made Octavia's heart ache. *Will she? Will she say yes? To her? Or me? Or both of us? Please let it be both of us. Or neither of us.*

"You do. You know. You wouldn't have come out here looking for us, dressed like this if you didn't." Vivian clasped Bridget's chin, forcing her head back, the skin blanching under her grip. "Showing off your lovely tits." She swept her hand up and cupped Bridget's breast. She squeezed the nipple, drawing a sharp yip followed by a deep moan from Bridget. "Taunting us. You want. You need. I see it in your eyes. You want to serve. Serve me. Serve us." She leaned down and brushed her lips over Bridget's mouth. "Don't deny who and what you are. Life is too uncertain. Don't deny yourself pleasure."

Bridget pulled her hands from her pockets and clasped them behind her back at the wrists. Vivian wrapped her hand in Bridget's hair and arched her neck. She lowered her mouth and kissed her. Bridget made soft noises in the back of her throat. Vivian savaged her mouth. The shift in Vivian's demeanor as she transformed into Mistress made Octavia's breath come fast and hard. She ached watching them. Her desire flowed, wetting her jeans. She shifted her stance, trying to ease the pressure building in her clit.

Bridget leaned into the kiss, her body bowing as she pressed against Vivian. She pulled back and looked into Vivian's face. "Yes. Yes." She brought her hands up and rested them on Vivian's hips. She twisted in her arms to look over her shoulder at Octavia. She held Octavia's gaze, her eyes wide. "Please. If it pleases you, Ma'am. Let me. Let me please both of you."

She's asking me. For permission. She gets it. Gets me. Us. Loves me. Still.

"Yes." Octavia shifted her gaze to Vivian's eyes. "If it pleases you." Made bold by Vivian's speech, she said the word she had longed to say since she had come to Vivian's house. "Mistress."

"It pleases me. Very much." Her eyes warm, a slight smile on her face, Vivian beckoned to Octavia to join them. "Come."

Yes. Let me serve you. Both. Give myself to you. With quick steps Octavia went to stand behind Bridget, pressing her more firmly against Vivian. She wrapped her arms around both of them, holding tight to Vivian's hips. Octavia's hands overlapped Bridget's fingers. She kissed Bridget's neck and under her ear. Her soft moans signaled her need as Vivian kissed her again, and she rocked against Bridget, the movement pushing her ass firmly against Octavia's clit. Vivian broke her kiss with Bridget. Breathing rough, she met Octavia's gaze.

Octavia studied the hunger in Vivian's eyes. *Want. She wants us. Now. Lust. Feral. Now.* "Let's move this party."

Vivian kissed Octavia and nipped her lip before she pressed a quick kiss to Bridget's lips. "Yes. Somewhere more comfortable." She broke their embrace and took Bridget's hand to lead her out of the door toward the house. Octavia stopped long enough to close the office door and followed after them.

OCTAVIA AND BRIDGET pulled their shoes off and placed them neatly on the boot tray. Octavia reached to unbutton her shirt.

"Wait." Vivian's voice was steel wrapped in satin. "Hands at your sides."

Octavia shivered, her soul responding to Vivian's command. *This. I need this. Need her.* She moved her hands to comply, holding on to her pants seam to still them.

Octavia caught her breath as Vivian stripped Bridget's clothes off, the buttons of the shirt flying as she ripped the silk in her quiet urgency. She bent her head and took Bridget's nipple in her mouth. She slipped her hand down, opened the button top of Bridget's jeans and unzipped them. Bridget shifted on her feet, trying to kick off her jeans. Octavia knelt and tugged the wet jeans from Bridget's skin. She kissed the tops of Bridget's feet, working her way up her legs but stopping shy of the junction of her thighs. *Not without permission. Not now. So hard to wait. I can't.* The scent of Bridget made her mouth water. She placed her nose against the soft curls at the top of Bridget's sex and inhaled. Her mouth watered. She wanted to push her tongue through the curls and lick Bridget's clit. To savor the taste of her and the way her clit would thicken under her tongue. Bridget pushed forward, thrusting herself into Octavia's mouth. Octavia wrapped her hands around her legs to steady her. Bridget's moans were loud in the tiled room.

Vivian's gentle hand on her head made Octavia stop. "Enough."

Octavia leaned into her touch, her command. Her kind, firm tone made Octavia want to obey, to fulfill Vivian's desires, to give her obedience as a gift. Vivian leaned down and traced her fingers over Octavia's cheek before cupping her face with both hands. She looked into Octavia's eyes.

"You've forgotten your training. We'll have to work on that." The sweet threat in Vivian's voice sent another wave of want through Octavia. "Stand for me."

Octavia stood next to Bridget. The heat of their bodies warmed the small space. Vivian held her gaze a long moment. *Do it. Please punish me. Please.* She slapped her face, and Octavia moaned with the sharp sting of the blow. She fought the urge to touch her cheek where Vivian had slapped her. A gush of wetness spilled from her core. Vivian held her gaze as she slowly unbuttoned the blue denim shirt Octavia wore. She pushed her hands under the shirt to slide it off Octavia's shoulders, her touch sending waves of heat through Octavia. Her nipples were hard from the slap and Vivian cupped her hands under Octavia's breasts before she caught both of her nipples in a tight grip. A deep moan rumbled in Octavia's chest. *Yes. Please. Hurt me. So good. Please give me your pain. Let me hold it. Give it back.* Vivian release her nipples, and Octavia groaned at the loss of her touch and the sweet sting as her body responded to Vivian's harshness.

Leaning close, Vivian kissed the side of Octavia's neck as she tugged the shirt off her arms and let it drop to the floor. She traced her fingers over the vine tattoos winding around Octavia's shoulders and flowing over her arms. She brought her lips close to Octavia's ear. "I've wanted to see how far these tattoos go since I first saw them."

The backs of her hands brushed the skin of Octavia's stomach as she unbuckled her belt. Octavia trembled as Vivian unbuttoned her jeans. With one finger, she teased Octavia's clit through her briefs before she unzipped her jeans and pushed them down. She knelt at Octavia's feet and slipped the pants the rest of the way off. She rose and stepped back. With one hand on her hip, she studied Octavia and Bridget, her gaze shifting from one to the other. She held her hand up and made a circular motion, signaling them to turn. As one, they turned their backs. Bridget reached over and clasped Octavia's hand. There was a slight tremor in her touch. Octavia squeezed her hand before she brought her hand to her lips and kissed it. "Okay, love?"

Bridget nodded a quick yes.

The whisper of Vivian's clothes as she removed them sent a bolt of desire through Octavia. *Let us see you. Let us touch you.* The sweet denial of seeing Vivian undress made Octavia's pulse race. She took a deep breath to steady herself.

"Remember, either of you can say stop anytime." Vivian placed a hand on the back of each of their necks. She dropped a kiss on Bridget's shoulder. "You're safe with me. We decided together what we want. I won't ask anything you can't give."

She pressed a kiss to Octavia's shoulder before she released their necks. She stepped in front of them. Her body was slim, all hard angles and long lines. Her breasts were small, topped with thick nipples. She turned her back to them. The graceful curve of her back and hips was limned in the light from the kitchen. Naked together, Octavia longed to touch both of them, to have them touch her. Vivian led them from the kitchen, through the dining room. In the hall, she turned left. They passed the entry to her bedroom and made another turn before stopping at a closed door. Vivian reached up and retrieved a thick black key from the doorframe.

After inserting it in the lock, she paused. She turned her head and closed her eyes. A moment passed before Vivian turned to them, her eyes dark. "No." She pulled the key from the lock and replaced it. She stood with her head down and her shoulders slumped.

Miriam. She hasn't had a lover since she lost her. First time. First for her. First for Bridget. Don't fuck this up. Be strong for her. For both of them. Octavia slipped an arm around Vivian's shoulders.

Bridget slid her arm around Vivian's waist. "If it pleases you, Mistress, could we go to our room?"

A long moment passed. *Please say yes. Please be with us. Let us in. Be with us.*

"Yes." Vivian looked up to meet their gaze. "Yes." Her voice was soft. "Your room would be perfect."

They walked together, arms tight around each other, lending their strength to Vivian. Their steps in sync, each lost in their thoughts, comfortable in the silence that surrounded them.

SOFT LIGHT FROM the bedside lamps bathed the room in cool white light. Vivian stood to the side of the bed. Whatever war she had fought inside herself was over by the time they arrived at Bridget and Octavia's room. "Down."

As one, Bridget and Octavia kneeled. Octavia watched Bridget from under her lashes. *She's okay. Vivian has this. Time to relax. Let go. Give in. Surrender. All of me.*

Vivian came to stand in front of them. Her bare legs were so close Octavia longed to cover the tops of her feet with kisses before she rested her head on them. She wanted to kiss her way along her legs, to feel her skin under her lips. To nuzzle her thighs and higher, to the tight curls between her legs, to taste, to touch, to hear the sounds of Vivian's pleasure. *Mistress. Obey. Serve. Let me serve you. Please.*

The scent of their arousal suffused the room. Octavia inhaled, taking in the essence of them. Honeysuckle, verbena, sweat, and desire.

"Bridget, here." She patted the bed. "Face up. Arms over your head. Spread your legs for me." Octavia dared a quick look when she was sure Vivian's back was to her. The trust on Bridget's face reassured her.

"Do you need me to tie you or can you be still for me?" Vivian passed a hand over Bridget's skin, brushing her nipples, before she dipped her fingers between her legs. The bedsprings creaked with Bridget's movement as she lifted her hips.

"Whatever pleases you, Ma'am."

The slap was quick, lighter than what she had given Octavia but sharp enough to make Bridget gasp. Vivian grabbed Bridget's chin, her eyes hard. "I am not your Ma'am. You will call me Mistress. I won't be as gentle with my reminder next time."

She snapped her fingers at Octavia and pointed to a spot next to her.

Octavia crawled forward to obey.

Vivian snapped her fingers again. "Stand up. Eyes to me."

Octavia rose and raised her eyes to meet Vivian's gaze.

"You've been lax in her training." Vivian frowned at Octavia.

"Yes, Mistress."

Vivian smiled at Octavia, a tight cruel smile that made Octavia weak with want. "We'll remedy that. What have you used for discipline?"

"Spanking, with my hand or a belt, denial of pleasure, light pain." Suddenly shy under Vivian's gaze, she looked down at her hands. "Mistress."

Bridget's breathing became louder in the room. The bed shifted as she squirmed on the bed. Vivian slapped the inside of Bridget's thigh, drawing a squeal from her. "Be still. What is your word?"

Bridget frowned and jutted her chin forward. "I don't have one, Ma—Mistress."

"No word?" Vivian rounded on Octavia. She flicked Octavia's nipple. The sting sent an electric shock of pleasure to Octavia's clit. "Mmm, another thing to punish you for. This will be a long night. What have you relied on?"

"My instincts. My sense of her as a person, nonverbal clues, Mistress."

Vivian pressed her lips in a thin line. "I know Rowan House has its own rules, but every submissive deserves a safe word and we will use them."

Octavia shifted, trying to relieve the pressure in her clit. "Yes, Mistress." *Please now. Punish me. Now. Give me the pain I desire. Now, please.*

Vivian shifted her focus back to Bridget. "You must choose. I won't play without one."

Bridget raised an eyebrow, her voice firm. "It's not play to me, Mistress."

Vivian pursed her lips. "Until I decide it's something more, it is to me." She cupped Bridget's face in her hands. "If you don't want to do this, say so now. I can't promise you more than tonight."

"Apples, Mistress. Apples will be my word." Bridget's voice held a quiver of tears.

Vivian leaned down and brushed her lips over her mouth. "Well done, sweet girl." She squeezed Bridget's nipple and drew a sharp intake of breath from her. "Apples it is." She straightened and turned to Octavia. "Bind her. I'll be back."

Vivian pulled the side chair near the bed before she left the room, and Octavia hurried to obey. She went to the armoire and pulled four of Bridget's scarves from the drawer. She brought the scissors from the desk and placed them on the nightstand. Turning her attention to the bed and Bridget, she worked carefully to secure her arms and legs. Octavia passed a scarf around Bridget's wrist, before knotting it to hold her without pulling tight if she struggled against her bonds. She worked her way around the bed and tied Bridget's legs wide. Bridget's breath came faster as Octavia moved to the other side of the bed and repeated the procedure with her arm.

Bridget turned her head, her gaze settling on Octavia's face. "What are the scissors for?"

Excitement. Want. Need. Trust. So much love. She leaned close and brought her lips to Bridget's ear. "Safety. In case we needed to release you quickly. Ready, love?"

"Yes." Bridget raised her head and kissed Octavia's cheek. "Are you?"

"Yes. Remember your word." She slipped her fingers under the last knot, making sure the bonds were safe and would hold.

Vivian returned to the room dressed in a long black silk robe. In one hand was a short flogger with wide leather tails, in the other a red-and-black crop. The braided leather alternated colors, ending in a thin red keeper. She placed the flogger on the nightstand. The robe swirled and swayed around her legs as she walked around the bed and checked Octavia's work. She sat in the chair facing the bed and leaned back before crossing her legs. The robe parted, revealing her thigh, and even though Octavia had seen her naked, the effect of the partial display made her press her legs together to stop the flow of her want from wetting the floor. Bridget's breathing was loud in the quiet of the room. Her gaze focused on Bridget, Vivian began to tap the crop against the side of the chair rhythmically.

She's assessing her. Making her plan. She'll test her. And me. That crop. Octavia's thighs were slick with want as she kneeled next to the bed, waiting for Vivian to speak. She longed for direction, ached to serve, to let go, to be in the moment, no worries, no fear, nothing to focus on but sweet pain and Vivian's desires.

Vivian stood. She placed the crop on the nightstand before she took hold of the thick braid at the base of Octavia's neck and pulled her head back, forcing her to meet her gaze.

She needs this. Wants this as much as I do. Octavia was unable to stifle her sigh of desire.

"Patience, my sweet. You'll have your turn." Vivian leaned down and kissed her before she released her. "Get on the bed. I want your mouth on her, edging her. Lips and tongue only, she's not to come until I say otherwise."

Octavia mounted the bed, anxious to obey. She kneeled between Bridget's legs. The soft curls of her sex glistened. Bridget's body was taut as she arched to meet Octavia's mouth.

Vivian stood next to the bed. She brought the flogger to Bridget's lips. "Show the proper respect." Bridget stilled, her breath rough and loud in the room. She looked at Vivian, an uncertainty in her eyes.

"The flogger is an extension of me. When you kiss the flogger, it is the same as kissing my hand." Bridget raised her head and brought her lips to the flogger. Vivian leaned over the bed. She pinned Bridget with her gaze. "Remember your word. You do not take your pleasure until I say. Your pleasure belongs to me tonight."

"Yes, Mistress." Bridget's voice was thick.

The sound of the soft flogger as it made first contact with Bridget's skin caused Octavia to moan. She lifted her gaze.

Faint red stripes from the wide tails marked Bridget's stomach and the underside of her breasts. Octavia kept her lips and tongue moving over Bridget's clit, sucking and licking. A surge of wetness poured from Bridget.

Vivian placed a hand on Octavia's shoulder and squeezed hard, digging her nails into Octavia's skin. "Stop."

Octavia obeyed even as every part of her wanted to bury her face between Bridget's legs and lick her until she screamed and came, unable to stop herself. She raised her head and watched as Vivian passed her hand over the marks she had made. Bridget shook and moaned.

Vivian leaned over Bridget's face. "That was a taste. Remember you must ask my permission to come. If you need to stop for any reason, say your word and we will both stop. Do you understand?"

"Yes." Bridget's tone bordered on insolent.

Vivian grabbed her nipple, squeezed hard, and Bridget squealed. The sound of her pain sent a rush of love and desire through Octavia.

"Answer properly."

"Ahh. Yes, Mistress. Oh." Bridget panted and thrashed, pulling against her bonds.

Vivian released her. She motioned for Octavia to resume her task. Octavia lowered her head and suckled Bridget's clit. She knew Bridget's body, knew how to keep her on the cusp of coming, make her crazy with want. The soft swish of the flogger cutting through the air before it made contact made Octavia ache for her own punishment. She knew the crop awaited her, when and if Vivian had her fill of Bridget's pain. She was crying now, a soft sound undergirded by the sound of her want, sharp sounds of pain blending with deep moans as Bridget struggled to hold back.

"Please, Mistress. Oh please. I can't. I'm going to come. Please, Mistress. I can't hold back. I can't." Her body shook with her effort, every muscle tight. The bed squeaked as she thrashed and bucked into Octavia's mouth. Anchoring her with her arms, Octavia held her down, keeping her from obtaining what she needed to come. Controlling her for Vivian. *For you, Mistress, holding her for you, binding her for your desires.* The sound of Vivian's soft pleased hum made Octavia's clit swell, and she shifted her legs. A puddle of her own need collected on the bed below her.

"Do you want us to stop?" Vivian paused in her strokes. She tapped Octavia on the shoulder, and she stilled while keeping her mouth on Bridget. Vivian ran the edge of her fingernail over the tight peak of Bridget's nipple.

"Oh no, Mistress. Please. I need. Please let me." Bridget's cheeks were red. She turned her face to the side, her eyes squeezed tight.

"Eyes to me. Ask me. Ask for what you want."

Bridget turned her tear-stained face to Vivian. "Please let me come for you. Let me come while you flog me. Let me come in her mouth. Let me please you. Let me come for you. Please don't stop. Please, Mistress."

"Are you going to call me Ma'am anymore? Are you clear what to call me?" Vivian's voice held a tremor, the only sign of her excitement, and it was enough for Octavia to moan as she waited for the signal to begin again. Vivian flicked the flogger over Bridget's breasts.

Bridget arched in response. "Oh. Oh. Mistress. Always. Please, Mistress, let me come for you." She panted, her breathing rough and sweet to Octavia's ears.

Vivian tapped Octavia on the shoulder. Octavia watched Vivian from under her lashes as she covered Bridget's clit with her mouth. Her robe had come open with her movement, and Vivian's breasts swayed with each stroke of the flogger. Her dark nipples stood erect, and her lips were pulled back in a feral smile. "Come as you wish." She brought the flogger down quickly, whipping it over Bridget's breasts and stomach.

Octavia matched her strokes, licking and sucking in time with the blows of the flogger. Bridget's screams became chest-rattling moans as she broke, and Octavia swallowed her sweetness as it filled her mouth. Vivian dropped the flogger on the bed. She leaned over Bridget and kissed her. Octavia drove her up again, making her scream her release in Vivian's mouth. A deep groan from Vivian sent a thrill through Octavia. *For us. For this.*

Vivian pulled back from the kiss. "Well done, sweet girl." She rested her hand on Octavia's head. "Enough." She reached over and tugged Bridget's bonds free of the headboard, leaving them knotted at her wrist. Bridget grabbed Vivian with both arms and pulled her down into a deep kiss. Vivian moaned into the kiss before she brought her hands up and caught Bridget's hands at the wrists and forced them down, pinning her on the bed. She broke their kiss and lingered for a moment before she pulled back. "No. No touching. Not until I say so. Next lesson." She stood up and pulled her robe closed and knotted it. "Water. And then—" She cupped Octavia's face with her hand and caressed her cheek with her thumb. "We begin again."

Chapter Ten

VIVIAN PULLED THE knots loose and freed Bridget's legs. She sat on the bed and gathered Bridget into her arms before she leaned back against the headboard. Octavia rested on her heels watching them, waiting for Vivian's command and admiring the way they looked together. Vivian's long elegant form draped in satin with Bridget's curvy body wrapped around her. Bridget glanced at her before she blushed and looked away.

Octavia met Vivian's gaze and shifted her eyes toward Bridget. Vivian silently mouthed, "Is she okay?" Octavia shrugged in response.

Vivian massaged the back of Bridget's neck. Octavia touched Bridget's foot. "You okay, love?"

Bridget brought her gaze to Octavia's, her cheeks a deep red, guilt on her face. "I don't know how to do this part."

"There is no one way." She pressed a kiss to the top of Bridget's foot and looked to Vivian's face.

"Join us." She held her hand out to Octavia.

Octavia clasped her fingers and squeezed them. She released Vivian's hand and moved up the bed and spooned Bridget from behind. Bridget reached back and cupped Octavia's face. She turned and planted a kiss on her cheek, before she snuggled back into Vivian's shoulder. Octavia squeezed Bridget's ass. "You were magnificent, love."

"I don't have words." Bridget caught Octavia's hand. She held it tight and kissed her fingers. "Thank you."

"For what?"

"For making me feel brave. For loving me."

Octavia turned Bridget's hand over and kissed her palm. "You are brave." She lifted her gaze to Vivian's face. "And you, Mistress."

Vivian reached over and squeezed Octavia's shoulder and held her gaze a moment before she spoke. "I'm also parched."

"I'll get water, Mistress." Octavia scooted out the door and hurried to the kitchen. She arranged three glasses and a pitcher of water on a tray. She collected a box of crackers from the pantry and a bunch of grapes from the bowl on the table. She hurried back to their bedroom. The sounds of pleasure greeted her as she opened the door.

Bridget was lying on her back between Vivian's legs as Vivian knelt over her face. Vivian's eyes were closed as she rocked her hips. Octavia closed her legs against the gush of wetness that spilled from her. She placed the tray on the nightstand.

Vivian opened her eyes and met Octavia's gaze. "Come here."

Octavia mounted the bed from the opposite side. Vivian reached up and cupped her head, bringing her in for a hard kiss. Her sharp teeth nicked Octavia's lips, and she moaned into Vivian's mouth.

Vivian leaned back from the kiss. Her eyes burned with need. "Fuck me."

Octavia scrambled behind Vivian. She straddled Bridget's body and clasped Vivian around the waist. She brought her hand up and pushed her fingers in deep. Bridget moaned under her, and the wet sounds of her licking and sucking Vivian's clit made Octavia shiver. She rubbed herself against Bridget's stomach, the firm pressure pleasing against her clit. Vivian shuddered, and Octavia pushed faster and deeper. "Now, my sweets, now."

She came with long low moan, her pleasure coating Octavia's hand and spilling into Bridget's mouth. Bridget's moans of satisfaction mixed with Vivian's soft groans. Octavia panted, cherishing the clutch of Vivian around her fingers.

When she was sure Vivian was satisfied, she pulled her fingers from her. Octavia clasped her shoulders and helped her off Bridget. Vivian lay down next to Bridget, and Octavia scooted up behind her, reaching over to touch Bridget as she turned to face her. Bridget lifted her head, and Octavia leaned over Vivian to kiss her, savoring the taste of Vivian on her lips. Vivian shifted so she could wrap her arms around both of them, bringing them in to snuggle against her shoulders. She kissed the tops of their heads. "And now I truly need a drink of water."

Octavia got up and poured three glasses of water. She passed a glass to Vivian and then to Bridget. She drank her own glass of water standing at the bedside and poured another and drank half of it. "Would you like some crackers? Or grapes, Mistress?"

Vivian smiled and extended her hand. "Yes, grapes." Octavia handed her a bunch of the blood-red grapes. Vivian pulled a grape free before she pressed it to Bridget's mouth. She smiled as Bridget took the food from her hand. She pulled another free and fed Octavia. "Eat, my sweets. It's been a long time, and I'm not done with either of you." The light in her eyes made Octavia shiver.

Vivian frowned. "Are you cold? Come here. Bring the grapes." She patted the bed in front of her. Bridget shifted her seat, pulling her legs ups and tucking them under herself. Vivian pulled her robe from the bed where it lay. She handed to Octavia. "Put it on."

Octavia slipped the robe over her shoulders, inhaling deeply the scent of Vivian's light verbena perfume that clung to the fabric. Vivian fed them each in turn until they finished the grapes. Octavia grew warm watching Vivian feed Bridget, the way her mouth looked as Bridget took grapes from Vivian's hand. *So long. When was the last time I was fed by hand?* She cherished the way Vivian fed her, her fingertips brushing against her lips as she placed the grapes in Octavia's mouth, holding eye contact until Octavia swallowed. The tender expression on her face as she attended to Octavia's needs made her want to kneel and ask to be hers forever.

They ate all the grapes, and Vivian laid the woody stem on the tray. She finished her water and placed the glass on the nightstand. She tilted her head at Octavia, sweeping her gaze over her body before she brought it back to her face. "Better?"

"Yes, Mistress."

Vivian caressed her, fingertips tracing a line down Octavia's cheek and over her lips. She clasped her jaw and leaned forward and kissed her, holding her still. Her lips were firm as Vivian took what she wanted. Small sounds of need flowed from Octavia. *Now. Yes. More. Give me more.*

A deep growl sounded from Vivian before she spoke. "Yes. You want. You need." She smoothed her hands under the robe and pushed it off Octavia's shoulders. She scraped a nail along the tender skin under her breast before she caught her nipple between her thumb and forefinger. "I love how thick your nipples are. I want to put clamps on them, but tonight I'm too impatient."

Octavia was aware of Bridget. She could hear her breathing as it increased and sensed her eyes upon her.

Vivian arched an eyebrow. "You're worried about her, aren't you? Distracted by her." She squeezed Octavia's nipple harder, making her cry out. "Relax. I'll take care her. And you. Eyes to me."

Octavia held Vivian's gaze. The pain of her squeezing her nipple focused her. Vivian was her world. *Trust. She'll take care of me. Of us. She'll make sure Bridget is included. It's okay to let go. It's safe to be me.*

Vivian released her nipple. "Get the crop. Stand at the end of the bed. On your elbows, legs spread. Display yourself for me."

Octavia slid off the bed. She brought the crop to her. She kissed it before presenting it with both hands, keeping her eyes down. Vivian took it from her, the brush of her fingertips igniting a fire that burned low in Octavia's belly. She moved to the end of the bed and bent at the hips and spread her legs.

"Bridget, slide down to the end of the bed, on your back. Spread your legs to give Octavia a view of how wet you are." Bridget moved to obey, and Vivian tucked the crop under her arm before she pushed a pillow under Bridget's shoulders. "There. Now I'll be able to see your face. And your other charms." She passed her hand over Bridget's body, stopping to dip her fingers between her legs. "So wet. Already. You can't wait to put on a show for us, can you?" Bridget did not respond, her face bright red. "Answer me, or use your word."

"Yes, Mistress." Bridget bit her lip.

"Put your fingers on your clit. Show us how you touch yourself when you're alone."

Bridget moved her hand down and swept the wetness between her legs up, slicking her fingers before she rubbed them over her clit.

Vivian moved to Octavia's head. "I've not done this for a long time." She pushed a wisp of hair that had worked loose from Octavia's braid behind her ear before she moved the thick braid to the side, exposing her back. She leaned down and brought her lips close to Octavia's ear. "What is your word, my sweet?"

"Eight. But I won't need it, Mistress."

Vivian slapped Octavia's ass hard enough she jumped. "Don't be so sure of yourself. Bridget, same as before. You don't come unless I command."

"Yes, Mistress."

She stepped behind Octavia. "Raise your head. Wrap your hands around her ankles, help her to keep her legs open, and keep your eyes on her. She's touching herself for us."

She raised the crop and brought it down hard across Octavia's shoulders. The biting sting made her groan. *More please. Harder. Missed this. Need this. Give it to me.* Bridget's eyes widened. Octavia met her gaze, letting her see she was okay. Another blow and she moaned as a tide of desire swept through her. Her nipples peaked, and she lowered her gaze, mesmerized by the beauty of Bridget's fingers rubbing and stroking her clit. Her mouth watered. She wanted to taste her, to have her face buried in her while Vivian beat her.

Vivian brushed her fingers over her back, caressing the raised welts. Octavia shivered. Her skin stung every place Vivian touched, and she whimpered, craving more. "Please, Mistress. More. Please." *Give me what I want. What I need. More. Harder. Break me. Make me beg.*

"I love the way your skin takes my marks."

"More. Please, Mistress. Please. Mark me."

Vivian stepped to the side of her. Octavia watched Bridget as she caressed herself and focused on the way she jacked her clit. She glanced to the side, trying to see more of Vivian. Forgetting her training, she made eye contact for a brief moment. Then the crop landed on her ass. A cutting blow, it was followed by more strikes on her hips and her back. Vivian spaced her strikes expertly, allowing Octavia to become lost in the sea of endorphins flowing through her. Sweet pain filled her, blotting out everything but Bridget's heavy breathing and the sounds of Vivian panting with effort and excitement as she marked her. She stopped and passed her hand over the welts again, drawing her nails across them. Octavia listened as Vivian's breathing shifted and she regained control.

"Eyes to me, Octavia." Vivian slipped the robe off her body and let it fall in an inky puddle at her fee. Naked, she reached between her legs and touched her fingers there, gathering evidence of her desire. She brought her fingers to Octavia's mouth and shoved them between her lips. Octavia sucked and licked, aching for more. Vivian thrust her fingers in and out of her mouth, a sweet torment, and Octavia shook with need. She pulled her fingers free and wrapped her hand around Octavia's throat. Octavia stilled, closing her eyes against the sensation of Vivian's hand collaring her. *Own me. Make me yours. Let me serve.*

Vivian tightened her fingers, and Octavia's heart raced. "Please me and I'll let you pleasure me."

Octavia groaned at her words. Vivian removed her hand. A moment, an eternity, then the blows of the crop rained down, the cutting sensation replaced by heavy, bruising, thudding blows against her skin. Octavia cried out with the pain. Her body shook, and she panted through the sensation, absorbing it, reveling in it. *Yes. More.*

Pleasepleaseplease. Break me. Make me yours. Break me and make me whole again. Tears then as she cried and begged. To be marked. To come. To touch herself. To touch Bridget. To be allowed to lick her Mistress's clit. To serve. Her clit throbbed and ached to be touched. Wet to her knees with desire, she shifted her feet, wanting to squeeze her legs together, to ease the pressure in her hard clit. She kept her legs apart, fighting her desire for relief, her obedience and denial a gift to Vivian. Her mouth was dry, and she ached as she watched Bridget become wetter, the thick shine of her excitement coating her fingers.

"Please, Mistress." Bridget's soft plea cut into Octavia's thoughts

Vivian's harsh breathing matched the fierceness of her blows.

Give it to me. Let me take your pain. Let me. Give it all to me. All of your pain. My gift to you. My body. My obedience. Octavia panted, struggling to control herself, desperate to hold on, to wait upon her Mistress's pleasure.

"Mistress. I can't. I'm going to come. Please. Let me come for you." Bridget's body was tense, and she trembled. Octavia dug her fingers into her ankles as she held tight, trying to hold herself back, trying to distract Bridget, trying to help her.

Vivian dropped the crop to the floor and stepped behind Octavia. She leaned forward, draping herself over Octavia's back. Her hard nipples pressed against the welts and marks that would bruise. She brought her hand up and fingered Octavia's clit. A deep groan shook Octavia. Everywhere Vivian's body touched her, she burned.

"Oh Mistress. Please. Let me come for you." Octavia bit her lip, trying to hold off the pressure building in her core. "Please, Mistress."

Bridget's fingers moved with a steady rhythm, and she rocked her hips up into her hand. "Please, Mistress. Let me come for you. For both of you. Please." The volume of her pleading increased as she shook with trying to hold her pleasure, saving it for her Mistress.

Vivian's body trembled against Octavia, and she brought her other hand up and thrust three fingers into Octavia. Fucking her roughly, she kept her other hand on her clit, fingertips rolling and squeezing, keeping pace with her hard strokes. She ground her hips against Octavia's ass. The sensation of her pressing her wet curls and flesh against Octavia's raw skin as she rocked her clit against her pushed Octavia closer to the edge.

"Ahh, yesyesyes. Please, Mistress, fuck me. Please. Fuck me. Harder please, Mistress." Octavia thrust her hips back, trying to take more of Vivian, to give her Mistress everything.

Vivian's breathing was rough on the back of her neck. Octavia groaned when Vivian thrust another finger in, spreading her wide. She gritted her teeth against the sweet sting and burn, fighting to control herself. Vivian's fingers thrust deeper and curled over the spot that sent her spinning over the edge. "Oh please. Mistress. Please. I can't... Eight!"

"Now. Come for me, both of you. Now." Vivian fucked Octavia ruthlessly, and she came hard, her pleasure soaking Vivian's hand. Her body shaking, she watched as Bridget rubbed faster. She came for them, legs open, showing them the deep pink and red of her center. She arched up into her hand, and Octavia held fast to Bridget's ankles and groaned as she came again, with Vivian's fingers deep inside her, stroking her to another orgasm. Vivian slowed her thrusts, and the soft sound of her release as she came against Octavia's ass sent a satisfying sensation through Octavia.

They stayed like that, her hands wrapped around Bridget's ankles, Octavia's head resting on the mattress, Vivian deep inside her with her body resting on Octavia's back until her breathing returned to normal.

Vivian eased her fingers from Octavia and stood up. "You can release Bridget." Octavia uncurled her hands. She smoothed her palms over the marks her nails had made when she came. Bridget closed her legs and lay on her side. Vivian helped Octavia to the bed and covered both of them with the duvet. She poured them each water. Octavia pushed herself up in the bed to take the glass from Vivian's hand. Bridget's eyes were closed.

Octavia tapped her on the shoulder. "Have some water, love." Bridget sat up and yawned. She took the glass from Vivian with both hands.

While she drank, Vivian ran her hand over Bridget's breasts and stomach. A few red marks remained from the soft flogger. Bridget drank her water quickly. She passed the glass to Octavia and lay back down. "You wore me out."

Vivian cupped her face and pressed a gentle kiss to her forehead. "Sleep well, sweet girl." Bridget curled on her side and drew her legs up. Vivian tucked the blanket around her. A soft sigh escaped Bridget, and she closed her eyes.

Vivian picked up her robe and put it on. She tied it loosely and collected the flogger and the crop before she left the room.

Octavia pulled the blanket up higher around Bridget's shoulders. "Good night, love."

Bridget caught her hand and pressed her lips to the back of it. "Love you. Night, Ma'am."

A tight curl of love wrapped around Octavia's heart and squeezed hard. *Mine. Hers. Still.*

Vivian returned with a washcloth, a towel, and a small blue jar. "I was not as light-handed with you. Let me put this salve on those marks." Her gaze was soft when she met Octavia's eyes.

Octavia placed her glass on the nightstand. She turned over on her stomach and pillowed her hands on her arms.

Vivian sat on the edge of the bed next to Octavia. "I broke the skin in a few places. This might sting a bit." She wiped the wet cloth over Octavia's back and hips, cleaning her skin before she dried it. Vivian's hands were warm and gentle as she rubbed the soothing ointment into Octavia's skin. She leaned over and kissed the back of her neck, the hollow at the base of her hairline, and Octavia's shoulder before she rested her cheek there.

The moment stretched out, and Octavia searched for words to tell Vivian all the emotions filing her heart and soul. *My safe word. I haven't said it in years. I used it with her. Will she know what a gift it is? How can I tell her what I want? Tell her all the things I feel?* She remained mute. Savoring the sensation of Vivian's tenderness.

"Sleep well, my sweet. Thank you." Vivian stood up. She rested her hand on Octavia's head.

Stay. Be with us. Sleep here. Lay down next to me. Let me curl around you. Let me hold you and listen to your heartbeat. Let me wake up to you. Octavia watched as she left, resisting the urge to run after her and beg her to come back to bed. *Not enough. It has to be. I want more. Will I ever have enough of her?* A delicious soreness settled into her body, making her wish Vivian had marked her breasts too, so she could see the evidence of their time together. She settled on her side and watched Bridget sleep, envying her peaceful slumber. *Will she be okay in the morning? Will I?*

Chapter Eleven

OCTAVIA HAD SLIPPED out of bed to care for the horses before Bridget woke. Her back stung when she tugged on her shirt, a sweet reminder of the night before. After feeding the horses, she turned them out and went back to the house. The smell of coffee brewing greeted her. She pulled off her boots and washed up in the mudroom sink. Their clothes from the night before were in a small pile. Hard evidence of their night of passion. *Need to wash those. After breakfast.*

Bridget met her at the door to the kitchen with a deep kiss. "There's hot tea for you. Do you want some eggs? I'm starved."

"Eggs sounds wonderful." Octavia nuzzled Bridget's neck. "Do we have any more of that bread you made? The rye?"

"Yes. You make the toast, I'll make the eggs." She squeezed Octavia tight to her before she let go.

"Deal."

Octavia cut thick slices from the rye loaf before she toasted them. The smell of butter melting in the pan made her mouth water. She smeared each slice with butter before passing the plates to Bridget for their eggs. They sat down across from each other.

Octavia took a bite of the bread. Chewing slowly, she savored the texture and taste of her toast. "This is so good. You never made this at Rowan House."

"I didn't make a lot of things at Rowan House. Cook set the menus." Bridget took a sip of her coffee and placed the cup on the table. She looked at the clock and the kitchen door. "Do you think she'll join us?" The uncertainty and longing in her voice made Octavia wince.

Octavia reached across the table and took Bridget's hand. "For breakfast? Yes, when she wakes up. If that's what you meant."

Bridget blushed and squeezed Octavia's hand. "I feel so awkward. How do you do it? You're so calm." She met Octavia's gaze.

"It's not my first time around the block." Octavia looked into Bridget's eyes. "And it will be what it will be. What happened was exquisite and perfect and beautiful."

"So we go back to how we were? Like nothing happened?" Bridget's mouth turned down at the corners. "Like it didn't mean anything?"

"No. It means we wait and see what happens. And it will always mean something to me that you were brave enough to try something new. Come here." Bridget let go of Octavia's hand. She walked around the table, and Octavia pushed her chair back so that Bridget could sit in her lap. Curling into Octavia, Bridget rested her head on her shoulder. Octavia wrapped her arms around her and pulled her close. "We all crossed a line last night, and we have to work out what it means for each of us."

"I don't know what to do with my feelings for her." Bridget kissed Octavia's neck under her ear.

"You feel them. Don't try to box them up."

"How do you feel about her?" Bridget raised her head to look in Octavia's eyes.

"I care about her. I love her."

Bridget chewed her lip. "Like you love me?"

Octavia met Bridget's gaze. "I love you like I love you and will always love you. I love her like I love her. No two loves are the same."

Bridget quirked her mouth. "Like you loved Martha? I can't give you what she did. Couldn't hurt you like that."

"Did it hurt when Vivian beat you with the flogger?"

"Yes. And no." Bridget rested her hand on the buttons of Octavia's shirt. "It was like when you spank me. I wanted more. But not too much more."

"A good Domme knows each submissive's limit and adjusts. I don't expect you to do what she does. I wouldn't ask you because I know it's not in you to be like that with me."

"But it's in you."

"It is, not as much as it's in Vivian, but it's there."

"I love that it's there." Bridget kissed Octavia, her lips soft and searching. She moved her hands down to Octavia's belt and fingered the buckle. "Does a good Ma'am know what her sub wants? Right now."

Octavia cupped the back of Bridget's neck. "I can guess." She pulled her closer and kissed her hard. She moved her hand up to cup her breast through her shirt and thumbed her nipple. Bridget made a soft needy noise, setting Octavia on fire. She leaned back and looked into Bridget's eyes. *Love. Want. Need. She needs to know we are okay. Wants to show me.*

She moved her hand to Bridget's neck and gripped the back of it under her curls. She brought her other hand up and traced Bridget's lower lip with her thumb before she pushed it between her lips. Bridget opened her mouth and sucked on Octavia's thumb. She maintained eye contact, eyes wide, open desire on her face. Octavia's clit was hard against the seam of her jeans. She squeezed the back of Bridget's neck, digging her fingers into her soft skin.

"I love your mouth." She pulled her thumb from between Bridget's lips. "Kneel." She forced her down to sitting on her heels before she took her hand from her neck. She stood and unbuckled her belt. The sound of metal against metal was loud in the quiet of the morning. Bridget's gaze was fixed on her face and she licked her lower lip. Octavia unbuttoned her jeans one button at a time. "You want this?" She dipped her fingers in and brought them out glistening with her desire.

Bridget moaned and leaned toward her. "Please, Ma'am. Please let me lick you."

Octavia pushed her jeans and briefs down and stepped out of them. She leaned forward and wrapped both hands in Bridget's hair. Pulling tight, she raised Bridget up on her knees and arched her head back. She kissed her and bit her lower lip, drawing a yip from Bridget. She broke their kiss and released Bridget. Octavia sat back in the chair, shifting her hips to the edge of the seat. "Lick me."

Bridget thrust her face between her legs, her tongue flat against her clit. The press and thrust of her tongue made Octavia groan. Bridget brought her hands up and rested them on the inside of her thighs, pushing Octavia's legs wider, giving herself more access as she worked her greedy mouth over her. Bridget thrust her tongue deeper, before she swept it up and over Octavia's clit. Aching pleasure soared through her. She clutched Bridget's head and buried her fingers in her curls. She rocked her hips, marking Bridget's face. The sounds of her mouth working and the soft moans of pleasure from Bridget as she licked her sent her over the edge, and she spilled into Bridget's mouth as she ground out her pleasure on Bridget's face. *Mine. Always. Mine.* She rode out her pleasure, grinding her way to another orgasm.

Sated, she released Bridget. With tender lips Bridget suckled her clit, sending another wave of pleasure though Octavia. She relaxed in the chair and let Bridget lick her fill, boneless. Bridget smoothed her hands over her thighs and wrapped her arms around her hips, digging her fingers in to pull her close as she worked her up again, sending Octavia into another long slow, pounding orgasm. She tugged at Bridget's curls. "Enough, greedy girl. I won't have strength to muck."

Bridget hummed her satisfaction and planted kisses along her thighs before she sat back on her heels. "Thank you, Ma'am. I needed that."

Octavia cupped her face and kissed her, savoring the taste of herself on Bridget's lips. "So did I." She pulled her up into her lap. "No matter what, you're mine. Always."

Bridget squeezed her arms around her tightly. "Yours, Ma'am. Always."

"HEY YOU! *VIETATO fumare*. No smoking anywhere near the barn."

The man spit his cigarette out and ground out the ash with the toe of his Armani loafers. He pushed his thick-framed black sunglasses up and rested them on his head. The practiced bored expression on his face made Octavia want to wipe it off with her shovel.

"Sorry." His mouth pulled into a fake smile as he swept his gaze over Octavia. "You must be the barn person Mother was talking about."

Let me guess. Octavia stopped herself from rolling her eyes. "Maybe. Who is your mother?"

"Sofia Abrami. I'm Carlo. She wanted me to drop off this file." He held out a thick folder. He dropped his gaze to her breasts. "You are as beautiful as she said."

Ugh, why didn't I wear something besides this tank top? I hate to think what she said. Octavia suppressed a shudder. The idea of Sofia discussing her appearance with her son made her stomach roil. She took the folder from his hand and leafed through it before she handed it back. "I don't need this. She can't bring her horses here. I've not time or space." *Or patience to deal with her.*

"Mother won't be happy." He tapped the folder on his leg. "She's used to getting what she wants."

"Not this time." Octavia leaned on her shovel.

"She's willing to pay any amount Vivian wants." He leaned back and raised an eyebrow. "She'll pay extra for your services."

He's not talking about the horses. What the hell? She's sending her son to hook her up? What the hell? She stared into his eyes and frowned at him. "It's not about the money."

"Everything and everyone has their price. What's yours?"

Octavia gripped the shovel tighter. "Nothing you—" She swept her gaze over him. "—or she could ever afford."

He stepped back and sighed. "Why does Vivian need this place anyway? It was too big when she was with that woman, and now she's alone she should sell it. Mother would buy it an instant."

"What Vivian does and does not need is no concern of yours. Or your mother's. She sells her crops to your mother. Why does she need more land?"

"She doesn't, but she is obsessed with owning this again."

Octavia frowned at him. "Again?"

"We had a few bad crops, ran into some loan problems a few years back. She needed cash, and Vivian's father bought it without even coming to see it. Mother didn't know about him, or she never would have sold it to him."

"What about him?"

"He's..." The man looked around before he leaned close. He whispered, "African."

Octavia was torn between hitting him with the shovel and punching him. She took two steps back. "Oh for fuck's sake. Get out." She raised the shovel, holding it across her body with both hands wrapped tight, the thought of time in jail the only thing keeping her from swinging it. "And tell your mother she can go fuck herself."

The man straightened and smiled a smile that did not reach his eyes. "I'll tell her. And tell Vivian you threatened me."

"Tell anyone any bloody thing you want. But get off this property now or you will find out my threat was a promise." She gripped the shovel and raised it higher, shifting her hands as if to hit him with it.

He backed away from her slowly, facing her until he was out of range of a shovel swing. He sauntered down the drive. She watched him until she couldn't see him anymore. Her hands ached from holding the shovel so tightly. She relaxed her grip on the smooth wooden handle. *What makes people assume I can be bought? Sofia doesn't even know me. What the fuck? Do I look like a whore? Still? What an asshole. I should have hit him. Does Sofia feel that way? Or is he an ass? She acted like Vivian was a friend. They seemed pretty close at dinner. But she wouldn't be the first person who was an ass about skin color behind someone's back.* She walked back to the barn and hung up her shovel. She washed up in the sink, wishing the soap and water could wash away her anger and disgust at Carlo's words.

Chapter Twelve

THE MORNING AIR was crisp, the ground still wet from the night's storms. She tacked up Carmel. *A ride will do me good. Air out my brain. Bridget's going to struggle if this was a one-off. Me too. Fuck, this is complicated. So good but so hard now.* She led the mare out to the mounting block. She gathered her reins, ready to step up.

"Care for company?" Vivian stood with her hands clasped in front of her. "I don't want to intrude if you want the time alone."

"I can wait. Do you want to ride Max? He's not brushed out. It will take me a bit to get him ready."

"No. I think Sassy is better for the trail." She smiled at Octavia.

The edge of formality between them made Octavia's heart ache. *Damn it. She's back in her shell. She doesn't want more. Or doesn't want us. It was play. A release, nothing more. She needed to have a time with training wheels. It's going to kill Bridget. Maybe we better start looking for new jobs. Fuck.*

"If you hold Carmel, I'll get her ready. She's brushed. I was going to exercise her this afternoon." She handed Vivian the reins. Carmel blew out a breath and tossed her head. "Steady, girl. We'll go in a minute."

Octavia went to the tack closet and pulled out Sassy's saddle pad, saddle, and bridle. Since she had reorganized the barn, she was able to get Sassy ready in minutes versus the half hour it had taken when she first arrived. She picked up Vivian's hard hat and tucked it under her arm. She led Sassy out into the area between the barn and the ring. Vivian's quiet smile made her want to pull her close and kiss her until the cautious look in her eyes disappeared.

She took Carmel's' reins from Vivian. *Will she ever let me take the reins? Is she like Martha? Never able to let go of her control? I want to undo her. Have her beg me. So much for fantasy. She'd never let go like that.* "I'll hold her for you."

"No need." She took her hard hat from Octavia and settled it on her head. After taking Sassy's reins, she led her to the mounting block and mounted the horse.

Octavia adjusted her riding helmet and mounted her horse. "I was going to ride the north trail."

"Lead on." Vivian held Sassy back, waiting for Octavia to ride out in front of her.

If only. If only she wanted me to lead her. Focus. They rode the trail that bordered the edge of the grape arbors. The vines were full, the grapes a pale green against the darker green of the leaves. "How do you know when to harvest?" she called over her shoulder to Vivian. *Talk about anything. Try to get back to normal. You were friends. Be friends again. Don't let one night fuck up what you were.*

"I don't know. I leave everything to Sofia." She sighed. "I'm a terrible farmer. I don't know what the hell my father was thinking when he gave me this place."

The trail widened out, and Octavia slowed Carmel so Vivian could ride next to her. The birds chirped and flitted ahead of them, scratching at the ground between the rows of vines. As they moved along the crest of the hill, the valley spread out before them. The Alps rose up in the distance, blue and gray with a scattering of white along their peaks. The creaking of their saddles and the sound of the horses breathing made Octavia's heart full, as she appreciated the beauty surrounding them. They stopped at a junction, the trail splitting off east toward Sophia's vineyard and west toward other vineyards in the valley.

"It's beautiful. And peaceful."

"You sound like Miriam. She loved it."

Octavia stifled the bit of sadness in her heart for Vivian, not wanting to give in to grief. "That's twice you've said I remind you of her."

"Does it bother you?" Vivian halted her horse.

"No." Octavia pulled Carmel around so she could face Vivian. "Does it bother you?"

Vivian looked down. "Not in a bad way."

"I'm still me, Vivian. No matter what happens going forward."

"I know. And some part of me feels I don't deserve it." She brought her gaze to Octavia's face. "I don't want to use you. Or Bridget."

Pain. So much pain. And fear. Octavia firmed her jaw. "We're grown women. We make our own choices."

"I'm your employer. I've never crossed that line before. I don't want to again."

Anger, slow and ugly, built up in Octavia's chest. "So it's the whore thing with you too? Fuck you, Vivian. I thought you would understand. I was with Martha because I loved her. Yes, I worked for her. Yes, she paid my salary. But I loved her. I didn't beg her to collar me because she was my employer."

Vivian pressed her mouth in a thin line. "I didn't say you did."

"But you think it. You think I did what I did last night out of obligation? That I'm acting like I want you so you'll give me a raise or better quarters?" Her anger took over then. "Fuck you, Vivian. I may have been a whore, but I was an honest one. My father wasn't around to give me a fucking vineyard or anything else. I made my choices. I've paid for them."

"Anna—I'm sorry, I didn't mean..." Vivian reached out and touched Octavia's arm.

Octavia pulled away from her touch. "You did. You said as much. And don't call me Anna. That young girl you knew is gone." She tipped her chin at Vivian. "I'm sure you can find your own way back." She turned her horse to the west and left her there, not bothering to look back.

She chewed her lip. *Fuck. Even Vivian. Fuck that. Fuck her. Fuck me, what I am I going to do? Can we stay? Do I want to? Bridget. She's going to flip. And be hurt. Fuck, why did we come here? Why did I say yes? Because I want her. Even now. She doesn't want me. Us. Fuck me.* She rode along the trail, the rhythm of the horse moving under her soothing. The heat of the sun had burned off the morning cool and a trickle of sweat rolled down her neck. *I should get back. Do the stalls. Ugh, I have to tell Bridget. Or will Vivian?* She stopped at the fork in the path leading to Sofia's farm.

"Out alone?" Sofia appeared from the row of arbors. She wore jeans and a white shirt. Her hair was pulled back, and in the morning light, the lines around her eyes were deep. She had a pair of clippers in her hand.

Octavia tilted her head and considered her. "Yes."

Sofia nodded. "It's a lovely morning for it."

"What're you doing?"

"I came up to inspect the vines. One of the workers was worried about mold after the rains." She held up a leaf covered in soft gray powder. "He was right." She frowned. "We had a decent harvest last year, but this mold may be the end of us."

"I met Carlo."

Sofia nodded. "He told me." Her voice was resigned.

"He said you wanted to buy the vineyard back."

Sofia laughed. "With what money? Carlo talks too much." She shoved the clippers in her back pocket. "I'm going to have to sell if this crop is ruined." The bold flirt from the other night was gone. "Carlo imagines himself the grand landowner. He spends money we don't have on things we don't need." She walked closer and rested her hand on Octavia's leg. "You won't reconsider? I'll have to sell my horses if I can't keep them at Vivian's. I can't afford the boarding fees."

"You son made it sound like money was no object."

"Carlo lives in a magic world where money flows like water. Please don't take anything he says as truth."

"I have to get back."

Sophia pulled her hand away. "Please think about it. I don't want to sell them." Her eyes held unshed tears. "They are more family to me than Carlo."

Is she lying? Maybe she's a good actress. "I'll think about it."

Octavia turned the horse back to the barn and rode at a fast walk back. She mulled Sophia's words over in her head. *Who to believe? Who to trust? The one person I want to talk to about this is too invested. I should tell Vivian about the mold. Keep it formal. Shut off my feelings. I can do it. Can she? Can Bridget?* She focused on the ride, pushing her melancholy thoughts away.

Chapter Thirteen

THE MURMUR OF voices from the kitchen caught her attention as she entered the mudroom. *Vivian. Bridget. What are they talking about? Did they hear me come in?* Octavia toed off her boots. She crept to the door to the kitchen, staying out of their line of sight, and edged forward to listen. Heads bowed over a cookbook, they stood hip to hip, Vivian's lean frame next to Bridget's curvy body. Bridget's shoulders were canted a bit as she inclined her body toward Vivian, close but not touching.

"I'd like you to prepare this. For eight. I'll choose the wine. What type of dessert will you make?"

"I don't know. Do you have a favorite dessert?"

Vivian rested her hand on the small of Bridget's back. Jealousy flared and burned through Octavia as she watched Vivian lower her head and kiss Bridget, taking her time. Her anger had fizzled on the ride back and after mucking the stalls, but this display reignited the coals of her fury. The small needy noise Bridget made fanned the flames of Octavia's jealousy into a burning rage. She turned away from them, clenching her fists and driving her nails into her palms. *Fuck. So that talk was about me? What the fuck? She wants Bridget. Only. Fuck, she could have been up front about it. Fuck me.*

She crept back and opened the door quietly before she slammed it shut. She picked up her boots and dropped them one at a time. "Hey, love, what's for lunch? I'm starved," she yelled as washed her hands in the sink.

Bridget's flushed face appeared in the doorway. "I've got some leftover chicken from last night. And bread." She handed Octavia a towel.

Octavia dried her hands and hung up the towel. "Sounds wonderful." She followed Bridget into the kitchen. Vivian was gone. The only evidence of her presence was the lingering scent of her verbena perfume. She didn't ask about Vivian, waiting for Bridget to say something. *Tell me. Tell me what you talked about. Tell me. Please want to tell me.* She chewed her lip, not wanting to let Bridget know she had spied on them. A smidgen of guilt kept her from mentioning what she'd seen. *She's not going to say anything.*

"Did you have a nice ride?" Bridget pressed a kiss on her cheek as she set the plate in front of Octavia.

"Yes." She forked a bite of the roasted chicken into her mouth.

"Vivian ride with you?" Bridget sat down opposite Octavia.

"For a bit." She sipped her water.

"She's planning a dinner party next weekend. Eight people."

Not going to tell me about the kiss. Ask her. Don't ask. Fuck. She doesn't have to tell me. "Will you need my help? I'm okay in the kitchen as long as I don't have to do fiddly things."

Bridget laughed. "No fiddly things. But I could use your help with prep if you have time."

"I'll make time." Octavia reached across the table and lifted Bridget's hand to her lips. She kissed her fingertips. "How is your afternoon? Care for a nap?" She gazed into Bridget's eyes, letting her know she was interested in more than a nap. *I need to know. Know she still wants me too. Does she?*

Bridget pulled her hand from Octavia's "I have so much to do." She looked away from her eyes.

So it begins. She's never refused me before. Fuck. She's gone from me.

"Okay. I've got some things I can do in the barn." She pushed her plate away before wiping her mouth.

"You're finished? You've hardly touched anything."

"You're busy and have better things to do besides feed me." Octavia stood up and picked up her plate.

Bridget frowned at her. "I didn't think not taking a nap would cause a problem."

"You know that is not what I was asking for. And you have every right to say no."

Bridget met her gaze. "I'm not saying no. I'm saying not right now."

"Understood." Octavia scraped her plate and put it in the sink. "Find me when you have time for me."

I'm being a bitch. I don't care. She's gone from me. What have I done? Why did I say yes that night? Fuck me. Fuck me, I'm an idiot. I should've known. She only picked me over Cook because I was available. She wants a real Mistress. Not me. Fuck. What am I going to do?

She sat on the bench in the mudroom and stuffed her feet into her boots. She leaned over and rested her head in her hands for a moment. Her throat was dry. The pain in her heart took her breath away. *So much for love. So much for always.* She scrubbed her hands over her face before she stood up. She gripped the doorknob. A hand on her shoulder stopped her.

"Talk to me. Don't walk away." Bridget squeezed her fingers, her grip tight on Octavia's shoulder. "Why are you so angry at me?"

"If you don't know it won't matter what I say." She pulled away from Bridget. She leaned her head against the door, avoiding Bridget's eyes, not wanting her to see the hurt she knew would show in her face.

Bridget's voice was loud in the tiled mudroom. "I'm not allowed to say no? It hurts your feelings? You think me refusing your advances one time in three years is unreasonable?"

"No. It's not unreasonable. I said as much." *Even if it kills me.*

"And then you dumped your lunch and left like a petulant teenager."

"Insulting me doesn't make this better. Leave me alone. I'll be okay. Right now, I need some space." *To make some plans. Figure this out. Get myself together.*

"Fine." Bridget's voice was brittle.

Octavia left, pulling the door closed behind her. She refused to let herself cry. *So she said no. So what? She didn't tell me anything about Vivian. Didn't say anything at all. If Vivian had given her the same talk she gave me, she would have been in tears. But she didn't. And that kiss. She looked guilty as fuck when she brought me the towel.* Octavia looked up at the sky, clear blue and cloudless. *It's okay. I'm okay. Things change. Things end. Damn, I didn't think this would end. It's not the end of the world, but it seems like it. I'll find another job. They deserve each other.*

The barn was cool after the midday heat, the overhead fans doing their job. Octavia went into the office. Sitting at her desk, she leafed through the monthly receipts, trying to distract herself from the ache in her heart. The gray tabby came in and brushed against her legs. She leaned over and scratched between his ears. "You don't care, do you? You'd let this old whore pet you all day long." She sighed as he pushed into her hand.

"He's not the only one." Vivian's lean frame filled the doorway to the office.

"It'd be funny if you meant it." Octavia turned her chair and tipped it back on two legs to meet Vivian's gaze.

Vivian looked away first. "I'm sorry about before."

"Sorry you said what you said to me? Or sorry you thought it?"

"Both." Vivian raised her head and met Octavia's gaze. "I was wrong on both counts."

Octavia said nothing, not willing to let go of her hurt. The silence between them stretched out tense as a bow string. *What to do? Accept her apology? Let her know you saw her with Bridget? Wait for her to tell you? Say nothing. Don't give in to her silence.*

"I know you're angry. Can I make it up to you?"

Octavia kept her gaze hard. "You can't unsay words. And you made yourself clear. As long as you're my employer, you don't want anything more than I was hired for. I'll do my job. Don't worry I won't say anything to Bridget. You can continue with her. I'll move my things out here."

"You want to sleep in the barn?"

"Seems the best place for ex-whores. Keeps me away from decent folk. Like you and Bridget." Octavia let the anger she'd been holding on to since their ride fill her voice.

"Anna, be reasonable."

Octavia stood up and crossed the room. She stopped, her face a bare inch from Vivian's. "Don't. Don't call me Anna. I never want to hear that name on your lips again. The past is past."

Vivian's eyes were bright. "I don't want it to be like this."

Octavia curled her lip at her. "Save it. I'm sure Bridget will be ready to listen. Or you'll be too busy letting her lick you to care."

Vivian's hand came up quick, but Octavia was quicker. She caught her by the wrist. "No. Not today. I'm not your sub for you to slap." Vivian twisted out of Octavia's grip. Her eyes were wet with tears.

"I saw you, Vivian. In the kitchen. Touching her. Kissing her. You heard me come in and you slipped out of the kitchen like a rat running off a burning ship. You said you didn't want more because you weren't sure I wasn't doing what I did with you because I work for you. But Bridget, she's honest, she's sincere, she's never been a whore. It must be true devotion from her. Fuck you, Vivian."

Vivian stepped back as if Octavia had slapped her. She looked down, avoiding Octavia's eyes. "I was going to talk to you. Tell you I was wrong. Ask your forgiveness. I was wrong. Bridget is yours."

"Not anymore." Octavia backed up and sat down in the chair. She was shaking from her anger and not enough to eat at lunch. "I've never collared her. She has made it clear she wants what you can give her." She worked to slow her breathing and struggled to focus on Vivian's voice. She sensed herself falling and tried to catch herself as she fell forward from the chair. Her hands, wet with sweat, slipped on the arm of the chair and her forehead connected with the edge of the desk. The last sound she heard was Vivian screaming her name.

SHE WOKE UP on the couch in the barn office. Her head ached. Soft hands touched her face. The sharp smell of ammonia stung her nose. She shoved the hands away. "Fuck is that? Get it away from me." She tried to sit up and strong hands pushed her back.

"No. You stay right there. I knew you didn't have enough lunch." Bridget's firm voice made her relax back onto the couch. "Lucky you don't need stitches."

Octavia opened one eye and looked up at Bridget. The worry on her face poked the guilty spot inside her. "I'm sorry, love."

Bridget leaned down and kissed her lips softly. "You scared me. And Vivian."

Vivian. The events leading up to her blackout came back into focus. She touched her forehead. A tender lump at her hairline made her wince when her fingers touched it. "Damn. That hurts."

Bridget rested her hand on Octavia's shirt. "Let me hold this ice on it."

"I can do it."

"Sh. You lie still. I'll hold it in place."

The firmness in Bridget's voice and concern on her face reminded Octavia of what she would lose if Bridget were not in her life. She gazed into her eyes. *Love. She loves me. Still.* She caught Bridget's hand and squeezed it tight. "I'm sorry I was an ass. I was jealous. I saw you and Vivian."

Bridget frowned at her. "When?"

"When I came in for lunch. You didn't hear me. I saw her kiss you."

Bridget lowered her eyes. "And then I refused you. No wonder you left." She raised her hand and touched Octavia's cheek. "I don't know how to do this. What's okay and what's not."

Octavia glanced around the office. "Where's Vivian?"

"She's on the phone to a friend who is a physician. She's worried you have a concussion."

"I'm fine." She tried to sit up. A wave of nausea forced her to lie back down. "Ugh. Maybe not. Do you have a bucket?" She swallowed the sour taste in her mouth.

Bridget got the office trash can and brought it close to the couch. "Lie still. Listen. For once."

"I listen."

"You don't always listen to me. I'm not a child."

Truth. I don't. She's not a child. I need to. Before I lose her. "I'm sorry. I'll do better. I don't think I know how to be outside of Rowan House. The rules were simple there. Here we have to make our own rules." She brought Bridget's hand to her lips and kissed her fingertips. "I'm listening."

"What happened between you two? Vivian wouldn't tell me. I could tell she'd been crying, and she was a wreck when she called me to come help her."

Octavia's face grew warm, the remnants of her anger surfacing. "On our ride she told me she didn't want any more of what happened between us because she was my employer and she was worried I was doing it out of obligation, like a whore."

Bridget's eyes grew dark. "She said that? Oh fuck no." Her face twisted in anger. "She has some nerve."

Bridget's anger on her behalf made Octavia's heart overflow. "She came to apologize, and we were arguing when I passed out."

Bridget leaned down and pressed a gentle kiss to Octavia's lips. "I didn't know. She didn't say anything to me. And that makes me even angrier. When she comes back, we are going to talk. Together. No more hiding. If she wants this, us, she's going to have to talk, not hide out in her office all day. Fuck that."

The conviction in Bridget's voice made Octavia see her in a new light. *Strong. Fighting for us. For me.* She touched Bridget's face. "I didn't know you had this in you."

"I might not be a Mistress, but you can't get through cooking school without believing in yourself. The head pastry chef at our school prided herself on how many students cried in her class." Bridget smoothed her hand over Octavia's shirt. "If you can sit up, I think if you had something to drink and some food you might feel better. Are you still nauseous?"

"No, it's better." Octavia let Bridget help her to a sitting position. She held on to the arm of the couch until a wave of dizziness passed. Bridget pushed a glass of juice into her hand. "I know apple is not your favorite, but you need the sugar. I told Vivian to bring some crackers and cheese down. My grandma had diabetes. This is what she ate when her sugar was low."

"You're awake. Thank God." Vivian entered carrying a tray with a box of crackers and slices of cheese. "Dr. Meloni will be here in fifteen minutes."

"He makes house calls?"

"She. And she does for me." Vivian placed the tray on the desk. She walked over to them.

Bridget pinned her with a look. "We've been talking. Did you tell Octavia you didn't want more with us because you thought she was doing it because you employ us?"

"I did." Vivian's voice was soft. "I spoke without thinking. I was wrong."

"You also spoke to her about us without me being there. And that's not okay. We are we, and we were we before we came here. I'm not interested in anything with you that does not include her." She walked over to Vivian and looked up into her face. "We either agree to this all of us or we don't do it. And if that doesn't fit with what you want, fuck off."

"Bridget!" Octavia set her juice down. "Easy. We don't need to get aggressive."

"No. She needs to understand. I may be a sub, but I'm not in this to have my life taken over. What we do in the bedroom is what we do in the bedroom. I'm not down with a 24/7 Domme/sub relationship." She poked Vivian in the chest. "And you need to know I will fight for what I want. And if you ever call her a whore or even suggest it again, we will be out of here so fast your head will spin, contract or no."

Octavia realized her mouth was hanging open. In her time with Bridget, she had never seen this, even when Bridget was angry with Cook or Martha.

Vivian clasped her hands in front of her. "Forgive me. Both of you. I was wrong. I want more with both of you. If you do. Can you forgive me?"

"Hello?" a woman's voice sounded from the barn.

"In here."

Dr. Meloni entered. She was a round woman with soft curls surrounding her face. "Hello, Vivian." She nodded a greeting at Bridget and smiled at Octavia. "You must be my patient." She came and sat next to Octavia on the couch. She picked up Octavia's arm and wrapped two fingers around her wrist and held it for a minute while looking at her watch. "Pulse is steady." She let go of Octavia's wrist and pulled a pen flashlight from her handbag. She shone the light in Octavia's eyes one at a time. "Pupils equal and reactive. Good. What day is it?

"Tuesday."

"What's your name?"

"Octavia Vargas."

"Where are we?

"Franciacorta, Italy. Vivian's barn to be exact."

Dr. Meloni touched the bump on Octavia's head. "That bump is going to take a while to go down. Have you ever had dizziness? Has this happened before?"

"No. I didn't eat much lunch. I've never had it happen before."

"I think you're going to be okay. I want you to rest for what's left of today. No strenuous activity. You need to have someone monitor you, hourly checks for the rest of the day and tonight."

"So I don't wake up dead?" Octavia couldn't resist. She had cared for more than one rider who had taken a fall.

"Exactly." Dr. Meloni patted her leg. "I do think you're fine, or I would send you to the hospital." She looked up at Vivian. "Call me tomorrow and tell me how she is." She stood up and nodded at Octavia and Bridget. "Nice meeting you. And eat your lunch next time."

"She will." Bridget tilted her head at doctor. "I'm Bridget and I'll make sure she does." And she held the doctors' gaze to make her point.

The doctor raised an eyebrow at Bridget and smiled. "Very good." She turned to Vivian. "I'll see you next week." She left them.

Bridget crossed the room and sat next to Octavia. "Do you think you could walk to the house?"

"Yes. Nothing wrong with my legs." Octavia slid forward on the couch. She looked from Bridget's face to Vivian's.

"Nonsense. You heard what Laura said. I'll bring the car around. At least we can get you closer to the house." Vivian turned and left.

Octavia rested her hand on Bridget's knee. "I think I like this side of you."

Bridget smiled at her. "You better. I'm not going anywhere." She cupped Octavia's cheek and kissed her gently. "I take care of what is mine. I'll do whatever I have to do to protect you."

"ARE YOU GOING to stay up all night watching me sleep?" Octavia shifted to her side and tucked her arm under her head. "I'm okay."

Bridget firmed her mouth. "Yes. And don't try to talk me out of it."

"We could set an alarm."

"No." She opened a thick book and placed a pad of paper next to it. "I need to do some planning anyway."

"Planning?"

"I want a kitchen garden like we had at Rowan House. Herbs and such."

"You're planning on being here long enough to plant a garden?"

Bridget tilted her head and met Octavia's gaze. "Even if we don't stay, it's fun to imagine. I've always wanted to be able to walk out and clip fresh herbs for dinner and flowers for the table. Cook was a tyrant about the garden. She planted the same things every year, refused to even consider flowers."

"Cook was a tyrant about everything. If she hadn't been Martha's sister, she would have never tolerated her behavior."

"Her sister?" Bridget paled. "No wonder she was so rude to me. I said so many horrid things about her to Martha."

Octavia laughed. "You and everyone else." She pushed herself up in the bed and propped the pillows behind her back. "Can you work over here? This bed is lonely without you."

Bridget stacked the pad of paper on top of the book and tucked the pen behind her ear. She smiled at Octavia. "Yes. But don't get any ideas. The doctor said no strenuous activity." She crossed the room and climbed into the bed and settled next to Octavia. "I wish I had a lap desk."

"I can lie down and you can write on my ass like in that movie." She shifted in the bed and pressed her arms together, stretching the fabric of her tank top to give Bridget a view of the swell of her breasts.

"You must be feeling better with all your frisky comments." She quirked her mouth at Octavia. "Settle down and help me lay this out. Where would be the best place?"

"What about part of the atrium? I'm sure Vivian wouldn't mind."

"No, it's too lovely to disturb. I can't wait to do a garden party there. The fountains are exquisite."

A knock at the door made them both jump and then laugh.

"For fuck's sake, Vivian, come in. You scared the hell out of us."

Vivian entered with a tray holding a coffee press and a small teapot, three cups, and a small tin of biscuits.

"I didn't want to intrude." She placed the tray on the desk. "I brought coffee for us, Bridget, and some rooibos tea for you." Vivian poured the coffee. She handed Bridget her cup. She fixed Octavia's tea, adding the perfect amount of cream before she passed it to her. *She knows how we drink our beverages. She's serving us. Caring for us. Both of us. She cares. I care. No. Love. Damn it. I love her. Still. After all this time.*

Vivian poured her own cup of coffee before she pulled the desk chair close to the bed. She sat down. "You appear to be feeling better." She took a sip of her coffee.

Bridget patted the bed. "Join us?"

Vivian brought her gaze to Octavia's face.

Wants to make sure it's okay with me. That we're okay. Octavia shifted to make room for Vivian. "Come on, join us. Let me hold your coffee for you."

Vivian smiled as she handed her cup of coffee to Octavia. She stood up and carefully climbed in the bed. She sat cross-legged. Octavia handed her cup back to her. "This tea is perfect. Thank you."

"You're welcome. I thought I'd keep Bridget company. I don't think I'd be able to sleep anyway."

"Perfect. I have questions for you." Bridget tapped the book in front of her. "I want to plant a kitchen garden. Where do you think would be the best place?"

Vivian smiled. "I'd put it to the right of the back door. Close to the kitchen and it will get at least seven hours of full sun." A wave of sadness passed across her features. "We always said we'd plant one, but we never did. Something always came up."

Bridget put her coffee cup down on the nightstand. She touched Vivian's wrist. "If it makes you sad, we don't have to talk about it."

Vivian straightened her shoulders. "No. I'm fine. She'd want me to." She eyed the two of them, her gaze shifting from Octavia's face to Bridget's. "You're planning on being here long enough to enjoy a garden?"

Octavia met Vivian's gaze. "Yes. If you want us to stay."

Vivian looked down. "I would like nothing more in the world than if you stayed. I wasn't sure you would want to. After..."

"Look at me."

Vivian raised her head.

"That's done. No more about it. You don't have to apologize anymore." She placed her cup on the table and took Vivian's cup from her hands. She clasped her hand before she reached back and caught Bridget's hand in her other hand. Bridget clasped Vivian's other hand. "If we are going to do this, we need to talk. We need to lay it all out."

Bridget squeezed her fingers in a quiet affirmation that she agreed with Octavia.

"Yes. All of us together." She brought Vivian's and Octavia's hands to her lips and kissed the back of their hands. She leaned in and rested her head on Octavia's shoulder. Bridget shifted closer to wrap her arms around Vivian, holding her tight.

They stayed like that until Vivian sat up. "I suppose it's real now I've cried in front of both of you. So much for the Iron Mistress."

"Well, I've passed out, acted an ass, and told you to fuck off, so I'd say it got real then." Octavia handed Vivian her coffee.

Bridget laughed. "And I threw a pan, yelled at you, and I poked you in the chest."

Vivian's eyes were bright. "The first time I met Miriam, I was with another woman. It was a date, nothing serious, but Miriam was so jealous she dumped a drink on the woman accidentally on purpose and made her think we were a couple."

"So you have a history of pissing women off?" Octavia lay back in the bed and pillowed her arms behind her head.

Bridget snorted. "You two have a lot in common." She stretched her legs out and leaned back against the headboard. She moved the book and the writing pad to the nightstand before placing her pen on top of the stack. "Going forward. What are the rules?"

Octavia met Bridget's gaze. "What is most important to you?"

"It's not play to me." Bridget looked at Vivian. "I need you to understand that about me."

Bridget held Vivian's gaze. "What is most important to you?"

Vivian pursed her lips. "I want to be able to be with you separately and together."

Bridget frowned. "I don't know if I can do that. I get terribly jealous."

"But you have been with Octavia alone since we were together."

"Yes." Bridget pressed her lips in a firm line. "And we were a couple before we came here. I know myself. I can't do this if we have that rule."

Octavia cleared her throat. "I think kisses and touches are fine. I don't want anything more than that to occur alone. Too many chances for things to be misunderstood and jealous feelings. At least for now."

Vivian nodded. "It sounds good in theory that no one would be jealous, but you two are probably right. Okay. Kisses and touches with me but no further unless we are all present or if the other gives permission."

Bridget frowned. "Then if I say no, I'm the difficult one. No."

"But what if one of us is not up for it?"

"Then the other two wait. I didn't say I was an easy person to be with."

Vivian nodded. "All right. I can agree to that. But you two should still take time with just each other. I don't want to interfere with that." She met Octavia's gaze. "And what is most important to you going forward?"

"Trust. I need both of you to let go of my past. I need to know you trust me."

Vivian leaned forward and rested her forehead on Octavia's forehead and cupped the back of her neck. "I do. I will." She kissed her cheek and sat back on her heels.

Bridget squeezed Octavia's hand. "Me as well, love."

"Shall we eat biscuits in bed to celebrate?" Octavia was ready for their serious mood to dissipate.

"Biscuits in bed might be a hard limit." Bridget pinched Octavia's thigh.

"Ow. Are you picking on an injured woman?"

"Vivian, what is your opinion on biscuits in bed?"

"It's a poor substitute for what I'd rather eat, but it will have to do until someone is cleared from her bump on the head."

Bridget laughed and scooted off the bed. She picked up the tin. She opened it and took a biscuit out before she passed it to Vivian. "I'm outvoted, but if you make crumbs, you are sleeping on the crumby side."

Vivian's laugh filled the room. "What makes you think I'm going to sleep here?" She arched an eyebrow at Bridget.

"You'll want to. No matter how much you want to play at Iron Mistress, I see how much you want to be with us."

Vivian snorted. "You know I have a flogger?"

"Yes. And when she's better, I'm going to ask you to show it to me again." Bridget made a show of licking the crumbs off her lip before she grinned at Vivian.

Octavia sailed a pillow at her head. "No fair teasing us when we can't do anything about it."

Bridget caught the pillow with both hands and laughed. "Maybe next time you'll be a good girl and eat your lunch."

She crossed the room and handed the pillow back to Octavia. She leaned down and pressed a kiss, full of promise and love, to her lips.

Chapter Fourteen

THE KNOCK ON the back door made Octavia frown. *Who the hell is at our door this early? What the fuck?*

Bridget looked at her and shrugged. "I don't have any deliveries scheduled."

The knock sounded again. Leaving her tea, Octavia went to see who was at the door.

Carlo stepped back when she opened it up. "Oh, I didn't... Uh, is Vivian here?"

Octavia leaned her arm against the doorframe, blocking his entrance. "Why do you want to know?"

"We had an appointment." He held his briefcase in front of his chest like a shield.

"You always come to the back door for a business appointment?"

"I knocked on the front door. No one answered."

"That's why there's a bell."

He wrenched his face into a smile that didn't reach his eyes. "Can I wait? Do you think it will be long?"

Fuck. I don't want him the house. But I can't leave him out here. "Come in. I'll check with her." She stepped back and let him in. Bridget turned as they entered the kitchen. "Bridget Murray. Carlo Benoit, Sofia's son."

"*Ciao, bella ragazza.*" Carlo inclined his head at Bridget. "Mother didn't say anything about you. It's a pleasure to meet you."

Octavia didn't stop herself from rolling her eyes at his attempt at being charming.

Bridget narrowed her eyes at Carlo before she turned her gaze to Octavia. "Why is he in my kitchen?"

"He says he has an appointment with Vivian this morning."

Carlo sniffed. "I do have an appointment. Not that it is your concern."

Bridget frowned. "She didn't say anything to me about it. I keep her calendar. I'll make some coffee." She turned her back to him.

"I'll go check with Vivian." Octavia leveled her gaze at Carlo. "Wait here." She pulled out a chair for him and left.

The door to Vivian's office was open. She tapped on the doorframe.

"Enter." Vivian was at her desk. She looked up from her computer screen. Elegant in a white blouse and a dark blue suit, Vivian pulled her glasses off, placed them on the desk and smiled at Octavia. "To what do I owe this welcome interruption? Come. Give me a kiss and take me away from all of this." She made a sweeping gesture with her hand.

Octavia crossed the floor and leaned over Vivian, clasping the arms of her chair. She pinned her in place with her arms. She kissed her long and slow, taking her time. Vivian slid her hands up and tweaked her nipples before she pulled back to look into Octavia's eyes. "I'll never get any work done if you keep kissing me. Did you need me?"

"Carlo is in the kitchen. Says he had an appointment."

"Idiot. It's tomorrow." She frowned. "You left him with Bridget?"

"Um, yeah." Octavia straightened up and pulled back from Vivian. "Is that not okay?"

Vivian stood up quickly. "We should go." She pushed past Octavia. Her heels sounded harsh on the tile floor. Octavia hurried to catch up.

As they passed through the dining room, a loud scream followed by cursing and a man's yelp shattered the quiet of the house. They bumped into each other as they both tried to push through the kitchen door.

Carlo was cowering in the corner, his hand over his nose, blood streaming between his fingers. Bridget stood at the counter, a skillet in one hand and large chef knife in the other.

Vivian crossed the floor and took the knife from Bridget's trembling fingers. "Did he hurt you?"

"He came up behind and ground his nasty self against my ass and grabbed my tits. I smashed his face. And if you don't get him the fuck out of my kitchen, I'm going to smash him again." She raised the pan, her knuckles white as she gripped it.

"I didn't do anything." He wiped at his nose with his hand. "She's lying."

Vivian spun around to face him. She leveled the knife at Carlo. His eyes widened. "Get out." He rose slowly. "Now." She gestured with the knife toward the door. He sprinted for the back door, leaving his briefcase behind.

Octavia picked up the case and bolted after him. He was running down the path leading to the barn. She hurled the briefcase at his back, hitting him between the shoulder blades. He stumbled and fell with the impact of the case. She walked to where he lay in the dirt. She kicked him in the ribs, and he rolled to his back. She grabbed the front of his shirt and twisted it to cut off his air. "I don't care who your mother is. If you ever lay a hand on Bridget again I'll kill you." She pulled her fist back to punch him.

"Octavia." Vivian's voice was sharp, cutting through Octavia's anger. She was standing in the doorway with her cell phone in her hand. "Let him go. Sofia will deal with him."

Octavia released his shirt and stepped back. Her breath was ragged, and she clenched her hands to stop them from shaking. She kicked him in the ribs again before she spit on the ground next to him. She turned her back to him and walked slowly back to the house.

BRIDGET PLACED THE bowl of soup in front of Octavia. A tendril of steam misted from its surface. Octavia leaned over to inhale the delicate sent of herbs from the dish. "The saffron smells heavenly. What is it?" She dipped her spoon in to the bowl and lifted it to her mouth. The delicate taste mirrored the scent.

"It's a Milanese chicken soup." Bridget sat opposite Octavia.

"Vivian joining us?"

"No." Bridget looked down at her soup. "She left early. Didn't say anything about when she would be back." She pressed her lips together.

Octavia spooned another mouthful of soup into her mouth. "She's private."

"I hate it." The hurt in Bridget's voice made Octavia's heart ache for her.

"She's used to coming and going as she pleases. We have no claim on her." Octavia buttered a slice of bread.

"I know I'm being silly, but I want to know. Do you think she'll go?"

"To the Onyx?" Memories of wicked fights with Martha spun out and made Octavia's chest tight. "Maybe. It's an honor to be invited." *How many times did I beg Martha not to go? Because she wanted what she could get there. Something she didn't want from me. Vivian's not her. I'm not collared.*

"I don't want to think about what it means." Bridget sat back and pushed her soup bowl away. "I can't stand the idea of anyone else touching her."

"What about when I touch her?" Octavia gazed into Bridget's eyes. "Do you hate that?"

"Not if I'm there." Bridget pursed her lips.

"Doesn't she kiss you when I'm not there? Touch you when I'm not there?"

Bridget looked down and away. "Yes." She blushed. The delicate color suffusing her face stirred Octavia. "Does it bother you?"

Octavia smiled at her. "Only because I like watching you together and I hate missing an opportunity." She reached across the table and clasped Bridget's hand. She rubbed her thumb over the back of her hand. "We don't belong to her, love. She may never want to be our Mistress."

Darkness filled Bridget's eyes. "I don't know if I can do this. I want her to want us. I want her to be ours." She pulled her hand from Octavia's grasp.

Octavia blew out a breath. "What are you going to do? She's like Martha. She'll go. And we will either have to be okay with it or we say we are done." She tapped the table, drumming out a rhythm with her fingertips. "I'm not going to ask her not to go."

"Why? Because a sub can't ask for what they want? Because what we want doesn't matter? Fuck that."

"Because I want her not to go to the Onyx of her own volition, not because we beg her not to go. I want her to choose us."

"You think she'll say no. You're afraid." Bridget's eyes were hard.

"I don't want to hear her say no." Octavia twisted her fingers together. "Living with the thought of her being with others is easier if I know it's how she feels. I can keep my heart safe."

"I'm not going to let her think we don't care. What if she wants us to ask? What if she thinks we are into this for fun or to spice up our relationship?" Bridget reached across the table and grabbed Octavia's hands. "What if I hadn't told you how much I wanted you? How I wanted to be your only?"

"What if she wants an only? And not two?" Octavia tilted her head at Bridget. "What if we're not enough?" She looked to Bridget's eyes. "What if she only wants one?"

Bridget squeezed her hands tighter. "I can't be silent about what I want. Don't you want her to be with us? To choose us?"

Anger spilled over into Octavia's heart and voice. "I don't understand why you need to force her to choose between us and an obligation you can't begin to understand."

Bridget snatched her hands away from Octavia's. "You're right. I don't understand why anyone would put their committed partner through the hell I saw you go through every time Martha left to go to the Onyx. Where is it written you can't expect a Mistress to respect you? To respect your relationship enough to listen to a sub?"

Octavia chewed her lip. "It's better to have what they give you than nothing."

"For how long?" Bridget stood up and picked up her bowl. "Until you meet someone else? Someone like me? If you had told Martha what you wanted, would we be here now?"

Octavia tilted her chin at Bridget. "I don't know. Would we? If I hadn't listened to you and what you wanted, would we?"

Bridget narrowed her eyes at her. "That's not an answer." She turned her back to Octavia and walked to the sink. She ran the water. The sound of the flow splashing against the metal was harsh.

Octavia picked up her bowl and brought it over to the sink. She placed it on the counter. "I love you, Bridget. I chose you. Isn't that answer enough?" She leaned her head against Bridget's shoulder. "I chose you. I still choose you."

Bridget turned the water off. "It is." She raised her hand and cupped Octavia's face. "It is, my love. I want her to choose us."

She turned and tucked herself into Octavia's arms. They held each other, the ache between them building. Bridget kissed her, her lips and mouth full of longing. Need rose in Octavia, and she answered her kiss. She held tight to Bridget, her curvy body solid in her arms. She grounded herself in Bridget's love for her.

Bridget brought her lips close to Octavia's ear. "What are we going to do?"

Octavia kissed her neck. "Hold on, love. We're going to hold on."

SHE ROLLED THE wheelbarrow toward the muck pile. The donkey followed close at her heels. His tiny hooves clattered on the stones of the path. After emptying the barrow, she stopped to wipe a trickle of sweat from her eyes. "I should teach you to pull a cart. You could help me. Victor the wonder donkey, I'll make you a cape." Victor came over and rubbed his head on her leg. She scratched him between his ears, and he leaned into her touch. "Come on. We have more to do."

She stopped petting him and pushed the wheelbarrow back to the barn. The quiet of the barn was disturbed only by the soft skittering of the doves as they scratched and fluttered in and out of the hayloft. *She doesn't want her to go to the Onyx. I don't either. Will she? What if we ask her? Bridget will say it. Equal. To belong equally.* She touched her neck. Not as bare as it once seemed but she still ached to have a collar around her neck. *I belong to Bridget. It's not the same. I want it all. Both of them. I want her to want me. To choose me. Us. To choose both of us.*

She finished loading the sawdust into the stall. She stopped and sat on the bench. Victor came over and laid his head in her lap. "You choose me, Victor." She stroked the soft fur around his ears and rubbed his neck. She looked at the clock. *Supper. I hope Vivian's back. Where does she go? To Sophia? What does she do? I want to know more. We are all so imitate and yet strangers. I'll say something. Or not. Maybe together with Bridget. We will. We can. Together.*

Octavia patted the donkey on the back. "Let me up, Victor. Help me get them in." He lifted his head. She stood and stretched before she walked the length of the barn with the donkey close behind. She loaded the evening meal buckets. Victor followed close. She clipped his food bucket in place and closed him in his stall. She clipped the rest of the food buckets in the other stalls before she unhooked the mesh gate. At the edge of the field, she whistled. Three heads looked up from the brown and pale green scruffy grass.

She unlocked the gate to the field and swung it open. The horses trotted across the field. She stepped out of the way as they bustled past her, headed into their stalls. It had not taken her long to train them to come in for their evening meal. She refastened the mesh gate and went down the line, closing their stall doors and locking them in. *Tonight. We'll talk tonight. If she comes home. Please let her come home.*

"THIS IS SPECTACULAR, Bridget." Vivian wiped her mouth.

Bridget smiled at Vivian, her face bright as her cheeks colored. "I'm glad you like it. I found it in the box of old recipes you gave me."

Octavia sat back in her chair. "Is this a family recipe?"

Vivian turned her attention to Octavia. A shiver ran though her under her gaze. *How does she do that?* "Yes. I brought back my grandmother's box of recipes the last time I visited my mother." She looked back to Bridget and raised her wineglass. "To your powers at deciphering my grandmother's handwriting."

"It wasn't hard. I love reading and making old recipes."

"I'm going to miss your cooking." Vivian placed her wineglass on the table. "I'm going away for two weeks." She looked from Octavia's face to Bridget's before she lowered her eyes. "I won't be available for anything but emergencies. I trust you will be able to entertain yourselves."

"Where are you going?" Bridget tilted her chin at Vivian.

Octavia knew the answer before Vivian spoke. She had marked the days on her calendar, not wanting to know, wishing time would reverse itself. *Bridget will not be down with this. She'll want to stop. Not be engaged. She'll be done. I don't want to be done. But I don't want her to go either. Fuck, this is hard.*

Vivian's voice took on a cool tone, a sharp contrast to her praise before. "The Onyx. It's an annual affair. I've never missed one. I don't intend to this year." She sat back in her chair. Her expression shuttered.

Bridget stood up. "What if we don't want you to go? What about us?"

"What about you?" Vivian arched an eyebrow. "I've been clear about my intentions and feelings."

"Oh yes, you've been clear. Crystal. But let me be clear." She leaned over and firmed her jaw, her face close to Vivian's. "I don't want you to go. Octavia doesn't want you to go, no matter what bullshit she wants to tell you."

Octavia twisted her napkin in her hands. "That's enough."

"No, it's not." Bridget's face twisted in pain and anger. "I'm not willing to go on with this, with us, if you go." She picked up her plate and left the room, the kitchen door banging closed behind her.

Vivian pursed her lips. She shifted her gaze to Octavia. "And you? Does she speak for you?"

Octavia swallowed hard. "I won't beg or threaten. I wanted you to choose us because you wanted us." She looked down at her hands. "I sat by and said nothing year after year when Martha choose to go to the Onyx. I want you to not go because you can't imagine anyone else but us giving you what you need." She bit her lip, the pain quelling the urge to beg Vivian not to go. The ache in her heart burned. *It won't matter what I say. She's not asked for our commitment. Doesn't want to be our Mistress. Fuck, this hurts.* She pushed her chair back quietly and gathered her silverware and plate. Keeping her head down, she avoided Vivian's eyes. *Don't let her see. Don't let her know how much she's hurt me. Us. Why did I think this was different? Why did I think she would be different?* She left Vivian at the table.

Bridget was at the stove stirring a pot. Her shoulders were slumped. Octavia placed her dish on the counter. Stepping close, she wrapped her arms around Bridget's waist. "I'm sorry."

"For what?" Bridget lifted the spoon and let the sauce flow from the tip. "Too thin still." She went back to stirring.

"Not speaking up when you did."

"I know you didn't want to. But she deserves to know. I meant what I said. I can't do this if it's not just us. I can't."

Octavia rested her head on Bridget's shoulders. "I don't want to either. But what are we going to do if she goes? How can we live here with her day after day and not want her?"

"I don't know. I don't want to think about it." The catch in her voice made Octavia's heart ache.

"We'll be together."

"Yes. But it will be like a piece is missing." She turned off the burner and moved the pot before she turned and pressed herself close to Octavia. "I know you feel the same. I see. I see how much she means to you."

Octavia kissed Bridget's forehead, her cheek, and her mouth. "You feel the same. We feel the same."

"We do. We'll get through this."

"We will."

"Help me clean up?"

"Yes. If you come out to the barn with me after." Octavia trailed a finger down Bridget's cheek. "I want to show you something."

Bridget tugged her belt. "Do you? I've got something to show you too." She nipped Octavia's lower lip. "I've been ready to show you something all day."

Octavia pulled her hand free and lifted it to her lips. She kissed her fingertips. "Do we have to clean up first?"

"You know I can't stand to leave the kitchen dirty."

"Just once?" She sucked one of Bridget's fingers into her mouth. A soft groan from Bridget made her clit ache. She raked her teeth over the skin on her finger as she pulled it out slowly. "Please?"

"Impatient woman." Bridget placed her hand on Octavia's chest. "No. You'll thank me later. Let's get the rest of the dishes."

Vivian's chair was empty. The only evidence of her presence was her place setting. Bridget picked up Vivian's wineglass and ran her finger over lipstick smudges she had left on the rim. "Do you think she'll change her mind?"

Octavia met Bridget's gaze. "I don't know, love. I don't know."

Chapter Fifteen

THE DOOR TO their room was ajar, and light poured through the opening onto the tile floor. Octavia reached back and clasped Bridget's hand. She pushed the door open with two fingers. Vivian sat on the edge of the bed. She had changed into a black silk vest and tailored pants.

"You want something?" Octavia raised an eyebrow.

"Forgiveness." She clasped her hands in front of her chest.

Bridget released Octavia's hand. "For what?"

"Testing our relationship." She met Octavia's gaze. "I'm sorry."

Octavia's heart squeezed in her chest. "You're not going?" She sank to her knees and crawled to the bed. She lay her head on Vivian's lap.

"No." Vivian stroked the back of her neck. "No, my sweet."

Octavia sat back on her heels and turned her head to look at Bridget.

She stood with her arms crossed in front of her chest. "Why?"

"You asked me not to."

"Not good enough." She took a moment to assess Vivian's words before she spoke. "I don't want you to stay only because I asked you."

Vivian raised her chin. "What do you want? I've said I wasn't going."

"You. I want you, Vivian. All of you. Not the parts you choose to give us. I don't want crumbs."

Octavia blew out the breath she had been holding. Vivian stood up and crossed the room. She clasped Bridget's chin in her hands. "Greedy girl." She kissed her then, the anger between them boiling up and melting away in the fierceness of their kiss.

Bridget locked her arms around Vivian's waist. She broke their kiss. "Yes. Greedy. Give me what I want. What I need, Vivian. What you need."

Vivian kissed her way along Bridget's throat, drawing a low sigh from her.

Octavia rose and wrapped her arms around Vivian and Bridget. She held tight to her hips, pinning Vivian between them. She scattered kisses on the back of Vivian's neck before she planted a kiss under her ear. "What do you get at the Onyx you can't get here?" Octavia whispered and moved her hands to cup Vivian's breasts. She rolled Vivian's nipples to tight peaks before she pinched them. Vivian's deep moan sent a rush of wetness to her core. "Give yourself over to us. Let us give you what you want. Let me." She kissed and nipped her shoulder, cherishing the taste of her skin.

Vivian leaned back against Octavia. She let her head rest on Octavia's shoulder. "I."

Bridget silenced her with a kiss as she unzipped her pants and slipped her hand inside. "So wet. For us. Trust us."

Octavia palmed Vivian's breasts and teased her nipples through her shirt as Bridget worked her fingers between her legs. Bridget kneeled to remove Vivian's pants. She caught the edge of her gauzy panties and pulled them off with her teeth before she stood up and unbuttoned Vivian's vest and opened it to display her delicate lace bra. She folded down the cups before she sucked her nipples.

Vivian groaned and arched back against Octavia, her breath ragged. "Oh. I can't. Please."

"You can." Octavia kissed the soft skin of her neck. "You want to." She brought her hand up, daring to clasp her Mistress's neck. Vivian shivered. "This is what you go for, isn't it? Two weeks a year, you don't have to think. You go to kneel to Madame Givernay. Nothing to do but feel. Obey. Cherished. Treasured. Adored." She tightened her fingers

"Yes." Vivian's voice was a whisper, her pulse rapid under Octavia's fingers. Bridget was on her knees now, her mouth between Vivian's legs with arms wrapped around her legs, holding her still as she devoured her. Vivian shook and trembled in her arms. "Yes. This. Oh. I..." Her voice harsh, she bucked into Bridget's mouth. "I...I'm going to—to... I can't."

"Come for us. Give us what we want." Octavia nipped her ear, and Vivian broke, and her scream of release filled Octavia's heart as her pulse hammered against her fingers. Bridget's satisfied sounds as she licked and sucked Vivian's clit, forcing her to come again, made Octavia tremble with need. She held on as Vivian shook and came with no sound as she tumbled again down the slope of pleasure. Bridget kissed her way up Vivian's body, stopping to suck each of Vivian's nipples in turn before she brought her mouth to Octavia's and kissed her, and they shared the taste of Vivian.

They held Vivian up between them. She trembled in their arms, and Octavia kissed the marks she had left on Vivian's neck. "We need to lay you down before you fall." They guided Vivian to the bed. She tugged off her vest and bra and tossed them to the floor. She lay back on the bed and spread her legs and stroked her clit. She smiled at them and watched as they stripped quickly.

"We're not done with you." Bridget knelt over Vivian. She kissed her way to her mouth. "Did you know Octavia is a master with a strap-on?" She brushed the back of her hands over Vivian's stomach, the curve of her breasts, the curve of her collarbone.

Vivian's eyes widened. "Um. I... No."

"No, you don't want to?" Bridget lowered her head and suckled each nipple. "Or no, you didn't know?"

Vivian panted. "Didn't know." Her hands clenched the sheets.

Bridget drew her fingers down Vivian's stomach. She traced a path down though the tight wet curls between her thighs and slipped her thumb inside Vivian. A deep groan rattled Vivian's chest and she closed her eyes, her face suffused with pleasure.

Octavia plucked the strap-on from the drawer. She put it on and tightened the straps. Vivian's thighs glistened with desire. *So wet. For us. For this.* "Slide your hips over the edge of the bed."

Bridget pulled her thumb out and smeared the wetness over Vivian's clit. "You heard her. Hips over the edge of the bed."

Vivian moved to obey. Her eyes were closed. She slid down until her feet were on the floor and her hips were resting on the edge of the bed. Her hands gripped the duvet.

"Open your eyes, look at me." Octavia kept her voice firm.

Vivian opened her eyes slowly and brought her gaze to Octavia's face.

"No hiding."

"Yes, Ma'am." Vivian's soft answer made Octavia swallow hard. *"Ma'am." She called me Ma'am.* She looked up and blinked back her emotion. *Get it together. Be what she needs. Be what you need.*

"Bridget, help her remember what to do with her hands."

Bridget moved behind Vivian, positioning herself at the top of her head. She leaned forward and kissed her gently before she clasped her wrists, pinning her to the bed.

"What is your word?"

Vivian's eyes were wide. "Sugar." Her body trembled, her voice a whisper. Her breath came faster.

Octavia smeared lube over the shaft. She touched her fingers to the wetness between Vivian's legs. She pushed her fingers into her silken center. Wet heat pulsed around her as she swept her fingers over the spot that made Vivian's body jerk with pleasure and soft moans spill from her mouth. She pressed the shaft into her, sliding deep, sinking into Vivian's body.

Vivian inhaled sharply. Octavia stilled. She stared into Vivian's eyes. *Mine. Ours.*

Vivian groaned and rocked her hips. She clenched around the phallus, the pressure and vibrations delicious against Octavia's clit. She held Octavia's gaze. "Please. Fuck me. Please, Ma'am."

Octavia growled deep in her throat and pulled her hips back almost to the tip and then thrust forward again hard and deep. "Like this?"

"Oh ah yes, Ma'am. Please. Oh. Please." The muscles in Vivian's arms were taut as she struggled against Bridget's grip.

Octavia fucked her slow and deep, the pressure on her own clit torture, as she edged Vivian, cherishing each deep groan and plea that came from her lips. Her own need won out, and she thrust faster.

"Help me, Bridget."

Bridget met her gaze, and she let go of Vivian's hands and straddled her to lick her clit as Octavia fucked her. She brought her hips lower, offering herself to Vivian's mouth, teasing her by keeping herself just out of reach, touching herself to torment Vivian.

"Oh. Please. I'm... Need... Please, Ma'am. Let me have Bridget. Let me taste her. Please." Vivian arched her neck, trying to reach Bridget.

"Later. Right. Now. I. Want. All. Of. Your. Attention." Octavia rotated her hips and punctuated each word with a thrust, bringing herself closer to coming.

Vivian's breathing was ragged as she arched into their touch. "Please. Oh please let me come. I can't. Don't stop. Please."

They worked in tandem to bring their Mistress off. To give her what she gave them. "Give it to us. Now. Come with us. Be with us. Now. Now."

Vivian's drawn-out deep groan as she came while Bridget brought herself off made Octavia speed up her thrusts, forcing Vivian to come again as Octavia came while fucking her. Their cries and moans blended into one. *Ours. Hers. We.*

"OCTAVIA?"

Octavia leaned her pitchfork against the wall. "In here."

Sofia rested her hand against the stall door. "I came to apologize for Carlo."

Octavia shook her head at Sofia. "I'm not the one you need to apologize to, and your spoiled rat bastard of a son is the one who needs to apologize."

"You're right." Sofia pressed her lips together. "I'm still sorry. Sorry I didn't raise him better."

"Raising kids is like herding cats. You can show them the way, but they're going to go where they want. Is there anything else?" Octavia picked up the pitchfork.

"Do you think Vivian would consider selling the vineyard?"

"Ask her yourself. I don't know. Why?"

"The real estate broker contacted me again. I put her off last time. A wine corporation wants both of our vineyards."

Octavia scooped up some dirty bedding and dumped it in the wheelbarrow. "Ask her."

Sofia shifted and stood up straight. "That's what Carlo was supposed to ask her."

"Why didn't you ask her yourself?"

"I don't want to think about it. It makes me sick. This vineyard has been in my family for more generations than I can count. Through wars, droughts, and bad crops." She looked away from Octavia's eyes. "I let my husband run it into the ground before I divorced him and took over. I've fought my way back from near bankruptcy. I've spoiled my son trying to make up for divorcing his father." Her voice broke. "The sale to Vivian's father was hard enough, and now I'm considering the one thing I never thought I would."

Octavia frowned at her. "Hard because you didn't want to sell or because you didn't want to sell to him?"

"I didn't want to sell at all, but it's been a blessing. Vivian is such a good person. Miriam was so lovely. I wept for days after she was killed."

Octavia turned Sofia's words over in her head. "I don't know her plans. You need to talk to her. And don't send Carlo on any more errands. "

"I won't." Sofia tilted her head at Octavia. "I want to apologize to you too. It wasn't right of me to treat you like I did. I'm sorry."

"Forget about it." Octavia leaned the pitchfork against the wall of the stall before she gripped the handles of the wheelbarrow. "If you'll excuse me, I need to empty this."

Sofia moved out of the doorway to let her pass. "If I said I would come and help with the mucking, would you take my horses? I asked Vivian. She referred me to you, again."

The softness of her voice and the desperation in her eyes made Octavia turn her head away. She blew out a breath. "I need to talk with Bridget. And you need to talk to Bridget. You need to apologize to her." She rolled the barrow out the barn door. She called over her shoulder, "And she's not as forgiving as me."

"SOFIA TALK TO you?" Octavia sipped her tea.

"Yes." Bridget placed a plate with an omelet and sliced fresh tomatoes in front of Octavia. She quirked her mouth. "She apologized. Made some promises I don't know if I believe."

"Vivian seems to trust her." Octavia took a bite of the omelet, the buttery softness melting her mouth. "You make the best omelets."

"Thank you, and Vivian is too trusting. I've gone over the accounts from the housekeeper and stable manager she had before us. They were stealing her blind." She firmed her mouth. "I told her, and she shrugged. Said it was water under the bridge." Bridget met Octavia's gaze. "Does she have so much money she doesn't worry? Or care?"

Octavia wiped her mouth. "I don't know. Her family was well off enough to send her to the Lyceum. With her horse."

Bridget reached across the table and touched Octavia's hand. "I can't even imagine not worrying about money. Your family had money like that, didn't they?"

"They did. My father's family owned a ranchero, cattle, over a hundred hectares. I got my own horse for my eighth birthday. We had so much. When things got bad politically, my father sent me to the Lyceum to keep me safe. I hated it.

We lost a lot of it because my father refused to use his newspaper to be part of a cover-up." She looked down at her hands. "My uncle never forgave him. My uncle was still rich as fuck, but he always wanted more. I saw how money can tear apart a family. I've had no use for it since." She picked up her tea cup. "Sofia is desperate. She's worried about the next crop. Some mold or something. Carlo wants her to sell the vineyard."

"Do you think that's why she cozying up to us? To get us to get Vivian to sell?"

"Maybe. I don't trust anyone when it comes to money."

"Even me?" Bridget looked into Octavia's eyes.

"Except you. I trust you about everything."

Bridget smiled at her. "You can, love. I'd never do anything to hurt you." She took a bit of bread and buttered it. "I don't want her to have to sell her horses. She had tears in her eyes when she talked about them."

"She told me they are more family to her than Carlo."

"She needs to kick him out. He's vile."

"She knows it. But like most mothers she doesn't want to believe it."

Bridget frowned. "My grandma was like that. My sister was hell-spawn. It cost my grandma her life. And ruined mine."

Octavia clasped Bridget's hand. "What happened? You say things in your sleep when you have nightmares."

"When the smoke alarm went off, I was so scared I froze. My grandma shoved me outside and went back to get my sister." She pulled her hand free from Octavia's grip and wiped tears away. "My sister was hiding in the bushes watching. When the roof collapsed, she laughed." Bridget looked up at the ceiling. "She was committed to a juvenile facility. She got in a fight and killed one of the other kids. She's been in jail since."

"I'm sorry." Octavia walked around the table. She wrapped her arms around Bridget. "I'm so sorry I asked." She held tight to Bridget and pressed her face to her cheek.

Bridget brought her hand up and cupped Octavia's cheek. "My grandma was my world. I don't remember my parents. My sister hated my grandma. Blamed her for our parents' death. My grandma was lenient with her. Tried to correct everything she'd done wrong with my mom. It only made it worse. I see Sofia going down the same path. She ignores what Carlo does. Makes excuses for his behavior."

Octavia held tight to Bridget. "We can still say no to the horses. We don't have to have them here. We don't owe her anything."

"We can say yes. I told her if I saw Carlo on the property ever, the horses would be out."

"I'll tell Vivian." She pressed a quick kiss on the side of Bridget's neck. "What made you change your mind about her?"

Bridget shrugged. "I don't know. Her eyes. I could see how much pain Carlo has caused her. Maybe because she reminds me of my grandma trying to fix my sister."

Octavia laughed. "Whatever you do, don't tell her she reminds you of your grandma."

Bridget caught her hand as she turned to go. "We're not making a mistake, are we? I trust you but I'm not sure she understands about us. All of us."

"It doesn't matter if she understands. We understand."

Chapter Sixteen

OCTAVIA ROLLED OPEN the barn door, and Victor ran up to her. "How did you get out? And what do you have in your mouth?" A soft whinny sounded from the south end of the barn. "And how did you let Carmel out?"

Victor trotted away from Octavia, a leg wrap dangling from his mouth. Bushes and blankets were strewn around the aisle. Clumps of hay, scattered buckets, and rags were everywhere. The donkey and horse had wrecked everything they could get their mouths on. Octavia swore softly to herself as she stepped around the piles of droppings in the aisle.

"Oh for fuck's sake, you two." She caught Carmel's halter and led her to her stall and put her inside. She locked the hasp on the door firmly. "You guys had a big party last night." Victor bolted out the door of the barn. "Victor! You come back here." Octavia sighed.

What a fucking mess. How the hell did he get out? She checked the door to his stall. *Must not have closed it all the way. Damn, he's clever to let Carmel out to play with him. I better get him before he gets in more mischief. He needs work to do. He's bored.*

She ran out the barn door after the donkey.

"*Komm jetzt hier.* Don't make me chase you." The donkey bolted around the corner of the barn. Octavia swore as she chased him. Rounding the corner, her boot heel hit a slick spot and she wiped out. She lay there trying to catch her breath. *Fuck. That little jackass is going in donkey jail when I catch him.*

She pushed herself up to sitting. Her hand was skinned, and blood began to well up under the mud on her palm. Soft wet lips nuzzled her neck. The donkey pushed his head against her shoulder. "Now you want to apologize?" The donkey lay down and placed his head in her lap. "Damn, it's hard to stay mad at you."

"You two bonding?" Vivian walked toward her.

"Did you see the barn? He and Carmel had a party in there last night."

Vivian laughed. "It's my fault. I came out to see him last night. I must not have pushed the lock down all the way. He's done it before." She kneeled beside them. Victor snorted and wedged himself between them.

"He may be a miniature donkey, but he is full-sized trouble."

Vivian clasped Octavia's hand and turned it over to examine her palm. "How bad is it?"

"Nothing a little soap and water won't fix. You come out here at night a lot?"

"I do. I don't sleep well. Victor never minds a visit."

"We wouldn't either, you know."

Vivian touched her fingers to Octavia's face. "I know. But sometimes I need this. He's a touchstone. A reminder of a perfect time in my life I didn't know was perfect until it was gone."

"If I had known how short my time would be with my family, I would have spent every second with them."

Vivian fixed her gaze on Octavia's face. "The more time I spend with you and Bridget, the more I realize this is a perfect time too."

Octavia chewed her lip, not saying the three words she was afraid to say, knowing her heart would break if she didn't hear them back. She leaned close and kissed Vivian, letting her kiss say what she was too afraid to give voice to. Vivian pulled away to look into Octavia's eyes.

Love. She loves me. As afraid to say as I am. Say it. Tell her how you feel. Tell her you love her. Don't let this chance slip away.

She took a deep breath in and opened her mouth to speak, only to be interrupted by the donkey's soft snore. The sound broke the tension between them and made them both laugh.

Vivian stood up and offered Octavia her hand. "Come on. Let's get him in his stall and your scrape taken care of, and then I'll help you put the barn to rights."

VIVIAN OPENED THE first aid kit in the office. "I have some antiseptic here."

Octavia washed her hand with soap and water, cleaning the scrape on her palm. "It's not bad."

Vivian handed her a bit of gauze. "Dry it off with that."

Octavia dabbed at her palm until it was dry. She sat on top of her desk. Vivian held her wrist and sprayed the antiseptic over her skin. "Ow. That stuff stings."

Vivian quirked her mouth. "I beat you hard enough to draw blood and you are whining about the antiseptic?"

Octavia laughed. "Yeah, well, it's all about the circumstances." She blew on her palm to ease the burn of the medication. Vivian released her wrist and put the antiseptic back in the kit.

Octavia tilted her head at Vivian. "Can I ask you about Sofia?"

Vivian's eyes took on a wary look. "What about her?"

"Is she...? Were you...?" She watched the change in Vivian's expression and knew the answer to her question before she finished speaking. "Never mind."

Vivian touched her face, drawing her eyes to her gaze. "Were. She's my best friend. And that's not going to change." She kissed Octavia's cheek before she tucked the first aid kit into the desk drawer next to the cognac.

VIVIAN CAME INTO the kitchen. Her long satin robe pulled open as she walked, giving Octavia a glimpse of her thigh and making her shift in her chair. Knowing her Mistress well enough to not speak until she had her first cup of coffee, she entertained herself by imagining all the ways she wanted to show her devotion. She traced her fingers over the edge of her tea cup.

Bridget pressed a coffee cup into Vivian's hand and turned back to the sink.

Vivian took a sip of her coffee. "Perfect." She sat down across from Octavia. "What do you to have planned for today?"

"The barn is done. I don't have to do anything until this evening."

"Bridget?"

"I've done my prep. I was going to go over the accounts."

Vivian waved her hand. "Let it go. I want to go shopping. And have lunch out."

Bridget rested her hand on her hip. "Tired of my cooking already?" She pushed her lips out in a pout.

Vivian wagged her finger at Bridget. "No. No pouting. I want you to take an afternoon off. You both have been working too hard since you got here."

Octavia raised an eyebrow. "We've taken some time for ourselves in the afternoons."

"Hmm, I know. Sometimes I can hear you. But today, I want to spend time with both of you. I need a break from this manuscript."

"Manuscript? Have you given up photography for writing?"

"Not given it up. I'm writing a memoir. Of my time as a photojournalist."

Memories. She's having to deal with her memoirs of Miriam. Of their life. Of the hard things she's seen.

"I can save my prep. What time do you want to leave?" Bridget pulled off her apron and came to stand next to Vivian. "Anything in particular you want to see us in?" She traced a finger over the line of bare skin exposed by the robe's neckline. Octavia watched the delicate flare of Vivian's nostrils as Bridget teased her.

Turning in her chair to look up at Bridget, Vivian reached up and tweaked Bridget's nipple. "Surprise me, my cheeky one. And don't stand over a Mistress."

Bridget yelped and stepped back. "Any Mistress?" She cocked her head and rested her hand on her hip. "Or you?"

Vivian placed her coffee cup on the table. She stood up and closed the distance between Bridget and herself and wrapped a hand in Bridget's hair. She forced her head back. "Me." Vivian kissed her way down Bridget's neck, before she stopped and pulled her head back farther, arching her neck into an elegant bow. "Do you need another lesson?"

Bridget voice trembled when she spoke. "Now?" She swallowed hard, the muscles in her throat taut.

Watching them together made Octavia's clit hard, and she sat back in her chair and spread her legs, trying to relieve the pressure on her clit.

Vivian traced a finger over Bridget's lips. "Maybe. Maybe not. Perhaps I'll make you wait." She pushed her fingers inside Bridget's mouth. With a soft, needy sound, Bridget sucked at her fingers until Vivian pulled them from her mouth and shoved them roughly into Bridget's pants. Bridget hollowed her body, giving her better access.

Octavia groaned. She wanted to touch herself. *Not without permission.* Vivian turned to stare at her and raised her eyebrow at Octavia. "You too? My, we are going to have an interesting trip." The muscles in her forearms rippled as she fingered Bridget.

Bridget shuddered and rocked her hips. "Ah. Oh. I'm…"

"No, you're not." Vivian pulled her hand free and released Bridget. She held her hand up. Her fingers glistened with Bridget's wetness. She licked her fingers. "Not now. Go get dressed."

Octavia's breath was as ragged as Bridget's. "Yes. Mistress." She was rewarded by a broad smile from Vivian.

"Wear something comfortable but nice. We are going have lunch in Milan. Leave your hair down for me. I like how it frames your face."

Bridget was leaning on the counter, bent over at the waist, resting her cheek on the cool marble. "I can't leave the house this way."

Vivian walked over to her and swatted her ass. "You will. And no touching yourself or each other until I say."

Vivian left them wet and aching with desire, walking away with her black robe swirling around her legs, her head up, the soft sent of verbena in her wake.

Bridget moaned. "Remind me not to do that again."

"Stand over her? Or test her?"

"Both. My clit is so hard it hurts." She stood up and slowed her breathing.

Octavia got to her feet. "Come on. Let's see what we can wear that will make her sorry we didn't finish this." She took Bridget's hand and led her to their room.

OCTAVIA STRETCHED IN her seat, arching her back. She adjusted her top so the soft fabric pulled tight and her cleavage was better displayed.

"Are you trying to distract me, wicked woman?" Vivian's large sunglasses hid her eyes, but her voice was full of affection.

"Maybe."

Bridget leaned forward and reached over the Octavia's seat. She cupped Octavia's breasts and thumbed her nipples through her shirt. "This is distracting, Mistress?" The playful tone in her voice made Octavia's heart squeeze in her chest. *Love her. Love the way she has embraced this. Love this. Being with both of them.*

"Don't make me stop this car." Vivian's voice was mock serious as she piloted the car toward Milan.

Bridget snorted. "Now you're making mom threats? Are you going to send us to bed without dessert?"

Vivian raised her chin and smiled at Bridget in the rearview mirror. "I wouldn't taunt me, little girl."

Octavia turned to watch as Bridget leaned back in the seat. She pulled her short skirt up revealing her lack of panties. She touched her fingers to herself, gathering a bit of wetness. She sucked her fingers into her mouth before she tugged her skirt back into place. "Is this taunting? Or teasing?" The cheeky expression on her face made Octavia want to kiss her until she couldn't breathe.

Vivian swore softly under her breath. She pulled on to a side street and stopped the car. She turned around in the seat. She pulled her sunglasses off slowly before she pinned Bridget with a hard look. "Didn't I tell you not to touch yourself or Octavia until I gave you permission?"

A chastened Bridget sat up. "Sorry, Mistress." She looked down at her hands.

"Pull your skirt up again without my asking and I will show you what happens when you disobey a direct order."

Bridget looked up, her eyes fierce. "Show me now."

"I suppose the only way I'm going to get to shop is to pacify you. Impatient girl." Vivian picked up her phone and scrolled though it. She pressed the button to dial a number. She spoke too quickly in Italian for Octavia to catch all of her conversation. Having ended the call, without a word, she pulled out into traffic.

Bridget was quiet in the back seat. Octavia turned to Bridget and she smiled at her, eyes full of mischief. *Does she know what she did? She's going to see what happens when you push a Mistress.* Octavia pressed her legs together and squirmed in her seat, earning a slap on the leg from Vivian. The sting sent a sharp wave of desire through her. *Where is she taking us?* Her palms were wet, and she wiped them on her pants. They turned down a side street. Row houses and small businesses crowded together on the narrow street.

Vivian pulled into a gated driveway, stopped the car, and opened the window. She lifted the cover on a black box and entered a code into a keypad. The gate rolled back, and she drove forward into a small paved lot. Octavia watched in the side-view mirror as the gate rolled closed behind them. Vivian parked next to a late-model Mercedes in the small cobblestoned lot. Octavia opened her door and walked around to Vivian's side of the car. She opened it for her Mistress. She took advantage of her position to admire the long length of Vivian's thigh exposed by the slit in her skirt. Vivian looked up at her. "Nice. I see someone has manners."

Bridget opened her door and shot Octavia a look. "Suck-up."

Brat. My beautiful brat. Begging for the spanking she deserves. I can't wait for Vivian to punish her. And me.

Vivian exited the car and pressed a quick kiss to Octavia's cheek before she leveled her gaze at Bridget. Bridget's lower lip quivered. "And now, my ornery one, let's see if we can take some of your edge off so we can enjoy ourselves later." She stepped away from them and walked toward the shaded courtyard without looking back to see if they followed. Octavia closed the car door and took Bridget's hand.

"What is this place?" Bridget frowned at the looming brick house. "There's no sign." She pushed herself closer to Octavia.

"I don't know. But it's not good to keep a Mistress waiting."

"Is it like when I stood over her?"

"Worse." Octavia kept her voice light in an attempt to soothe Bridget. "It gives them more time to think of ways to drive you mad with pleasure." She clasped Bridget's hand and brought it to her lips. She scattered kisses over her knuckles. "It will be all right, love. You trust her, right? She won't do anything to hurt us. At least not more than we want her to."

Bridget squeezed her fingers. "I'm frightened. Of what I want."

"I know." Octavia looped her arm around Bridget's waist. "Nothing will happen you don't want. I'll be there." She moved them along the walk in the direction Vivian had taken. "We better go."

THE DOOR TO the house was open. The foyer was tiled in small octagon-shaped black and white tiles. A wide stairway spilt the hallway. Vivian stood in the narrow hall next to the stairs with her arms crossed, waiting for them. Her face had transformed. She was a Mistress, power embodied, a queen to be served. She raked her gaze over them. "Kneel." Octavia sank to her knees, tugging Bridget with her. She let go of Bridget's hand, lowered her head, and rested her hands on the tops of her knees, assuming the position of service. After taking a deep breath, she blew it out slowly. *Settle. Focus. Obey. Serve.* She watched as Bridget copied her position. Her uncertainty and apprehension were palpable in the short distance between them.

Vivian walked forward, her steps measured. The sound of her heels on the floor sent a wave of desire through Octavia. She stopped in front of them. Her black-and-white spectator pumps were so close to Octavia she leaned forward and kissed the toe of her Mistress's shoe. *Mistress. Mine. Ours. Please be ours.* From under her lashes, she could see the ends of a short quirt Vivian held in her hand and her desire flowed.

"Follow me. No talking."

Bridget stood up.

"Did I tell you to stand?"

"No. I thought..."

The slap was short and sharp, the sound of it making Octavia wish it were her face that now bore the red mark of Vivian's displeasure.

"No. You don't think. You obey. And answer correctly."

Bridget's eyes were wide and her breathing rapid. Her nipples tented the soft fabric of her sheer shirt. "Yes, Mistress." She lowered herself to her knees.

Vivian turned and walked away from them. Bridget crawled after her, and Octavia followed. Watching Bridget's ass as she crawled down the halls toward Vivian made her want to kiss and lick the soft curves of her cheeks and the inside of her thighs and bury herself between her legs. The image of Vivian, striding down the hall, the two tails of the quirt brushing the edge of her skirt as she walked, Bridget behind her, crawling on her knees, sent a wave of desire through her, and she moaned softly.

Vivian stopped in front of a narrow door. Her whisper broke the silence. "Wait." She pulled a key from the top of the door frame. After unlocking it, she turned a light switch on the wall and opened it. The damp smell of a cellar wafted into the hall. "Rise. Follow me. Be careful. The steps are narrow and steep."

Cool air flowed over Octavia's skin, and the hairs on her arm stood up. The cellar was dimly lit. Wine bottles lined the walls in racks. A rough-planked thick-legged table with two straight-backed chairs was centered in the middle of the room. An oil lamp and a box of matches rested on the table. A ruby-red glazed pitcher and three glasses were on a silver tray. A wine barrel lay on its side, held in place by a rack, and took up most of the space in the cellar. A pair of leather cuffs were attached to the frame on the side facing them.

Vivian pulled a chair out and sat down. She spread her legs wide, the split in her skirt showing off her toned thigh. "Bridget, stand here." She pointed to the space between her legs.

A quiet Bridget moved into position. Vivian slid a hand under her skirt. "My, you are wet." She forced a deep groan from Bridget before she pulled her hand out. "We will take care of that, but first a lesson. Take off your skirt and blouse. I want you to be presentable when we go to the restaurant."

Bridget stepped back she kept her head down. "Here?"

Vivian pinned her with her eyes. "If you want to stop, use your word."

Bridget stepped back and chewed her lower lip.

Will she say it? Don't say it. Please don't stop. Trust her. Trust me. Octavia looked down and watched Bridget from beneath her lashes. *Can't help her. She has to choose. Her decision.*

Bridget blew out a loud breath before she unzipped her skirt. She tugged it down over her hips and stepped out of it. She picked it up and folded it neatly and placed it on the table. The whisper of the fabric of her blouse against her skin as she pulled it off sent a shiver through Octavia. Bridget toed off her shoes and arranged them neatly under the table. After adding her sheer bra to the pile, Bridget trembled as she stood naked in the small space between the chair and the barrel.

Vivian crooked her finger at Octavia, and she hurried to her side. Vivian reached up and pinched her nipple through her shirt. Octavia trembled under her touch. Vivian tugged and rolled her nipple before she tightened her grip and jerked her down. She cupped the back of her head and kissed her. Lips hard, she savaged her mouth. Octavia's hands opened and clenched at her side as she fought her urge to touch Vivian. She groaned her frustration. *Not now. Not without permission. Focus. So good.*

Vivian pulled back and looked in Octavia's eyes and dug her nails into the soft skin of her neck. "Take her to the wine barrel. I want her draped over it facedown. There are cuffs attached to the other side to hold her in place. Leave her legs loose." She released Octavia and settled her frame in the chair and crossed her arms. She held the quirt up right across her chest, and in the dim light, Octavia was reminded of every image she'd ever seen of ancient queens wielding a staff and flail. *Yes. This. Let me serve you.* Overwhelmed, she knelt and pressed kisses to the top of Vivian's shoes. *Worship. Let me kneel at your feet. Let me serve you. Feed me your pain.* The sting of the tails of the quirt across her shoulders stopped her.

"Enough. There will be time later. Do what I asked."

Focus. Serve. Forcing herself to move away from Vivian's lash, she took Bridget's upper arm and led her to the wine barrel. It had been sanded smooth and varnished, the wood like satin to the touch. She boosted Bridget up so she could stand on the frame holding the barrel. She set her feet wide and bent at the waist to lay facedown over the cask. Octavia placed her hands on her back and assisted her as she stretched over the curved wood. She slid her fingers down her arm and took her wrist. She buckled the cuff. Bridget's eyes were closed, her breathing rapid as Octavia buckled the second cuff that would help to keep her in place.

Bridget rested her cheek on the glossy surface. She met Octavia's gaze. *Fear. Want. Need. Trust.* Her face was twisted in fear and passion, and Octavia squeezed her shoulder, trying to reassure her. Forbidden to speak, she focused her gaze on Bridget's eyes. *You're okay, love. It will be okay. You're safe with us.* She turned away before Bridget could see how much she wanted to be in her place. She closed her eyes, remembering the times she had been flogged at Rowan House, bent over a table. Memories of being exposed and helpless ratcheted up her excitement. Her pants were soaked through with her need.

Vivian walked to them. She smoothed her hand over Bridget's ass and her back. "So helpless. Vulnerable. At my disposal." She slipped a finger between Bridget's legs and gathered the wetness there. She held it out to Octavia in an invitation. Octavia opened her mouth and sucked her fingers deep. *So sweet. More.* The taste of Bridget ignited the banked coals of her passion. Vivian pushed her fingers in and out of Octavia's mouth, teasing her. *Please give me more. Please I want more. So good. So sweet.*

"Enough." Vivian pulled her hand from Octavia's mouth.

Bridget's eyes were half-lidded, and the raw desire etched on her face sent rills of excitement through Octavia. Vivian reached out and gripped Octavia's chin. "Strip."

The pressure of her fingers forced a groan from Octavia. "Yes, Mistress."

Vivian released her before she grabbed a handful of Bridget's hair and tugged. Bridget yelped. Octavia stripped her clothes off fast and folded them. She stacked her pants and shirt on the chair in a neat pile.

"Watch and learn. That is how one acts when a Mistress commands. Without hesitation." She lowered her mouth to Bridget's lips. She kissed her, teasing her with her tongue. Octavia watched them, desire pooling between her legs and coating her thighs.

Keeping her hand wrapped in Bridget's hair, Vivian motioned for Octavia to come forward. "Remove my skirt." Octavia sank to her knees, the rough floor digging into her skin. She raised her hands and unzipped her skirt and lowered it with care. Vivian stepped out of her skirt, and Octavia folded it and placed it on the table. She crawled back to her side and sat back on her heels to wait for her Mistress's command. Vivian wore a red suspender belt and black patterned stockings. Her matching red panties were dark between her legs with her need.

"Lick me."

Octavia licked her lips and crawled forward until she was centered between her Mistress's legs. She pressed her thumb under the edge and pulled Vivian's panties to the side. She touched her tongue to the hard bud of Vivian's clit. *So sweet. Hard. Wet for us. For me. For this.* Vivian's palm on the top of her head was firm, holding Octavia in place. She worked her clit, sucking and rolling it on her tongue. She wanted to push her fingers inside, to have Vivian clench around her fingers, bury herself in Vivian, to touch all of her. *Wait. Not without permission.*

Vivian rocked her hips hard against Octavia's face. Her chin and cheeks were wet as Vivian marked her, holding her in place as she took her satisfaction. Octavia's clit ached. She wanted to squeeze her legs together to relieve the pressure, but she kept her legs wide to show Vivian, to hold her pleasure for her, a gift, a tribute to her. A tug on her hair and she pulled back. Hating the loss of Vivian on her tongue. *Mine. My Mistress. Please. Be Ours.*

Vivian pulled her up for kiss. "That mouth of yours." She cupped Octavia's cheek. "Stand in front of her. Touch yourself." She stepped behind Bridget. She trailed her fingers over her spine and teased the dimple at the top of her ass. "Such a lovely sight." She thrust her fingers into Bridget and fucked her slowly. "I can see how much you want this. I can feel it. Keep your eyes open. Watch."

Bridget panted, her breathing rough. "Please let me come, Mistress. Please let me come for you." She squirmed on the barrel. Held in place by the cuffs, she strained against them.

"No. Not until you learn the proper way to follow my directions." Vivian stepped back and brought the quirt down hard. Bridget screamed. She scattered the line of the strikes, and Bridget wiggled, trying to avoid the blows. Her breath came in short pants. "Ow, oh too much. Stop. Mercy, Mistress."

Octavia's chest was tight. She slowed her touches, worried she would not be able to hold back if Bridget screamed again. "Mistress. Please. Let me come for you." She stroked her clit, keeping herself in check. Holding on for her Mistress.

"No." Vivian's harsh tone filled the small room.

Octavia bit her lip and continued to stroke her clit, bracing her legs wide to steady herself. She could come from the sweet sound of Bridget's squeals and the snap of the quirt on her skin.

Vivian stopped and scraped her fingernails over the marks on Bridget's skin. "I love how your skin shows my marks so quickly." Bridget moaned. Octavia focused on Bridget, trying to hold off her pleasure.

"That was a sample of what happens when you test me. This is your punishment." She stepped back and brought the quirt down hard across the parallel lines that marked Bridget's back. Once. Twice. Three times and Bridget broke. "Oh please. I can't, Mistress." The sound of Bridget crying filled the room. "I'm sorry, Mistress." Vivian brought the quirt down again.

Her breath came in short pants. A thin line of sweat beaded on her brow, and Bridget begged. "Ow. Oh, too much. Stop. Mercy, Mistress. Please."

Another blow from Vivian. Octavia shuddered, close to losing control. *Hold on. Breathe. Wait.*

"Come for me. Show Bridget how a well-behaved sub is rewarded."

She kept her eyes focused on Vivian's face and spilled her pleasure, wetness spurting from her body and soaking her hand.

Vivian's broad smile was her reward. "I could watch you squirt for me all day. Again."

Octavia kept stroking her clit, shuddering, making herself come again, her desire to please Vivian the only thing keeping her on her feet.

Vivian stepped behind Bridget and thrust her fingers inside her. Bridget moaned and squirmed over the barrel. "Please, Mistress. Let me come for you. Please. I can't..."

"Are you going to test me again?"

"No, Mistress. Oh no. Please. I can't. Please let me come for you. Please."

Vivian kept thrusting, her arm muscles flexing as she pushed Bridget closer to the edge.

"Pleasepleaseplease, Mistress. I can't... I'm going to... Oh please." Tears gleamed on Bridget's face and the distress in her voice pushed Octavia closer to the edge.

"Come then, my sweet brat. Pay tribute to your Mistress."

Bridget screamed, the sound loud in the small cellar. Vivian was relentless, drawing every bit Bridget had to give to her from her body, tormenting her with pleasure. She writhed on the barrel, her breath ragged, as she came a third time before she whispered, "Apples, Mistress. Apples."

Vivian pulled her hand from Bridget before she walked around to the front of the barrel. She pushed back Bridget's hair and cupped her neck. Bridget lifted her tear-streaked face. Her eyes were closed. Vivian stroked her fingers along her cheek. Bridget leaned into her touch and sniffed. "Sorry, Mistress."

"For what?" Vivian carded her fingers through Bridget's hair. "Surrender is a gift. I treasure it. Eyes to me." She leaned down to look in Bridget's eyes before she pressed a kiss to her lips. "I treasure you."

She straightened and placed her hand on the crown of Bridget's head. "Come here." She held her arm out in invitation, and Octavia stepped into her embrace. She fit her body against her. The silky drag of her shirt made Octavia's nipples hard.

Vivian pulled her close, her arm banded about Octavia's shoulders. She looked in Octavia's eyes. "And you. I treasure you too, my sweet."

Octavia held Vivian's gaze. *Truth. Love. She loves us. Treasures us. Me.* "Please, Mistress, may I serve you?" Want pooled in her belly, a desperate ache to taste and touch her Mistress.

Vivian tilted her head. "Release Bridget. She'll be dizzy from having her head down so long. And then—" She reached out and rubbed her thumb over Octavia's lower lip. "We'll go upstairs and I'll take my pleasure from your gorgeous mouth."

Together they unbuckled the cuffs. Octavia moved to stand behind Bridget to support her when she stood up. She swayed, and Octavia gathered her in her arms, lifting her and holding her close. Bridget snuggled her head under Octavia's chin.

Vivian bought a chair over, and Octavia sat down and held Bridget on her lap. "The stairs are too narrow for you to carry her." She poured a glass of water and held it for Bridget while she drank. The heat from Bridget's body warmed Octavia. The cellar air was cool as the sweat dried on her skin. She shivered.

Vivian frowned. "I should have asked Martin for blankets."

"I can walk." Bridget lifted her head and shifted in Octavia's lap. "Mistress."

Vivian touched her face. "You'll be no use to anyone if you fall down the steps."

Bridget snorted. "I was a line cook for five years. I'm not frail." She stood up and poured herself a glass of water and chugged it down. She placed her glass on the table and smiled. She shifted her gaze between them. "And I'll crawl up the stairs if it means I get to watch the two of you together."

Vivian shook her head. "You are a menace and have learned nothing." Her tone was playful. "Very well. Get up the stairs before I decide to persuade you." She picked up the quirt and pulled the tails through her fingers.

Bridget quirked her mouth. "Not sure that's motivation to behave or not." She picked up her clothes from the table. She turned her back to them and sashayed up the steps swinging her hips.

Octavia laughed.

Vivian looked at her and raised an eyebrow. "That woman is incorrigible."

"Totally, Mistress. And totally worth it." Octavia gathered their clothes and waited for Vivian to lead the way up the stairs.

BRIDGET WAS STANDING in the hallway at the top of the steps. She held her clothes in one hand and rested the other on her hip. Octavia closed the door to the cellar. Vivian took her hand and guided them back to the foyer. The stairs leading up were wide enough for two abreast, and Bridget trailed after them.

"Whose house is this?" Bridget's voice was loud in the quiet space of the stairwell.

"Mine. And Sophia's."

Octavia swallowed her jealousy. She closed her eyes against the images of Vivian and Sophia together. *Theirs. They were lovers. Maybe they still are. She said "were."*

"Is this where you go when you don't come home?" The edge in Bridget's voice made the hairs on Octavia's arms stand on end.

Please let it go, Bridget. Don't start. Please. Don't start. Enjoy what we have. Enjoy now. Octavia held tighter to Vivian's hand, holding on to her words to them in the cellar. *Treasured. She treasures us. Loves us. I saw it in her eyes.*

"Time for questions later." Vivian's voice was firm. "I'm not done with you yet."

At the top of the stairs, Vivian pointed to a narrow door to the right. "Toilet is through there." She kept her grip on Octavia's hand as she walked to the end of the hallway. The door was open. A massive four poster bed, the canopy barely clearing the ceiling, was centered on one wall. The windows were topped with heavy dark green drapes. Sheer curtains softened the sunlight that streamed in. Thick carpet cushioned their steps. A wingback chair with a small side table and dark mahogany chest of drawers finished the room off.

Vivian let go of Octavia's hand. "On the bed, my sweet. Face up, legs spread."

Octavia placed her clothes on the side table. Bridget hung back, her shoulders slumped and her chin resting on her chest. She held her clothes in front of her body. Vivian crossed to her. She tipped her chin up with her fingers and kissed her. Octavia lingered as Vivian took her time kissing Bridget. The color rose in Bridget's cheeks, and she dropped the clothes from her hands and wrapped her arms around Vivian's waist and molded her body to her.

Vivian leaned back from their kiss. "Pick up your clothes and join Octavia on the bed. Lay between her legs. No touching until I return." She left though the door they had entered.

Octavia climbed onto the bed and lay back and spread her legs wide. The sensation of the cool air on her wet clit made her shiver. Bridget gathered her clothes and placed them on the chair before she joined Octavia on the bed. She settled herself between Octavia's legs, and because she was Bridget, she blew her warm breath over Octavia's wet thighs and the space between them. Octavia looked down at her. Bridget's mouth was poised over her body.

A sly smile crossed her face, and she puckered her lips and blew out again, making Octavia ache for her mouth. "Does this count as touching?"

"It should." Octavia gripped the headboard to keep from burying her hands in Bridget's hair and grinding her hips against her. A frown passed over Bridget's face and disappeared so fast if Octavia had not known Bridget for as long as she had she would have let it go. "Are you okay, love? Does your back hurt?"

"No. My heart." Bridget rested her head on Octavia's thigh. "I don't like thinking of them together."

"I know, love. I know." Octavia brought her hand down and touched her cheek. "But she's with us now. Let's enjoy it."

The sound of Vivian's footsteps in the hall made them assume their places. Vivian had changed into a short deep green robe. She stood next to the bed. Her gaze settled on Octavia's, and she held out a pair of nipple clamps connected by a silver chain. She mounted the bed. She shoved Bridget's face between Octavia's legs. "Feast on her. Take your time."

Octavia arched her back as Bridget made contact, surrounding her with wet heat. Vivian's hands were on her, stroking the undersides of her breasts with the backs of her knuckles. She lowered her head and took her nipple in her mouth, sucking hard and teasing it with her teeth, sending a sharp wave of need through Octavia. With a firm grip, she pulled Octavia's nipple into a tight point before she placed the clamp and tightened the screw. Octavia groaned and arched into her touch. Vivian lowered her head and did the same with the other nipple. Once the clamps were in place, she tugged gently on the chain. Octavia's breath came in short pants as the pleasure of Bridget's mouth on her and the pain of the nipple clamps blended into a sweet torture. Vivian shifted on the bed and kneeled over her, her face toward Bridget, her knees on either side of Octavia's face. The delicate scent of her filled Octavia with desire, and saliva pooled in her mouth.

"Tap my thigh if you need air." Vivian lowered herself onto Octavia's face.

Pressing her tongue to Vivian's swollen clit, Octavia licked and sucked hard. A deep groan rattled her chest as Bridget worked her, teasing her. Vivian tugged the chain linking the clamps in a rhythm. Her sounds of pleasure were loud in the room, her moaning goading Octavia to bring her off. The press of Vivian's flesh against her face made Octavia desperate for air. Timing Octavia's ability to go without a breath perfectly, Vivian lifted her hips, giving Octavia space to breathe. Gulping air, Octavia worked to slow her breathing. Bridget increased her pace and Octavia panted. "Please, Mistress, may I come for you?"

Vivian tugged the chain between her breasts. "After me." She lowered her hips and ground herself against Octavia's face. Thrusting her tongue deep, Octavia worked hard for her Mistress's release. Vivian came with a deep groan, filling Octavia's mouth. Octavia lapped and sucked, gorging herself on her Mistress's essence. Vivian lifted herself from Octavia's mouth. Her breath was ragged as she pulled the chain taut. "Make her come for me. Now."

With a wide sweep of her tongue followed by a deep suck on her clit, Bridget pushed Octavia into a pool of pleasure. Octavia screamed when Vivian yanked the chain and the nipple clamps pulled free. Blinding pain and pleasure twined as she came, spurting, filling Bridget's mouth. She closed her eyes against the spirals of sensation and relaxed on the tide of endorphins that swept over her. The bed shifted, and Vivian's mouth covered her nipple. She swirled her tongue over her tender flesh. The sensation was sweet, and Octavia came again, lifting her hips, arching off the bed. Bridget moaned against her, licking with slow strokes.

Boneless, she relaxed under their touch as Vivian and Bridget worked together, easing her down before coaxing another orgasm from her. Eyes closed, she relaxed under their hands. *This. Forever under both of them. Safe. Cherished. Wanted. Loved.*

Vivian moved to lie next to her, and Bridget rose from between her legs. She dragged her body over her sensitive nipples and dropped a kiss on her mouth before she snuggled under her arm. She cupped her breasts and thumbed her nipple. With a firm touch, Vivian smoothed her hands over Octavia's stomach and down through the wet curls over her clit.

"Mmm, that was exquisite." Vivian kissed her under her ear and pushed her fingers in deep. Octavia groaned and opened her legs wider, craving her touch. Raising herself on her elbow, Vivian leaned over her to look in her eyes. "Look at me. Come for me. Eyes open. Let me see you."

She worked her fingers in and out slowly, pressing deep, and Octavia bucked into her strokes, wanting more. Vivian slow-fucked her, the heel of her hand grinding into her clit, relentless, until Octavia came again. Eyes wide open, unable to hide from her Mistress, showing her everything, how much she wanted to belong to her, how she loved her, all of it as she came under her touch.

Vivian gazed into her eyes, and Octavia gazed back, seeking what she craved, rewarded by what she saw there.

Chapter Seventeen

"SHE OWNS A house with her. Still." Bridget worked, the muscles in her forearm flexing as she aggressively kneaded the dough.

"We can't change the past. She said it was over between them." Octavia leaned a hip on the counter.

"I know." Bridget stopped and brushed the back of her wrist over her brow, leaving a bit of flour behind.

Octavia reached over and wiped the flour away. "We're in deep."

Bridget sighed and shaped a loaf out of the elastic dough in front of her. "Slide the basket over, please."

Octavia moved the towel-draped basket closer to where she was working. Bridget scattered flour over the towel and gently placed the round loaf in the basket. She gathered up the ends of the towel and covered the dough. "I know. I can't stop thinking about what she said."

"Which part?"

"Treasured. It's how I feel about you. And how you make me feel." Bridget washed her hands.

Octavia picked up the bowl. "Where do you want this?"

Bridget pointed to a cabinet next to the stove. "In there. It's the perfect temperature for the second rise."

Octavia placed the bowl in the cabinet. She moved behind Bridget and wrapped her arms around her waist and pulled her close. Bridget lifted her hand and cupped her cheek, leaning her brow against the side of Octavia's face.

"I saw a letter from the realtor. It was on her desk." Octavia pulled Bridget closer to her.

"Do you think she'll do it?"

"I don't know. She has a lot of memories here."

"That can be a good thing or a bad thing."

Octavia kissed the side of Bridget's neck. "Are you worried?"

Bridget turned in her arms. She gazed into Octavia's eyes. "What will it mean for us if she sells? She won't need us if she sells and moves to Milan."

"Do you think we're like furniture? We're something she'll leave behind if she can't fit us into her life if she moves?"

"I don't know. I worry we could have been anyone. That it's for now, not forever."

The pain in Bridget's eyes made Octavia's heart hurt for both of them. "It will be what it is. We have each other. That won't change no matter what happens with Vivian."

Bridget kissed her. "I know, love. I know." Tears tracked their way down her cheeks. "I love her. I love it here. I imagined we would be home here."

"Wherever you are is my home." Octavia wiped her tears with her thumbs. "We will get through this whatever she decides. We can't force her to choose us. She has to do what is right for her."

"I know. I want her to want us. I'm old enough to know you can't force someone to love you. I want what's best for her too. But I'm selfish enough to want her to choose what we want."

"I don't think she'll sell."

"Why?"

"Victor. And Max. And Carmel. Although I think there is little love lost between her and Sassy."

Bridget laughed. "So we are saved by her love of the donkey?"

Octavia hugged her close and brought her lips close to her ear. "And us. I think she loves us. And I know she knows how much you like it here."

"DO YOU EVER think she'll want to sleep with us? Like in our bed? I hate how she always leaves us to go sleep in her room." Bridget lowered her book, keeping her finger between the pages to mark her place.

"I don't know." Octavia stretched before she pillowed her hands behind her head.

Bridget frowned at her. "She's so damn mysterious. I want to know her. She gives us bits and pieces. What she wants us to know."

"Doesn't everyone?"

"Hmm. Don't remind me. I'm still pissed you didn't tell me about your past."

"I was honest. About my feelings. And things that mattered."

"Your past matters."

"What about your past?" Octavia rolled her side and rested her head on her hand.

Bridget narrowed her eyes. "What about it? I've told you everything I remember."

"Not everything." Octavia touched Bridget's hand. "You've never told me about your first kiss. Or high school. Or why you ran away from your foster home."

Bridget huffed out a breath and placed a bookmark in her book. She placed it on the nightstand. She turned to face Octavia and lay down on her side, mirroring her position. "Okay. My first kiss was from Wanda Thompson. A drunken slobber fest that lasted all of thirty sloppy seconds. I quit high school and ran away. I lived in a shelter for queer teens and got my GED. I ran away from my foster home because they wouldn't take me to see my sister."

Octavia reached out and touched Bridget's shoulder. "That's awful. Why the fuck wouldn't they take you to see her?"

"They insisted the drive to the detention facility was too far away. Mind you, they had relatives about ten miles from the place we saw on the regular."

The pain in her eyes made Octavia sorry she had asked. "I'm sorry. We don't have to talk about it if you don't want to."

"No. You started it. Now it's your turn. Why weren't you and Vivian lovers in high school? And why didn't you go to college?"

Octavia laughed. "I'm not sure I like this game. All right. I was too afraid she'd reject me and I'd get kicked out of school. My uncle controlled the money after my father died, and he didn't think women needed to go to college."

"Wasn't it family money? Wasn't some of it yours?"

"Yes. I was eighteen and didn't want to fight with him about it. I was madly in love with a woman who took me on as a groom on the international dressage circuit. It seemed like a good idea at the time."

"You say that a lot."

"I tend to go with the flow."

"And not ask for what you want."

Octavia sat up and pushed Bridget onto her back, using her body weight to hold her down. The flare of heat in Bridget's eyes made her hungry for her submission. She kissed her hard and pushed her knee between her legs. "I think I'm pretty good at asking for some things."

Shifting seamlessly into her role, Bridget relaxed under her. "Yes, Ma'am."

Octavia sat up and kneeled between Bridget's legs. "Open your shirt and show yourself to me."

Bridget unbuttoned her shirt and pulled the shirttail loose from her pants. She took it off and tossed it over the side of the bed.

"Bra too."

She held Octavia's gaze as she sat up and reached behind her to unhook her bra. She threw it on the floor next to her shirt. She tilted her head and raised her chin. "Anything else, Ma'am?"

Octavia sucked a nipple into her mouth. She bit down, savoring the sharp squeal from Bridget. She released her nipple. "The rest of it."

Bridget shoved her pants down and pulled them off before she added her panties to the clothes on the floor.

"Mmm. Perfection." Octavia clasped Bridget's upper arms and held her down. She lowered her mouth and drew each nipple in turn deep, forcing Bridget still as Octavia took her time teasing her nipples into hard peaks.

Bridget's breathing shifted. She arched her back, seeking contact with Octavia. "Please, Ma'am. More. Please."

Octavia kissed her way down Bridget's stomach and nibbled at her flesh. Bridget squirmed and squealed with the harder nips. The scent of her excitement made saliva well in Octavia's mouth. She licked a trail down her stomach before she took Bridget in her mouth. Bridget arched to meet her, thrusting her hips up and pushing herself into Octavia's mouth. As she teased her with her tongue, Octavia slipped three fingers inside before drawing them back slowly. She raised her mouth from Bridget. "I love you, my beautiful brat. I love the way you taste." She licked a firm line over her clit and thrust harder, making Bridget groan. "I love watching you under me. The way your face looks when you come for me." She licked Bridget's clit again and drew it into her mouth, teasing the hardness with her tongue. "And I love the way it feels when you come under my tongue. Come for me." She lowered her mouth and swirled her tongue over Bridget's clit, pushing her fingers deeps, curling them over the spot that would send Bridget over. She held tight as Bridget bucked her hips into her mouth and clenched around her fingers, a surge of salty sweetness filling her mouth.

Bridget rested her hand on the top of Octavia's head. The pulsating waves of her pleasure rippled over Octavia's fingers. Bridget's breathing slowed, and Octavia kissed the soft skin over her stomach, each nipple, and the delicate hollow of her throat as she made her way to Bridget's mouth. A tug at her hair made her lift her head to look in Bridget's eyes.

Bridget held her gaze and brought her other hand up to touch her cheek. "I love you, Ma'am." She kissed Octavia hard and nipped her lip. "Always."

Chapter Eighteen

VIVIAN PUSHED HER glasses up on top of her head and rubbed her eyes. "I don't know why I said yes to this." She tossed the binder holding her manuscript on the table.

Octavia looked up from her book. "Because no one else can write the story but you."

Bridget stacked up the recipe cards she was sorting and placed them back into the wooden file box on the table. She stood and moved behind Vivian and placed her hands on her shoulders. The muscles in her arms flexed as she rubbed and massaged her neck and shoulders.

Vivian leaned back in her chair. "Mmm, that's good." She reached up and touched the back of Bridget's hand. "Your hands are so strong. They are divine."

"All the bread she makes." Octavia placed her book on the table before she kneeled at Vivian's feet. She pulled her shoe off and wrapped her hands around her foot and used her thumbs to massage the delicate arch. Vivian groaned. "You two are melting me. I won't be able to do any work if you keep it up. "

"You've been working on that manuscript for hours. Take a break with us." Bridget massaged her shoulders, working her fingers deep.

Octavia looked up from Vivian's feet and met Bridget's eyes. Bridget's smile warmed her. With a light touch she trailed her fingers up Vivian's leg under her loose skirt. "Please." She pressed a kiss to the top of Vivian's foot.

Bridget looped her arms around Vivian's neck and nuzzled her neck. "Let us serve you, Mistress. Please."

Vivian leaned back in the chair and placed her other foot on Octavia's chest. "Yes. I think a break would help." Twisting her hand in Bridget's curls, she pulled her in for a kiss. She opened her legs and placed one on the floor next to Octavia and lifted the other to rest on her shoulder. With soft hands Octavia pushed Vivian's skirt higher, exposing the emerald-green lace thong that graced the space between Vivian's thighs. She slipped a finger under the edge of her panties. Vivian shifted and lifted her hips for Octavia to remove them. She inhaled the scent of Vivian's desire mixed with the soft smell of verbena that clung to her skin. Octavia lowered her mouth and licked her firm clit. The salt honey filled her mouth as she licked and sucked. She worked her Mistress's clit, striving to please her, desperate to hear her pleasure.

Vivian brought her leg up and wrapped it around Octavia's shoulder, trapping her between her legs. The sensation of being held in place to pleasure her Mistress made Octavia squeeze her legs together. Her body trembled with need. The soft sounds of Vivian's release and the surge of wetness that coated her lips and tongue filled her and made her want more.

She softened her strokes. Licking gently, she swept her tongue over her Mistress, collecting her sweetness, wallowing in want and desire. A tap on her shoulder made her stop.

"Look at me."

She looked up. Bridget was naked, and Vivian had her arm around her waist. Bridget's nipples stood up and glistened a dark red against her freckled skin. A sharp smile split Vivian's face, and she pinned Octavia with a look that made her swallow hard. "Strip." Vivian toyed with Bridget's nipples.

Octavia fingered the buttons on her shirt and held Vivian's gaze as she undid each one. She pulled the tail of her shirt loose from her jeans before she unfastened the top button of her jeans and unzipped them. She thrust her hand into her briefs and pulled it out. Her fingers shone with her desire, and she bought them to her mouth and sucked them. Vivian's eyes widened. Naked desire shone on her face.

Vivian arched a brow. "Tease. I think Bridget is a bad influence." Bridget yelped when Vivian pinched her hip. "I think a lesson is in order."

Lesson. Yes, please. Please. I need a lesson. Octavia pulled her shirt off her shoulders and let it drop to the floor. She stepped out of her jeans before she added her briefs to the pile of clothes on the floor.

Vivian crooked her finger at her and Octavia went to her as if she were on a leash. She stopped in front of Vivian's knees. Bridget's breathing was loud in the space between them. With a hand on her arm, Vivian pushed Bridget into place next to Octavia. She raked her gaze over them. Octavia fought the urge to lower her eyes under Vivian's intense scrutiny. *Does she see? See how much I want to give her? How much I want her to own me?*

"We need more room for what I have in mind." Vivian stood up and pushed her skirt in place. "Down." They lowered themselves to their hands and knees. Eyes on the floor, they crawled after Vivian.

THE TILE WAS hard and cool under Octavia's knees. The pain of crawling on the floor drove her desire. Already turned on from pleasuring Vivian, her clit ached as she crawled. She was so wet she pressed her thighs together to keep herself from dripping on the floor. Vivian stopped outside the door that was never open, the door Octavia touched each time she walked by, fighting with her curiosity and powerful desire to know what lay beyond the locked door. She had held the key once, tempted to open it, but her better nature and fear of offending Vivian had led her to replace the key and turn away. Octavia heard the click as the key turned in the lock. Vivian walked across the threshold, and Octavia crawled after her into the dark room. Bridget's breath was warm on her hip as she followed close, her fear palatable to Octavia. *Wish I could see her eyes. She's afraid. She has to trust. Trust Vivian.*

The strong smell of sulfur filled the room. The match Vivian held illuminated her face briefly before she lit an oil lamp. The room filled with light as she replaced the globe. She moved around the room and lit three more lamps, each one providing more light until a playroom to rival Rowan House was bathed in a yellow glow. A leather-covered kneeling bench occupied one corner. Striking implements covered an entire wall. Crops, canes, quirts, floggers, and whips hung neatly arranged by type. Metal manacles, leather cuffs, and spreader bars filled another wall. A steel surgical cabinet stood next to a sink. A Saint Andrew's cross was at the far end of the room. One wall had large rings set at various heights. A large table, rough-hewn and wide with rings at each corner, made Octavia groan. Each device, each element, filled her thoughts with desire. *This. Oh please. Give me all of this. All of it.* Overwhelmed, she leaned forward and placed her face on the cool tile floor. She squeezed her eyes tight, pushing back the tears of want and need that threatened to fall.

Bridget's voice, full of fear, broke the spell. "I'm not... I..." Octavia turned to watch her, keeping her head down. Bridget's face was twisted in conflict. "I don't know if I can..."

Vivian crossed the floor. She reached down and pulled Bridget to her feet. She pushed aside a stray curl that had fallen across her cheek. "Nothing will happen to you that you don't want. You're in control. Your word stops everything." She rested her hands on her shoulders. "I'll keep you safe. You have to trust me. I know heavy pain is not your thing." She kissed her gently.

Bridget raised her hands and rested them on Vivian's waist. "I know she needs this. I don't know if I can watch."

Vivian tilted her head. "Have you watched her like this?"

Bridget looked away. "I only saw the aftermath. The welts, the deep bruises, the cuts."

"Did you see the peace? The way it filled a need in her?"

Bridget's voice was a whisper. "Yes."

"Like when I used the quirt on you?"

"Yes."

Vivian pursed her lips. "I'll leave the door open. If you need to leave, leave. I won't deny myself or Octavia this because you're afraid."

Bridget's eyes grew hard. "I'm not afraid."

"What is it then?" Vivian stepped back and crossed her arms.

Bridget chewed her lip. "I'm jealous."

Vivian frowned and narrowed her eyes. "Of me?"

"I can't give her this." Bridget's expression was fierce.

Vivian closed the distance between them. "And she can't give me what you give me. That is why and how this works. We give to each other as we can." She cupped Bridget's face in her hands. "I need pushback. To conquer. To mete out punishment. You give me that. And sometimes I need complete obedience. To cause pain. To hurt and heal with pleasure. We complete each other. You have to trust *me*."

Bridget leaned into her touch. "I do. I don't trust me."

Octavia fought the urge to go to them to wrap her arms around them, to help them process this. *They need to do this. To sort this.* Love for both of them made her chest ache.

Octavia waited, counting her breaths, focusing herself. *Please let her say yes. Don't leave us, Bridget. Stay with me. Us.* The moment spun out until Bridget stepped back and squared her shoulders. She lowered her eyes and kneeled at Vivian's feet. "How can I serve you, Mistress?" The boldness and bravery in her voice made Octavia remember why she had fallen for her beautiful brat in the first place.

"Well done, my sweet." Vivian rested her hand on Bridget's head. "Go stand at the end of the table." Bridget rose and obeyed. Vivian turned her attention to Octavia. "Eyes to me."

Octavia looked into her Mistress's face.

Vivian pointed to the table. "There. Face up. Hands on the rings."

Octavia rose and walked to the table. She climbed up and lay back. She clasped the rings set into the end of the table, the metal cool against her sweaty palms.

Vivian cupped the back of Bridget's neck and pinched her nipple. The soft sound of her reaction made a trickle of desire flow from Octavia. "Watch her face. Don't look away. Examine the light in her eyes. See the truth there."

Bridget leaned over the table and looked at Octavia, making eye contact with her.

Fear. Afraid for me. Love. She loves me. Enough to give me this. Octavia wanted to reach up and touch her, to comfort her. The sound of the medical cabinet opening made her breath come faster. She spread her legs, opening herself to whatever her Mistress wanted. Her desire pooled under her. *Breathe. Focus. Obey. Serve.* She heard the cabinet door close.

"So many things I want to do to you. But today I think something more personal is in order." Vivian's hand on her calf demanded her attention. She pinched the soft skin on the inside of Octavia's leg with her nails, making Octavia groan. Soft lips, followed by Vivian's tongue, caressed her before teeth, sharp and bruising, in the same spot made her arch her hips. *Mark me. Please mark me.* Vivian growled low in her chest and moved to the other leg. Another pinch, another bite. Octavia wanted to close her eyes lose herself in the pain, but the look on Bridget's face made her keep them open, letting Bridget see and understand her desire. Vivian placed the next bite close to the first. The sensation of her teeth and lips on her as Vivian rolled the flesh between her teeth, stopping shy of breaking the skin, sent another wave of desire and need through Octavia. *Yes. Mark me. Yours. More.* She groaned with the sweet pain, pleasure building in her core. She kept her body still, her arms pulling on the rings, offering herself to her Mistress, a willing feast for her pleasure. Working her way along Octavia's legs, Vivian marked her. She took her time. Each delicious bite increased Octavia's need. Vivian bit her inner thighs, and the back of her hand made casual contact with her clit and Octavia had to pant to keep from coming. Vivian worked her teeth over her outer thighs, biting her flesh and rolling the muscle below in her teeth. Deep growls and satisfied noises from Vivian contributed to the sensation of being devoured, consumed by her Mistress. Tiny nips over her hips, the teeth sharp against the hard shelf of bone there, and on to her stomach. The press of lips and teeth moved over her belly, creating a pattern with her bites, and up to the underside of her breasts.

Vivian was naked, and she pressed herself against Octavia's thigh. As she savaged Octavia with her teeth, she ground herself against the bites she had left on Octavia's thighs. The scratch and pull of the curls between her legs was another torture for Octavia. Then Vivian's hand was on her, pinching and tugging at her clit. Octavia bucked into her hand, and Vivian pushed deep. She fucked her as she marked her, biting the soft undersides of her breasts and teasing the taut tendons of her neck. Vivian put her mouth on the top of each shoulder, biting hard enough Octavia was sure she had drawn blood. The thought made her thrash under her Mistress. She forgot her orders and closed her eyes. "Please let me come for you. Please."

Bridget pinched her earlobe. "Eyes open, love," she whispered as she stroked Octavia's hair. Her eyes had a feral look.

Octavia was floating on a sea of endorphins. Vivian raised her head. "Eyes to me." She fucked Octavia hard, her fingers thrusting deep, the heel of her hand against her clit. "Bridget, come here. Put your hand under my hand. Fuck her with me."

Bridget moved to obey, and Octavia took a breath and spread her legs wider. Bridget slid her fingers into her, and she groaned with the sting and burn. Vivian set the pace, and they stroked slow and deep. Octavia looked down. The vision of both of them thrusting into her, owning her, together made her bite her lip to keep from coming. This, she wanted this, always. To be a vessel, to be owned, to serve. She didn't want it to end. She fought herself, fought to keep control. Bridget reached up and pinched her nipple hard, and Octavia lost the battle. Unable to stop herself, she shouted her release as they took her over the edge together.

THE SMELL OF rosemary surrounded Octavia as she trimmed the overgrown herb crowding the other plants in the bed. The sound of gravel crunching made her stand up. A white sedan pulled into the circular drive. Octavia shoved the plant clippers in her back pocket and wiped her hands on her jeans. The woman who emerged was small, her petite frame mismatched with the oversize briefcase she carried under her arm. Her bleach-blonde hair was pulled up into a jaunty ponytail. She wore a bright red scarf draped around her neck, a navy-blue blazer, and white pants.

"Hello. I'm here to see Vivian." The woman walked over to Octavia with her hand stuck out. Octavia shook her hand, surprised by the strength of her grip. "I'm Sylvia Derutchi. Vivian's expecting me."

The front door opened, and Vivian stepped out. "Please come in, Sylvia. Octavia, would you ask Bridget to bring us some coffee?"

Octavia hurried around to the back of the house and entered through the mudroom. She pulled off her boots and washed her hands. "Hey, love. Can you make some coffee for Vivian and her appointment?"

"I've got it ready. That's the real estate agent. What's she like?"

"Aging cheerleader."

Bridget snort-giggled. "Will you take it to them? I'm not sure of the time on these cookies, and I don't want to burn them."

"Sure." Octavia pressed a kiss to Bridget's cheek and picked up the tray with the coffee press, two cups, cream, and sugar.

The door to Vivian's office was open. Sylvia was talking fast, her voice reminding Octavia of a used-car salesman. She slowed her pace and lingered in the dark hallway, unable to stop herself from eavesdropping on their conversation. She crept closer to the doorway.

"This is the deal of a lifetime. You'd never have to work again."

"Is that supposed to appeal to me?"

"Everyone needs money."

"I've got money. This is my home."

"Vivian, please listen to me. You will clear enough in this deal to have ten homes, wherever you want."

"And Sofia? How will she fare?"

"She will clear enough to get out of debt. Beyond that, I don't know."

Guilt won out and Octavia knocked on the doorframe.

"Come in." Vivian smiled at Octavia. "Thank you. I was getting desperate."

Octavia placed the tray on the desk and poured Vivian a cup of strong black coffee. She handed it to her before she turned to Sylvia. "And you? How would you like your coffee?"

Sylvia smiled at her. "Same, thank you."

Octavia poured a second cup and placed it in front of Sylvia.

"If someone offered you enough money you would never have to work again in your life, would you take it?" Sylvia picked up her cup and took a sip.

"Me?" Octavia tilted her head and smiled at Sylvia.

"Yes. Would you take it?

Octavia held Sylvia's gaze, startled by the avarice she saw in her eyes. "I don't know. I like to work. Gives me a reason to get out of bed in the morning."

"Only fools work when they don't have to." Sylvia waved her off. "You'd take it. Anyone with sense would."

Vivian cleared her throat. "Let's not involve Octavia in our discussion."

Sylvia turned back to Vivian. "Please, Vivian. They won't wait too much longer. What do you say?"

Taking the cue, Octavia left the room. She closed the door behind her, not wanting to hear Vivian's answer.

VIVIAN PUSHED THE stack of papers away from her and tossed her glasses on top of the pile. "That is where it stands. I've no interest in selling, but Sophia has her back to the wall and the company won't buy her parcel." She pinched the bridge of her nose. "They want the whole valley."

Octavia took a sip of her tea. "Could Sophia get a loan? To make it until next year's crop?"

"She's maxed out. That's part of the problem. When she sold this piece of land to my father, she took out a huge loan against her property. The payments are outrageous."

"Hasn't her family owned the vineyard for years? How can she owe anything on the land?"

"She was cash poor. The year she sold this acreage, they had had two bad crops in a row. And Carlo doesn't understand a damn thing about money." Vivian sat back in her chair and looked around the living room. "Miriam and I spent so much of our time remodeling and designing this house." She placed her palms flat on the table. "Part of her ashes are spread here. I don't want to leave this house." Their normally stoic Mistress's eyes were bright with tears. "It would be like losing her all over again."

Bridget cleared her throat. "So what happens if you say no?"

"I'd most likely lose Sophia as a friend. She'd stall the creditors, or find new ones, but in one year, she'll go under and the bank will foreclose or force a sale of the property. She'd be left with nothing. And I know nothing about running a vineyard. I'd be forced to sell too."

Octavia touched the back of Vivian's hand. "Sofia doesn't want to sell. Carlo is driving this, as well as driving her bankrupt."

"Yes. But family is family. She won't cut him off or kick him out."

"Fuck that." Bridget stood up. "I won't feel sorry for stupid. He's an idiot."

"Yes. But he's her son. I can't talk to her about him. She shuts me down."

"What are you going to do about this?" Bridget tapped the pile of papers.

"I don't know, my sweets. I don't know."

Chapter Nineteen

"HOW DO I look?" Octavia tugged at the black bow tie she had agreed to wear.

Bridget smoothed her hands over Octavia's shoulders. "Good enough to eat. Which makes me wish we had more time." She flattened her hands and dragged them down the front of the shirt and cupped Octavia's breasts before she thumbed her nipples, bringing them to hard points.

Octavia grabbed Bridget's hips and pulled her close. She ground her hips into her. "You're rotten. Now all I want to do is drag you into the pantry and have my way with you."

Bridget shoved her and backed away. She grinned at Octavia. "Later. We have to serve dinner." She turned her back to Octavia and added the finishing garnishes to the appetizer plates. "Go see if they're ready to eat."

Octavia swatted her ass as she walked by. "That's a down payment."

"Promises, promises." The mock pout on Bridget's face made her chuckle to herself as she pushed through the dining room door on her way to the atrium.

The garden was still lush, the walls of the house functioning as a greenhouse. It was warm enough the retractable roof was open. Vivian was dressed in pair of tight black pants and a burgundy-colored loose tailored shirt. Black leather pumps completed her outfit. Sofia was talking loudly, her voice dominating the imitate space. Octavia made her way around the edges of the patio until she stood close behind Vivian. She leaned close to Vivian and whispered, "Are you ready for us to serve, Mistress?"

Vivian turned and favored Octavia with a smile. "Yes. I'll herd them to the dining room. Herding butterflies would be easier." She handed Octavia her empty wineglass and met Octavia's gaze. "You are divine in that outfit." She rested her hand on Octavia's forearm and pressed her breast against her arm. She brought her lips close and brushed them over the shell of Octavia's ear. "I can't wait to watch you take it off for me."

"You and Bridget. I'm going to spill everything, you have me so distracted."

Octavia laughed. "I'll take the risk. Tell Bridget we'll be there in five minutes."

VIVIAN SAT AT the head of the table, with Sophia sat on her right. The other women arranged themselves around the table. They all appeared to be close to Vivian's age, some wearing forty better than others. Octavia caught bits and snippets of their conversations, from the book they all were supposed to have read to the latest fashions and if they were going to Milan for Fashion Week. Octavia did not miss Vivian's bored expression she failed to hide during most of the discussion. Sophia carried the conversation, inspired by her frequently empty wineglass.

Standing with her hands behind her back, waiting to clear the dishes or refill wine as needed, Octavia remembered how many times she had served at Rowan House. The bow tie was constrictive and reminded her of her collar. *My collar. Will I ever have another?* She stared at Vivian, taking advantage of her distraction to look her fill of her Mistress. Under the dining room lights, the fine bit of gray gave her short-cropped hair a frosted appearance. She had gained some weight with Bridget's cooking and her face no longer held the sharp angles of too little food and too little sleep. Vivian laughed at something, and Octavia's heart squeezed with how much she loved her.

Bridget opened the kitchen door a crack and made eye contact with Octavia. Nodding in acknowledgment, Octavia began clearing the small plates. She brought the first load to the kitchen. Bridget was plating the main course, and Octavia hurried back to clear the rest of the plates.

When she returned, Bridget had a tray loaded. "Mind my plating when you set them down."

Octavia delivered the main course, taking care to keep the garnish in place as she set the dishes before each diner. She placed Sophia's plate last and a hand on her arm stopped her.

Sophia's blood-red nails contrasted with Octavia's white shirt. "Tell Bridget the first course was perfect."

"I will."

Vivian cleared her throat. Her eyes were focused on Sophia's hand. "You can tell her yourself. After dinner." She picked up her fork and started eating.

Sophia released Octavia's arm before she picked up her wine. "As you wish." She looked in Vivian's eyes over the rim of her glass as she sipped.

The way she said it made Octavia flush. *Oh hell no.* She hurried back to the kitchen.

Bridget was at the stove stirring a pot. "Sit a minute. Have some water. You don't need to stand over them."

"That bitch makes me want to slap her."

Bridget turned and raised an eyebrow. "Which bitch? And I'm thinking you don't mean slap in a good way."

"Fucking Sophia. She answered Vivian like she was her sub."

"Don't you think she was? They had something. Even if Vivian is not forthcoming about it. I feel it every time I'm near them."

"It shouldn't matter so much to me."

"Why not? It bothers the fuck out of me."

"I don't know. I want to think I'm beyond it. I mean, it's past."

"But whenever she's here, she goes out of her way to make a point about it."

Octavia took a sip of water. "I don't want it to bother me. It never bothered me with Martha."

Bridget held her gaze. "Can I remind you of how you wanted to beat Cook's ass? Your being with Martha was hard for me. And maybe you didn't care about Martha the way you care about Vivian."

Octavia placed her water glass on the counter. "Maybe." She sighed and straightened her shoulders. "I've got to go back."

"Hey, love?

"Yes?"

"Don't slap her. It'll ruin dinner and I've got a great dessert planned."

Octavia laughed, grateful for Bridget's ability to raise her spirits no matter what else was going on in their lives.

"WILL YOU GO get the rest of dessert from the guest house refrigerator?"

"What if I drop it?" Octavia stood with her hands on her hips. "You'll kill me."

Bridget quirked her mouth and sighed. "All right then, you stir this. Don't stop because I will kill you if you burn this also."

Octavia kept her face grave. "I won't fail you."

Bridget pinched her cheek. "I'll make a good sous-chef out of you yet." She patted her pockets. "Where did I put those keys?"

"These keys?" Octavia picked up a key ring from the kitchen table and held them up.

"Thank you." Bridget took the keys from her hand and left Octavia at the stove. She called over her shoulder, "Wish me luck. If I trip and fall with it, I'll hate myself."

Octavia focused on stirring the vanilla-scented sauce in the pan, manipulating the spoon to keep it from burning. Lost in her focus, she was startled when Vivian called her from the door.

"Is everything okay?"

Octavia turned to look at her. "Yes. Do you need more wine? Bridget went to get the dessert from the guesthouse refrigerator. I can't leave this sauce."

Vivian frowned. "No. I just... How long has it been?"

Octavia looked at the clock. Fifteen minutes had passed. "It shouldn't have taken her this long." She turned off the burner and shoved the pot onto the center grate.

Vivian was already pushing through the back door. Octavia hurried after her. As soon as she stepped out the door, the smell of burning wood surrounded her. Vivian pulled off her pumps, tossed them aside and ran. Thick black smoke was seeping from the guesthouse. Octavia ran after Vivian and caught up with her. The acrid clouds of gray smoke thickened and filled the air.

"Bridget! Bridget!" Vivian's voice was shrill. Octavia dropped to her knees and crawled up the steps to the guesthouse, staying low. The door was open and she crawled inside, ignoring Vivian's screams and her fear. She couldn't see. Her eyes stung from the acrid smoke. She coughed as tears and snot streamed down her face. *Bridget.* Her hand bumped into a shoe. *Bridget.* She fought the urge to stand up and run. She crawled forward and clutched Bridget's legs and reversed her course, crawling backward and dragging Bridget with her. She was sweating, fighting her panic. Each breath she took burned her chest. The way back seemed longer and she was dizzy. Hands clasped her legs, sharp nails digging into her flesh. She locked her hands around Bridget's ankles. *Hold on, Bridget. God, please. Bridget.*

Her chin bumped over the threshold, and she bit her tongue, the sharp pain focusing her mind. *Out, we're almost out.* More hands on her, trying to pry her grasp from Bridget's ankles. *No. No. No.*

"Let go. We've got you. Let go. We have to get off this porch." Vivian's voice was close.

Octavia released her hands from Bridget's legs. She turned her head and gulped air, breathing in spite of the pain in her chest. Sofia was there, her face twisted in fear. She grabbed Octavia's hands and pulled her up. "We have to get away." She pulled Octavia's arm over her shoulder. Octavia leaned on the smaller woman. Her lungs burned, and she coughed. "Bridget."

"Vivian has her." They made it to the drive. Sophia eased her down. "Stay here. I'm going to help Vivian."

Octavia lay down on her side. Too exhausted to help, she watched as Vivian and Sophia dragged Bridget to the grass near her. She crawled over to them and placed her head on Bridget's chest. The soft thud of her heartbeat was reassuring. She closed her eyes. *Alive. She's alive.*

Vivian's hands, firm and gentle, touched her face. "Lie back, love. The ambulance will be here soon."

Octavia struggled to sit up, giving up when dizziness forced her to lie still.

"IF ONE MORE person tells me I shouldn't have gone in to get Bridget, I'm going to hit them."

Vivian's fingers worked over her scalp as she gathered and separated the strands of her hair. The tug and pull as she braided Octavia's hair was soothing. "You are a brave woman. I stopped. If you hadn't..." She rested her hand on Octavia's shoulder.

Octavia clasped her hand. "You saved us. I was done. The smoke was so bad. We wouldn't have made it. When can I see Bridget?"

"Hand me the elastic." Vivian finished off the braid. "They were going to do another chest X-ray this morning. I asked the nurse to let us know when she was back in her room."

Octavia pulled her braid over her shoulder and inspected the intricate weave Vivian had accomplished. "Nice. I remember when you would do this for me in school."

Vivian pressed a kiss to her cheek. A tap at the door made them shift away from each other. The nurse entered and spoke to Vivian in Italian, nodded at Octavia, and left.

"Did she say the police want to talk to Bridget?" Octavia touched Vivian's arm.

"Yes." Vivian rested her hand on Octavia's shoulder.

Octavia frowned. "You better be there. Her Italian is limited to ordering food and reading cookbooks. And she hates cops. What do they want to talk to her for? She was out when I found her."

Vivian frowned. "That's why. She has a nasty cut on the side of her head."

Searing anger bubbled up in Octavia. "Someone tried to kill her?"

"They don't know. Something about the angle was wrong for a blow to the head. She most likely hit it when she passed out. I think she surprised whoever set the fire."

"She was inside the house facing away from the door. Whoever set this had keys."

"Or broke in. We don't know."

"If Bridget saw signs of the house being broken into, she wouldn't have gone inside. She's not stupid."

"No. She's not."

"What are we waiting for? I want to see her." Octavia shoved the covers off her legs.

Vivian pressed down on Octavia's shoulder. "I'll talk to the nurses. We need to get you a wheelchair."

"Oh hell, I don't need..." Octavia pushed herself up in the bed, and a fit of coughing made her lie back.

Vivian said nothing and raised an eyebrow.

"Okay. Maybe it would be a good idea." She chewed her lip as she waited for Vivian to bring a wheelchair. Vivian returned with a nurse, and they assisted Octavia into the wheelchair. "Fuck. How long am I going to feel like this?" Her voice was hoarse.

"*Inhalation fumo e' difficle non sei stato esposto a lungo, ma abbastanz a lungo.*" The nurse tucked the sheet around Octavia's legs. "*La signora Murray e' tornata nella sua stanza. Non rimanere a lungo.*" She held Octavia's gaze for a moment. "*Capire?*

They don't know. For me or Bridget. They don't know how badly Bridget's been affected by breathing in the smoke. That's why they're only letting me see her for a little while. "*Capisco.*" Octavia shifted her hips in the wheelchair as she confirmed that she understood.

Vivian rolled the wheelchair to Bridget's room. She opened the door and they entered. Bridget's eyes were closed. An oxygen mask covered the lower part of her face. She slept. A thin line of her hair was shaved out and gauze covered the wound on her scalp. Monitors glowed with numbers flashing. Octavia swallowed hard. Vivian pushed the chair close to the bed. Octavia reached over and touched Bridget's hand.

Bridget's eyes opened, and she curled her fingers around Octavia's hand and squeezed. "Did you burn my sauce?" Her voice was rough but strong even muffled by the oxygen mask.

Octavia laughed to keep from crying. "No. But I don't think we'll need it now."

Bridget opened her eyes and met Octavia's gaze. "My hero."

"Vivian pulled us clear. The smoke got me too."

Bridget lifted her other hand and gripped Vivian's. "My heroes."

A knock at the door startled them. Bridget looked over Octavia's shoulder and frowned. "What is he doing here?"

Octavia turned in the wheelchair to see what making her frown. A large man in a dark suit stood in the doorway. *Policia. Why do they all dress like that?*

"Ms. Murray? *Buongiorno. Sono ispettore di polizia Giamiattorio. Mi piacerebbe farle un paio di domande, se non le dispiace.*"

Bridget looked to Vivian. "I don't understand him. Will you help me?" She pressed her lips in a thin line.

Vivian inclined her head at the police inspector. "Ms. Murray *si scusa, non conosce l'italiano. Tradurrò ogni singola parola che dirai, perfettamente.*" She smoothed her hand over Bridget's hair and addressed her. "This is Inspector Giamiattorio. He only wants to ask you questions about what happened. I've told him that you don't understand Italian and I'll translate."

He nodded at Vivian and began speaking in Italian.

"Do I need a lawyer?" The fear in Bridget's voice made Octavia's heart ache.

"No, love. They want to see if you remember anything."

Tears filled Bridget's eyes. "I don't. The last thing I remember clearly is the moment I turned the key in the lock."

Inspector Giamiattorio asked his questions through Vivian, and Bridget answered. He typed notes into his phone. Octavia followed the questions. She held tight to Bridget's hand throughout, rubbing her thumb over her knuckles. He finished with his questions and stepped close to the bed. He pressed his card into Bridget's hand. "*Arrivederci*, Ms. Murray. If you remember anything else, call me." His English was perfect.

Bridget frowned at him. "Why the hell did you ask all those questions in Italian if you speak English?"

The man flushed. "I'm sorry. I wanted to see if Ms. Abiola was translating your answers correctly."

Vivian's voice cut through the room. "Are we all under suspicion? Someone has set fires at my house three times now and almost killed this woman, and you are playing games."

"No. Sometimes people need insurance money and they make fraudulent claims." At Vivian's glare, he lowered his eyes. "I'm sorry. That is not the case this time, I'm sure. My apologies."

"Stop wasting our time, Inspector, and find out who is doing this." Vivian's voice was hard and sharp.

Inspector Giamiattorio flushed bright red. "*Ciao*." He left the room.

Bridget relaxed her shoulders and closed her eyes. After a few minutes she fell asleep, the soft sounds of her breathing filling the quiet of the room. Octavia held on to her hand, not wanting to leave her. Vivian touched her shoulder. "We should get you back to your bed."

"No. Please I need to be with her." Octavia pushed away Vivian's hand, ignoring the tiredness making her own eyes heavy.

"You can't sleep in the wheelchair. It's only for tonight. They'll let you go home after the doctor sees you in the morning."

Octavia looked up into Vivian's face, meeting her gaze. "You'll stay with her?"

"I'll come back and stay with her, but we need to get you back to your room first."

Octavia gave Bridget's hand one last squeeze. "Sleep well, love," she whispered.

Chapter Twenty

"I'M NOT AN invalid." Bridget sighed.

"I know, but until Laura clears you, you are going to sit still and behave." Vivian turned out a perfectly cooked omelet onto a plate. She placed it in front of Bridget. "Now be good, or I'll let Octavia cook."

Octavia laughed. "That is a threat. Unless you like horse chow or hay, I'm lost when it comes to food." She picked up her fork. "But I am very good at eating it."

Vivian sat next to them and picked up her cup of coffee.

"Are you seeing the insurance adjuster today?" Octavia wiped her mouth.

"Yes. He's going to walk me through where we go from here. We can't start clearing the remains until the fire department and police finish their forensic investigation."

Bridget grimaced. "So we have to live with that reminder?" She rested her fork on her plate.

"I hate it too." Vivian touched the back of her hand. "As soon as we can, we'll have it cleared."

Octavia finished her omelet and pushed her plate to the side. "I want make some changes in the barn. We are lucky the asshole who torched the guesthouse didn't choose the barn."

"I don't think whoever is behind this will." Vivian pursed her lips. "Each time it has been an empty structure. Something that would cause damage but not hurt anything or anyone."

"What about Bridget?"

"I think that was panic. The horses were all inside the barn the night the turnout shed was burnt. When the equipment shed was burnt, it was empty."

"But the fires are getting closer to the house."

"I don't think we have to worry about the barn or the house." Octavia placed her fork on her plate.

"Why?" Bridget took a sip of her coffee.

Vivian sat back in her chair.

Octavia rested her hands on the table. "I've been thinking about the two fires since we've been here. Sofia was here both times. And that seems too coincidental. One common denominator has occurred. Sofia."

Vivian raised her eyebrows "She can't be setting them. At least the last two she was with me when the fires were set."

"But each time she has been a guest in your home. What about the other time?"

The room grew heavy with the silence between them.

"You're right." Vivian sighed "The first time a fire was set she was a guest in my bed." Vivian looked down at her hands.

The guilt on her face made Octavia shift in her chair. "It's past."

Bridget set her cup down in the saucer, making the china ring with the force of it. "Is it past, Vivian?"

Vivian looked up and held each of their gazes in turn. "Yes. Since we've been together, yes."

"So the first time with us wasn't the first time after Miriam?" Octavia chewed her lip.

Vivian pursed her lips. "Sofia is vanilla through and though. I took comfort from her when no one else in the world seemed to understand what I lost when I lost Miriam."

"Who do you think is behind this if not Sofia or that rat-faced son of hers?" Bridget's voice rose.

"Carlo may be lot of things, but I don't think he's an arsonist." Vivian frowned at her.

"Who else is interested in scaring you so you sell? Who else so desperate for money? Who else would try to kill me?" Bridget voice was sharp and loud.

"I don't know!" Vivian shouted. "I don't know." Quieter this time, her face a mask of despair. "I almost lost both of you. I don't know what to do. Carlo is Sofia's world."

"If he did do it, they'll catch him. He's not smart enough to be a successful arsonist. The fire department has discounted the other fires. They won't this time because of me. Attempted murder is not simple arson." Bridget's voice was cold, her eyes dark. "And you and Sofia won't be able to protect him."

Vivian sat back as if slapped. "Is that what you think? You think Sofia's friendship means more to me than you? If I thought Carlo did it, I would drag him to the police myself."

Bridget firmed her mouth. "I'm not so sure. We've never been guests in your bed."

Vivian stood, her chair scraping loudly on the tile. She opened her mouth as if to speak, closed it, and walked out of the kitchen. She slammed the door behind her.

"Aren't you going to run after her?" Bridget's face was red, her eyes dark.

Octavia lifted her shoulders and squared them. "I came here with you. I turned my whole life upside down to be with you. Why do you still ask me shit like that? For fuck's sake, I ran into a burning building for you. No matter how obstinate you are, I love you." Octavia pinned Bridget with her eyes. "I wanted to die when I thought I had lost you. Don't question my love."

Chastised, Bridget sat back in her chair. "You love her too. You would have gone in for her too."

"Yes. And it doesn't mean I love you less. You love her too."

Bridget looked up. "I shouldn't have said what I said."

"No. It was rude. And I don't think it's Carlo either. He's too stupid."

"I need to talk to her."

"Yes."

Bridget stood up. "Wish me luck. She was pretty mad."

Octavia pushed her chair back and patted her lap. "Sit a minute with me."

Bridget walked around the table and sat down, fitting herself into Octavia's arms. They sat in silence, holding on to each other, each lost in their own thoughts.

"IS THIS WHERE you want it?" Octavia leaned on her shovel. "I can move the stakes if it's not right."

Bridget walked around the edge of the sticks and string marking out the plot. "This is just right. I've watched how the sun moves over this spot and it will be perfect." She leaned in and kissed Octavia's cheek. "You sure you feel up to it?"

"Yes. I'm fine. Sit there and supervise. Dr. Meloni said one more week for you to rest."

"It's been two weeks. She's overcautious."

"Laura knows Vivian will have her ass if she's wrong."

"Did she tell you where she was going?" Bridget sat on the chair Octavia had placed for her.

"No. She said she'd be back and would bring us lunch." Octavia used her foot to force the tip of the shovel into the earth. She moved along the outline of twine using the sharp edge of the spade to cut into the earth.

"I wish I could help you." Bridget crossed her arms.

"I'll rest when I'm tired. I want to mark it out. Once I turn the ground, I'm going to bring some of composted manure over to mix in with the soil."

"Won't it stink?" Bridget wrinkled her nose.

"No. I won't bring the fresh manure. That would stink and burn up the plants. The composted stuff won't smell once I mix it with the dirt."

"You think we'll be here to plant this?" Bridget's voice was soft. "Really?"

Octavia stopped and leaned on the shovel. "I want to be. But I don't know. She's been quiet since the fire."

"You mean since our fight." Bridget stood up and walked to Octavia. "I'm afraid we've lost her. It feels like she's avoiding us since the argument in the kitchen." She wrapped her arms around Octavia's waist and rested her head on her shoulder. "She treats me like I might break if she looks at me."

Octavia let the shovel fall to the ground and pulled Bridget tight to her chest. "I know you won't break." She kissed the top of Bridget's head before moving her hands to her ass and squeezing hard. Bridget relaxed into her touch. "What did Dr. Meloni say about returning to your previous duties?"

"She said nothing too strenuous," Bridget murmured against Octavia's chest.

Octavia kissed her way down Bridget's neck, the light scent of the honeysuckle perfume filling her nose. "Come inside with me. You look like you need to lie down."

Bridget cupped her ass and pulled Octavia's hips into hers. She looked up into Octavia's face and kissed her, her mouth hard and hungry. "Yes, Ma'am."

THEY PUSHED THROUGH the door together, stopping long enough to take off their shoes. Octavia pulled Bridget close and kissed her again. "Are you sure you're up for this?"

"I am." She kissed her neck, nibbling at Octavia's collarbone. "Are you?"

Octavia groaned as Bridget cupped her breasts and squeezed her nipples though her shirt. "Do that again and I will strip you and fuck you on the kitchen table."

"You say it like it's a bad thing." Vivian's voice startled them. "Don't stop. I'll put this in the refrigerator."

They turned as one. "Join us." Bridget lifted her chin. "Mistress." She looked down at the floor. "If it's still okay to call you that."

Vivian placed her purse and the bag she was holding on the floor. She reached out and lifted Bridget's chin with two fingers and pinned her with her gaze. "Always."

Vivian looked to Octavia and raised her eyebrow. "And you?"

Octavia flushed. "If it pleases you, Mistress."

Vivian placed her hand on the back of Octavia's neck, her fingers firm, and squeezed. "It pleases me very much." Her voice had a breathy tone and Octavia's already hard clit ached. "The mudroom seems a bit small for all of us." She smiled at them. "My room. Now." When they hesitated, she lifted her chin and arched an eyebrow. "Do you need motivation?" She swatted Octavia's ass.

"No, Mistress." She clasped Bridget's hand and Octavia followed their Mistress to the one room in the house they had never seen.

VIVIAN'S ROOM WAS lit by skylights. White fabric shades filtered the sun and gave the room a soft glow. Vivian turned to them, her hands clasped in front of her. Octavia looked around the room, wanting to take in Vivian's private space. Huge photographic prints of flowers, erotic in tone and texture, covered the walls. A small desk and matching chair graced a corner, and on the wall facing the floor-to-ceiling windows of the garden was a king-sized bed. White sheets with a dark burgundy duvet covered the bed. On a small shelf was a picture of what had to be Miriam and Vivian, dressed in matching linen suits, holding hands and facing each other under a chuppah. Next to the photo was a small black-and-gold urn. The joy on Vivian's face in the photograph was sublime and cut through Octavia's excitement.

Vivian held her gaze and studied Octavia's face before she shifted her gaze to Bridget. "Does it bother you?" She gestured to the shelf.

Octavia looked down at the floor before she brought her gaze back to Vivian's face.

"You don't have to prove anything to us." Bridget's words echoed Octavia's thought. "We can go to our room or the playroom."

"No." Vivian's gaze was steady. "I want you with me here." She pointed to the photo. "I was blessed with an amazing relationship. The kind people write books about." She cleared her throat. "I never expected to love anyone again after Miriam died. And certainly not two people."

She loves us. Loves us. Like that. Octavia had no words. Bridget made a small sound and launched herself into Vivian's arms. Vivian held her with one arm wrapped around her. She met Octavia's gaze and held her hand out. Octavia crossed the floor and wrapped them both in her arms. Kisses and nips, sighs and words flowed between them. The whisper of their clothes as they shed them filled the room.

When they were naked, Vivian led them to her bed. She climbed up and sat on the bed and patted the mattress. Bridget and Octavia joined her. She smoothed her hands over Bridget's shoulder. "I know Dr. Meloni said nothing strenuous." Vivian pushed on Bridget's shoulders, lowering to her back. "We'll go slow."

With a sigh Bridget put her hands over her head and gripped the headboard. "As you wish, Mistress." A sultry smile spread across her face.

Vivian turned and looked at Octavia. "Top or bottom?"

Octavia cocked her head at Vivian. "Pardon, Mistress?"

Vivian reached out and stroked her thumb over Octavia's lower lip. She pushed her thumb into Octavia's mouth as she gazed into her eyes. Octavia sucked and licked as Vivian teased her with soft strokes until she pulled her thumb free slowly. "What do you need? To be controlled? Or to control?"

Octavia swallowed hard before she answered. "Let me serve you. Both of you. Please."

Vivian lay down next to Bridget, hip to hip, pressing the length of her body alongside Bridget. After draping her leg over Bridget, she placed her hands on the headboard overlapping Bridget's hand.

Desire welled up in Octavia. She kneeled and trailed her fingers down their bodies, stroking their breasts, enjoying the way each of them responded to her touch. She watched their faces, marveling at the way pleasure suffused their features, each in their own way. Their stomachs were a contrast, Vivian's flat belly and prominent hips so different to Bridget's curves. The softness of their skin, the scents of their desire filled Octavia with an overwhelming need to taste each of them. She slipped her fingers between their legs. She closed her eyes against the sensation of having her fingers inside each of them at the same time and their hot wet heat. She opened her eyes to watch them. They clasped hands on the side that touched, their fingers entwined. Octavia pushed forward slow and gentle. They arched up to meet her thrust. She bent her head and licked Bridget's clit, maintaining her slow strokes. She lifted her head and treated Vivian's clit with the same attention. *Mine. Always. My loves.* Octavia's clit was hard and she straddled Vivian's calf, pressing herself against her leg in a slow rhythm. Their breathing synced as they rose higher. Octavia managed their pleasure, parsing out her attentions, determined to have them both come around her hand at the same time. She rocked on Vivian's leg, seeking her own satisfaction. She thrust deep and slow, curling her fingers over their sweet spots as they arched to meet her thrusts.

Bridget's breath was ragged. "Please, Ma'am. Please let come for you. For both of you."

Vivian's fixed her gaze on Octavia's eyes. "What do you want, my love?" She tightened around Octavia's fingers.

Octavia edged herself closer with the sensation of having both of them, and she rocked harder on Vivian's calf. *So close. Now all of us. Now.* "Ahh. Please come for me. Now."

With deep groans, they arched as one, their pleasure coursing over Octavia's fingers, and she came with them. The slick slide of Vivian's and Bridget's flesh around her fingers made her desperate for more, and she brought them both off again as she ground out her pleasure a second time.

Rocking together, they came down from their high, and Octavia slipped her hands free. She swept her palms over their hips and stretched out over them, lying between and on top of them. Vivian and Bridget shifted, making room for her between them, and she sank into the welcoming space of them. Hands and fingers, lips and tongues, they melded together as one as they explored each other's bodies. No rules. No roles. Just love and the overarching desire to know and be known and to hold on to what was almost lost.

Chapter Twenty-One

"WHAT THE HECK are you playing with, Victor?" The donkey tossed his head. A scrap of dirty red fabric fluttered from his mouth. He shifted right and ran from Octavia. "Don't make me chase you." She went back to shoveling manure out of the stall. She emptied the barrow and walked back to the barn. Victor was in the center aisle, the scrap of fabric between his hooves. "I don't have time to play right now." He stamped on the cloth and brayed at Octavia before turning his back and trotting out of the barn. "Crazy little jackass."

She bent to pick up the rag. *Not a rag. A scarf.* A faint whiff of petrol emanated from the cloth. *Where the hell did he find this?* The scarf was muddy and torn in places from the donkey's teeth. Octavia turned it over in her hands. She looked at the edges. "SLD" was embroidered in navy-blue thread. *Sofia? She'd never wear anything so tacky.* She tried to remember the names of the women who had been at the dinner the night of the fire and came up empty. *Bridget made the place cards. She'll remember.* She shoved the scarf in her back pocket and ran back to the house.

"NO ONE HAS the initials SLD." Bridget held the scarf in her hands as she stared at the script. "I've gone over the guest list twice."

Octavia paced the kitchen. "It's connected with the fire. It has to be."

"Even if it is, it doesn't prove anything." Bridget sat back in her chair.

Octavia turned Vivian's appointment book around. "Maybe we aren't looking in the right place." She flipped the pages, scanning the notations in Vivian's daybook.

Vivian entered the kitchen and placed her cup on the counter. "Why are you two so fascinated with my planner?"

Octavia picked the scarf up from the table. "This. Victor was playing with it." She held it out to Vivian. "Smell it."

Vivian cocked an eyebrow. "I know what things usually smell like after Victor has played with them."

Bridget laughed. "No. What she's trying to say is it smells like petrol. We think it's connected with the fire."

Vivian leaned close and sniffed. She leaned back. "That's lamp oil."

Octavia met Vivian's gaze. "Do you know anyone whose initials are SLD?"

Vivian pursed her lips. "No one I can think of." She turned the planner and ran her finger down the list of entries on each page.

Bridget fidgeted with a pen, turning it over in her hands. "Even if we find out who it belongs to, we don't have anything to connect it. It could have blown into the field."

"If the scarf didn't smell like that, I might agree." Vivian tapped her finger on an entry in her daybook. "Sylvia Derutchi."

"Money!" Octavia shouted.

Bridget and Vivian looked at her.

"Follow the money."

Bridget arched an eyebrow and placed the pen on the table. "This isn't one of those cozy mysteries you're addicted to."

"Listen to me." Octavia tapped the planner. "Who would get money if Vivian got scared and sold this place?

"Me. And Sophia and by extension Carlo." Vivian met her gaze, brow furrowed.

"And Sylvia would get a big fat commission." Bridget sat forward and picked up the scarf. "That little bitch."

Vivian pulled her phone from her back pocket. "I'm going to call Inspector Giamiattorio."

Octavia held up her hand. "Wait."

"What for? That woman almost killed Bridget." Vivian's voice was harsh.

Octavia sighed. "Because this doesn't prove anything."

Bridget nodded her agreement. "Octavia's right. Sylvia will lawyer up and nothing will ever happen." A sharp bitterness in her tone underlined her words.

Vivian frowned. "So what do we do? Sofia is screwed if we don't sell. And if she goes out of business, I'll have to sell. I don't know anything about making wine and I don't want to learn."

"What if Bridget and I loan her the money she needs?"

"What money? I know I pay you well, but where would you get the money to pay off her loans?"

Bridget stood up and looked at Octavia like she had gone crazy. "We've been good at saving, Octavia, but we don't have millions."

"We do. Martha invested the money from my mother's estate and my salary for me while I was at Rowan House."

Bridget's eyes narrowed. "And you didn't tell me?"

"I kept it separate from our money here. I was afraid you would think it was tainted." Octavia looked away, avoiding Bridget's eyes. She heard a chair scrape on the floor. Bridget wrapped her arms around her waist and pulled her close.

"Look at me, love." Octavia met Bridget's gaze. "I may be a judgmental brat at times, but I'm not stupid. How much?"

"About nine million."

Bridget eyebrows rose. "Wow. I think I need to sit down." Vivian's laugh filled the kitchen.

"What?" Bridget looked over her shoulder at Vivian.

"I can't wait to see Sylvia's face." She picked up the scarf. "After we tell her why we are refusing the offer and that we gave this to the police."

SOFIA SIGNED THE last page of the contract in front of her and placed the thick black fountain pen in its holder. "Done." She picked up her glass of Franciacorta and lifted it in a toast to Octavia. "Thank you." She took a sip. "And thank you, Vivian." She took another sip and held Bridget's gaze. "And thank you, Bridget, for pushing me to do what I needed to do with Carlo."

"You're welcome." Bridget sipped her wine and raised her glass. "Thank you for helping to drag my ass out of the guesthouse."

Sofia tipped her chin at Bridget. "I would do it again."

Vivian slipped her arm around Octavia's waist and pulled her close. She looped her other arm around Bridget's waist. "And now we have to make the most important decision."

"What decision?"

"What are we going rename the vineyard?"

Chapter Twenty-Two

"WILL YOU HELP me with these?" Octavia held out the onyx-and-gold cuff links.

Bridget took the cufflinks and folded back the cuffs on Octavia's shirt and fastened them. "This shirt is so elegant and you look divine in it."

"Thanks, love." She kissed Bridget's cheek.

"What do you suppose she has planned?" Bridget turned her back to Octavia. "Zip me."

Octavia teased her fingers over the bare skin of Bridget's back before she zipped her form-fitting dress. She swept her hands over Bridget's curves. "I don't know. She shooed me inside before she would unload the car." She looked at the clock on the bookshelf. "She said to be ready by six."

Bridget stepped back and tugged at the hem of her dress before she slipped her feet into her shoes. A sharp rap on the door sounded.

"Right on time." Octavia opened the door.

Vivian stepped in and pressed a kiss to her cheek before she walked to Bridget and did the same. "You're so lovely. Both of you. Come with me." She stopped at the threshold. "Close your eyes, you two. Don't open them. Hold on to my arms. I won't let you bump into anything,"

Octavia held tight to Vivian's arm, savoring the sensation of her firm muscles under her fingers. She knew they had reached the door to the atrium from the path they walked. She heard the door slide open, and they followed her outside into the cool night.

"Now open them."

The retractable roof was open. Octavia looked up at the night sky full of bright stars. Small brass candle lanterns lit the courtyard. Bouquets of white and red roses in vases filled the space, and their scent perfumed the air. A small table was set with three place settings. The china and silver gleamed against the black tablecloth. A champagne stand with an ice bucket stood off to the side of the table.

"What are we celebrating?" Bridget smiled at Vivian.

"Us." Vivian held out her hand. In the center of her palm were three simple gold bands with vines engraved on them. She lowered herself to one knee. "If you'll have me."

Octavia kneeled and Bridget followed. With a firm grip, Bridget clasped Octavia's hand and interlaced their fingers. "Yes." She held the other hand out to Vivian. Vivian kissed her knuckles before she placed one of the rings on her finger.

She turned her head to look at Octavia. *Love. She loves us. Wants us. Yes. Say yes.*

"Yes." Octavia extended her hand. Vivian's grip was cool and her lips were warm as she kissed Octavia's hand before she pushed the ring over her knuckle and onto her finger.

They both looked to Vivian and placed their hands in hers. She placed her other hand on top of the pile. "Always, my sweets."

"I CAN'T BELIEVE how much it looks like him." Bridget traced her fingers over the wooden sign next to the drive.

"Laser carving is amazing. As long as you give them a good picture, they can do anything." Vivian patted Victor on the neck. "What do you think, Victor?"

The donkey snorted and rubbed his head on Vivian's thigh. She scratched between his ears.

"He doesn't seem impressed." Octavia tamped the last shovel full of dirt around the sign and stepped back to judge her work. "That should hold it. I still think Lil' Jackass Winery would have been better."

Bridget and Vivian turned as one to look at her. "Victor's Vineyard is much classier."

"When people ask who Victor is, I tell them he's the silent partner." Vivian patted the donkey's back. She shielded her eyes from the bright sun and her ring glinted in the sunlight. "I think we need to celebrate." Her voice was cool and commanding.

Octavia shivered and smiled as she took Bridget's hand. "As you wish, Mistress."

About the Author

Brenda Murphy writes short stories and novels. She is a member of Romance Writers of America. When she is not loitering at her local tea shop and writing, she wrangles one dog and an unrepentant parrot. She writes about life, books, photography, and writing on her blog, writingwhiledistracted.com. She also guest blogs at Queeromanceink.com.

I hope you enjoyed reading this book as much as I enjoyed writing it. Let's connect:

Website: www.brendalmurphy.com

Facebook: www.facebook.com/Writing-While-Distracted

Other books by this author

Dominique and Other Stories

Sum of the Whole

One

Coming Soon from Brenda Murphy

Knotted Legacy

Excerpt

"Black suit? Wedding or funeral?" Elaine shifted her weight on the bed and plumped the pillow with her fist.

Martha tilted her head and looked at her sister. "Madam has a thing for suits." She folded her shirt and placed it in her packing cube. "I miss the way Sarah ironed my shirts. So meticulous."

Elaine snorted. "Another one that left us. Are you going to see Vivian? I wonder how things are going with Bridget. What a succulent little brat." She sucked her teeth.

"Miss her?"

"Do you miss Octavia?" Elaine smiled a sick smile, the one guaranteed to start a fist fight when they were children.

Martha frowned at Elaine. "Let's drop this. I'm not going to see Vivian. She messaged me last week. Something's come up. She won't be attending."

Elaine raised her eyebrows. "Something? She's never missed one. Even the year she lost Miriam."

Martha sighed. "She said the three of them were—involved and she was not attending."

Elaine's expression changed, the teasing look on her face gone. "I'm sorry. Are you okay?"

Martha pursed her lips. "I will be. I love Vivian. I want her to be happy. I can't believe Bridget is okay with it. She's such a tight-ass."

Elaine left the bed. She moved behind Martha and hugged her hard before she released her. "I'll get out of your hair and let you finish packing. Anything special you want for lunch?"

"Is Myfanwy busy?" Martha chewed her lower lip, longing for the comfort of Myfanwy's sweet submission.

"She's scheduled with a client until tomorrow night." Elaine rested her hand on her sister's forearm. "Should I have Robin bring it to you? You haven't even looked at her since I hired her."

Maybe something new. Who knows? It might fill this empty place inside of me. Martha patted her sister's hand. "That sounds delightful. Is there any of the soup we had last night?"

Elaine squeezed her hard. "Yes. I'll send her up in an hour."

Also Available from NineStar Press

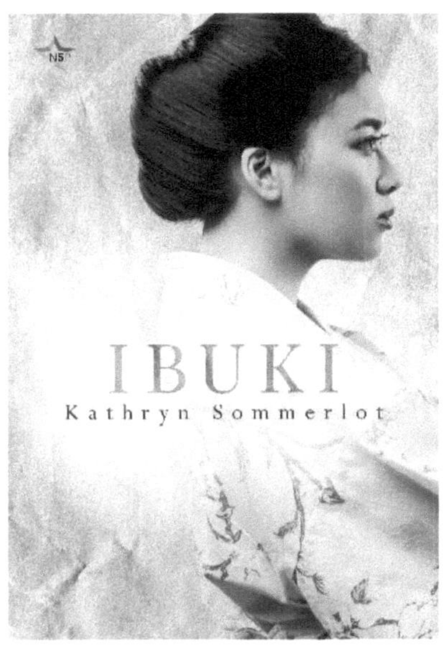

Connect with NineStar Press

Website: NineStarPress.com

Facebook: NineStarPress

Facebook Reader Group: NineStarNiche

Twitter: @ninestarpress

Tumblr: NineStarPress